THE R.E.M. EFFECT

J.M. LANHAM

The R.E.M. Effect
Trade Edition, November 2016

ISBN-10: 0-9973460-3-5
ISBN-13: 978-0-9973460-3-9

Cover design by 2Faced Design

Keep up with the latest J.M. Lanham news and releases by visiting www.jmlanham.com.

For Megan.

Dreams must be heeded and accepted. For a great many of them come true.

–Paracelsus

Chapter 1: Ham

Claire's eyes panned the interior of the stonewall chamber, searching for traces of light in the pitch-black room. The holding cell was dank and humid; a makeshift prison in some long-forgotten jungle somewhere. She had been strapped and bound to a chair for countless days without food, water, or any sign of deliverance. IV fluids hung from a stainless-steel pole nearby, providing her only source of nutrition during her cryptic stay. The hunger pangs were sheer agony, but the liquefied sustenance gave Claire a reason to believe she might make it out of this scenario alive.

If they want me hydrated, then they must want me to live, she reasoned. The hopeful assumption had become her survivor's mantra, and was just enough to preserve her precarious level of sanity through the days-long ordeal. She fought to keep her mind busy, but even an exercise as simple as recalling her own phone number had become an arduous task. It was as if the neurons in her brain were engulfed by a thick fog, obscuring connections and clouding her thoughts, all courtesy of the chemical cocktail being served to her by an unknown host.

The man with the needle. Although several people were likely involved in her kidnapping, Claire knew her short and scruffy tormentor was the one responsible for her current mental state. He was the man who flipped the lights during his daily visits. The man who dosed her with hallucinogenic concoctions delivered intravenously that sent Claire's mind to harrowing places without ever leaving the discomfort of her ill-fitting chair.

Claire had been through the crucible of torture, but that didn't stop her from trying to solve the mystery of her imprisonment. She searched for clues in a veil of darkness, hanging on to every fleeting trace of light that came from the crack at the bottom of the holding cell's only door.

The last thing Claire remembered before her kidnapping was dozing off on a flight from Boston to Los Angeles. Everything after that was a haze–a telltale sign of her recent drug-induced amnesia. She hadn't the slightest clue what her flight number was, but for some reason she *did* remember washing down her meds with overpriced scotch just before falling asleep in coach.

She decided to focus on the basics. She knew her name was Claire Connor, and she knew she was employed–a journalist, perhaps. She didn't think she was married, but she rubbed the base of her ring finger with her thumb just to be sure. Nothing. She tilted her head forward to observe her chin-length, burgundy-red hair. The split ends dangling in front of her signaled the stress she had been under, but provided little else in the form of meaningful intel.

It was clear her investigation had little to go on. There were, however, a few sketchy memories following her high-altitude nightcap; a collection of snapshots leading up to her capture. First, there was a blurry picture of the terminal at LAX. Another shot portrayed a man in a long, dark overcoat. He watched Claire as she walked through the terminal while he pretended to talk on his cellphone. The last snapshot came with a soundtrack, and was by far the most disturbing: a dingy white shroud pressed to her face and muffling her screams.

In an instant, it hit her: *a handkerchief. At the airport. A man grabbed me from behind and held a damp cloth to my face . . . I was drugged.*

"Son of a bitch," Claire muttered. She looked around the room again. The light from under the door was constant now, creeping across the floor and outlining two stainless-steel arms that reached up and out like metallic crab claws from each side of her chair. Both arms were wielding ominous instruments she pretended to ignore.

She turned her attention to a symbol on the IV bag hanging from one of the arms. It looked familiar. She tested her restraints, rocking her chair from side to side as she watched the metal arms move ever so slightly. The chair was firmly attached to the floor, but she was able to exert just enough force to swing the front of the affixed IV bag around to the dim interior light. That's when she noticed a logo, a stylized, silver letter *A*.

She knew she had seen it before, but the pharmacological roadblocks in her mind were inhibiting the connection. It was déjà vu in the worst sense. She glared at the logo, but nothing came to mind. She knew the answer to her kidnapping was written on the front of the bulging bag slowly spinning back and forth between the light and the shadows–but she had no idea what the symbol meant.

Claire furrowed her brow in frustration. She would have rubbed her temples to relieve the headache that was setting in, but her five-point restraints wouldn't allow it. She considered closing her eyes, but the sound of footsteps getting closer broke her concentration. Her attention was drawn to the door, where she noticed the shuffling of feet breaking up the light at the bottom. Her heart dropped. There was a loud clank of the exterior lock, and then the door swung open. In walked a short, stocky man dressed like a seasoned government official with cheap black-rimmed glasses, a starched white button-up, and a five-o'clock shadow that spoke to long working hours with little regard for personal hygiene.

The man flipped the light switch next to the door. Claire winced and turned away, seeking protection for sensitive eyes that had long been adjusted to the dark. The man was cheery and smug.

"Jesus, Ms. Connor. A little light never hurt anyone." He walked over to the detainee.

"You're going to do it again, aren't you?" Claire asked. The man didn't respond. She tried to keep her composure, but there was no hiding her trembling hands.

"Why are you doing this to me? Please . . . just tell me *something*. Anything."

"We've been over all of this before, Ms. Connor. We just have to keep you awake for a little while longer." He moved to a set of cabinets on the wall and pulled a syringe from one of the shelves.

Claire knew what was coming. The scruffy man had a fetish for administering some sort of hallucinogen into her IV, the components of which were still a mystery. Had it been something a little more mainstream like LSD or peyote, Claire's worst fear would have been a bad acid trip. One full of melting faces. Reptilian party-goers. Rock concerts officiated by the Lord of Darkness himself. This concoction, however, was nothing of the sort.

The man stood next to his involuntary patient and prepared her for the procedure. He flushed the IV line with saline. Then he brandished the syringe, giving it a flick as a drop of fluid rolled down the needle.

Claire begged, “Please. You don’t have to do this.”

“That’s where you’re wrong, Ms. Connor,” the man said, never taking his eyes off the syringe. “This has to be done.” He injected the solution into her port with a sadistic smile. “Just . . . think about the greater good.”

Claire watched as the opaque yellow fluid clouded the IV line, quickly moving toward the crease in her arm. She could see her vein, plump and pulsating right where the needle went in. The amalgamation of fluids felt cool under her skin. The meds hit her bloodstream and her heart went into overdrive.

She gripped the armrests, bracing for the kind of pain that could only come from a nefarious toxin coursing through every blood vessel in her body. She told herself not to worry, that it wouldn’t last long. The pressure in her head was intolerable. Sweat drenched her body as once-lost memories began pouring back into existence. Memories of her friends, her career, even her childhood rode in on a powerful wave of consciousness, separating her from her tormented body while washing away her pain and angst in one fell swoop.

Suddenly Claire found herself standing in a field. She looked down at her wrists, then to her ankles. The restraints she had worn for almost a week were gone. The grass she stood in came up to the pockets of her jeans, making it tough to see the sandspurs that were prickling her legs from the knees down.

She rubbed her wrists and looked over the landscape, assessing her surroundings. She was in the middle of a clear patch of land, closed in by a wall of jungle two hundred yards out in all directions. Huge ferns were scattered across the clearing. Honeycreepers fluttered around the tall ceiba trees in the distance. The noonday sun was intense and unrelenting, leading Claire to believe she was in the tropics.

She tied her jacket around her waist and started walking. She could see a hill high on the horizon, no more than a mile or two away. It would be a good vantage point, she supposed, and would hopefully lead her to a road or a nearby town. She hadn't thought about how she had escaped her holding cell. It didn't feel important, nor would it serve to help her out of the jungle. All Claire could think about was finding a way out.

She was almost to the southern edge of the clearing when she heard a commotion coming from the wood line to the north. She turned to zero in on the noise while crouching in the grass, confident the high weeds would keep her concealed. The ruckus grew louder and more obnoxious with each passing second.

Footsteps. Erratic and offbeat, but human footsteps nonetheless. The sound of bipedal creatures barreling through the jungle in the distance was unmistakable. Claire could make out voices, but she couldn't decipher any words.

Finally, the men reached the clearing, stepping out of the shadows and into the full afternoon sunlight. There was no mistaking their attire.

Soldiers. A group of heavily armed men, a dozen or so, all dressed in camouflage fatigues and walking in formation. Each soldier was easily packing eighty pounds of tactical gear. Claire noticed the apparent leader of the group front and center. He was pointing over Claire's head and motioning for the others to move forward.

They were heading straight toward her.

Claire looked back toward the south end of the field. She was almost a quarter mile away from the tree line. She turned her attention back to the soldiers at the nearest end of the clearing. At their current pace, they would be swarming her position in two, maybe three minutes, tops. It was an impossible distance to close without being noticed, but she had no choice. She had to make a move.

She rose into a sprinter's stance, setting her feet while keeping her body just below the tall grass, and then she waited. She peered up toward the soldiers once more, hoping to catch at least a few of them looking the other way before she made a run for it.

That was when she noticed something was wrong. The soldiers had stopped advancing. Not only had their forward march been halted, they were now shuffling in place. Claire squinted, trying to understand what she was seeing in the bright sunlight. The soldiers' movement was sporadic. No one was talking–only distant stares and blank faces.

"What the hell?" she muttered. The soldiers had effectively transformed from an elite military unit into a stumbling herd of drunkards. A dozen fighting men were locked in a zombie-like trance, capable of standing upright, but little else. The leader caught Claire's eye. Something was eerily familiar about him, aside from his current demeanor.

Claire looked harder. Heat radiated from the tall grass in the field and obscured the man's face, but she could just make out his salt-and-pepper hair, cut high and tight in true Marine Corp fashion, with a rugged expression that would send chills down any foreign combatant's spine . . .

"*Dawkins?*"

The name had barely left her lips when Claire felt it on her left. A bullet whizzed by her head, missing her by mere inches. She flinched as she hit the deck, lying flat and shielding her head while shots fired from a barrage of high-powered assault rifles downrange. Bullets cut through the field, sawing vegetation into a flurry of grass clippings raining down on Claire from above.

The shooting was ferocious. Round after round was coming from the south end of the field, aimed directly at Dawkin's group of bumbling targets. Had Claire made a mad dash for the tree line a moment sooner, she would have run right into enemy fire. She wondered who was firing on the halted soldiers, and why they were shooting at soldiers in distress, but her questions went unanswered. The shooting stopped as suddenly as it began, leaving behind a trail of deafening vibrations that echoed off into the hot still air.

It was quiet again. Claire uncovered her ears and patted her body down, checking anxiously for bullet holes. She moved from her chest down to her legs. It was nothing short of a miracle she hadn't been shot. She breathed a sigh of relief before remembering whom the bullets were intended for.

Claire rose up from the ground slowly, staying in a crouched position with her attention now focused on the well-being of her old friend Teddy Dawkins. She knew the man leading the team of soldiers from her time covering the Middle East for the Associated Press. Claire remembered running into Teddy about two years ago while on assignment in Costa Rica. But while she had only been in country temporarily, it appeared Dawkins might have taken on a permanent role.

She carefully searched above the tall grass for the group of soldiers. No sign of them. She pivoted to the south; the aggressors had apparently made their exit, too. Reluctant to raise her head any higher above the cover of grass, she sat back down, staying low to evaluate the situation.

"Jesus, my head!" Claire yelled. Her excruciating headache had returned. She looked to the sky, desperate to identify the source of her pain. It felt like the sun's rays were penetrating her skull, torching nerve endings and searing her mind. Her heart started racing again. Finally, she heard a resounding voice calling from the heavens above.

"Claaaire. Wake up, Claire."

Claire stood up and looked around, eager to locate the source of the voice.

"Time to wake up now . . ."

She looked to the sun. The light was blinding and cold, taking her away from the clearing, away from the soldiers, and most importantly, away from the fucking heat. There was nothing else to be seen or felt–there was only the light. In a fast and fluid transformation, the light turned into a single white-hot globe at the end of a long metallic arm.

Claire was back with her captor in the stonewall chamber. The man swiveled the examination light away from his subject before leaning down to speak to his patient. It was the first time the man had looked Claire directly in the eyes.

"Ms. Connor. I think it's imperative you know how well you performed today."

"What are you talking about?"

"The experiment you've been participating in. For all intents and purposes, it was a clinical success."

"Does this mean you're letting me go?"

The man paused, then said, "Yes. Yes, Ms. Connor. I don't see any reason why you can't go home." The man walked over to a desk below the cabinets and began searching through one of the drawers.

Claire watched him carefully. She wanted to believe him, but his assurances weren't appeasing her gut feeling that something was amiss.

"Will you tell me what this was all about?"

The question amused him. "Yes, of course. Why not." He faced Claire. "Tell me, Ms. Connor, have you ever heard of Ham the astronaut?"

She hadn't.

"Ham was the first hominid sent into space, flying solo during NASA's Mercury program in the early 1960s. Naturally, Ham's contribution to the space program was overshadowed by mankind's achievements, but the importance of his space flight cannot be stressed enough. Chimpanzees are our closest living relatives, with ninety-six percent of their genomes identical to ours. They are a living testament to the undeniable link between humans and apes. No other candidate was more qualified to go into space in our stead than the chimp. Ham was our biological proxy; the living proof the government needed to demonstrate to the American public that space flight was safe for human beings."

He resumed his search through the drawer. "Basically, Ms. Connor, Ham cleared the path for the space race, and look how far we've come since. Think about everything we have accomplished that can be attributed to the space program. Microchips, MRIs, advancements in solar technology, robotics, healthcare, global information systems . . . all byproducts of the Space Age. All beginning with a brave chimp named Ham."

He closed the drawer and returned to Claire's side. He leaned over and whispered in her ear. "You see, Claire . . . *you're* Ham."

The heavy fog was rolling in once again, cloudy and confusing. "I–I don't . . ."

" . . . I wouldn't expect you to grasp the significance of our findings today, Ms. Connor. After all, the drugs do take some time to wear off. But the good news is that you've proven to me, as well as my associates, that our theory regarding the neurological amplification of electromagnetic radiation in a controlled REM sleep-state is valid."

The man produced another syringe. Claire tried desperately to put together a cohesive sentence.

"What . . . what are you g-going to do?"

The man spoke softly as he reached for her port and pumped in the drug. "I already told you, Ms. Connor. I'm going to send you home."

Claire tried to withdraw her arm, but it was no use. Panic quickly succumbed to a feeling of warmth and peace, flowing into her body and calming her mind. Her breathing slowed and her head fell to the side. Her eyes grew heavy, and then everything faded to black.

Chapter 2:
The American Dream

Light broke between the downtown high-rises forming the Atlanta skyline, warming frigid towers of glass and steel as the sun made its grand entrance on a chilly winter morning. It was barely daybreak on a Monday and already the interstate was jam-packed with thousands of cars, creeping along at a snail's pace in the cold morning air. Restless commuters played with their radios and drummed their fingers while they performed the usual stop-and-go dance that had become a trademark of the bustling Southern city.

Paul Freeman was one of those commuters.

"Shit!" Paul said, lifting his forearm to block the sun. The truck shading his windshield had made an abrupt lane change, sending a sunbeam into his eye like a splinter without warning. Driving to work took resilience in the metro area, where coffee-juggling white-collars battled drowsy college kids for highway supremacy. A typical morning for Paul meant a combination of ritualistic prayer and superstitions, reciting supplications and crossing fingers in the hopes he would make it to work in one piece. Blowing horns. Cursing drivers. Multitudes of middle fingers, brake checks and false starts . . . it was enough to drive anyone mad, and Paul figured he could use all the help he could get.

The rush-hour circus was worth it, Paul believed, because at the end of the day he got to come home to a beautiful wife and a newborn baby boy. Michelle stayed home with their young son Aaron, choosing to spend her days raising her child while taking an extended break from a career in nursing. She had been on the brink of burnout when she discovered she was pregnant, leading the young couple to decide that now was the perfect time for her to take some time off and focus on their growing family. While changing diapers and feeding a nine-month-old eating machine were a far cry from the excitement of the emergency room, Michelle could still rely on Paul's detailed Atlanta traffic updates to get her adrenaline fix.

"Some jerk cut you off again?" she asked, twirling her sandy blonde hair.

"Not exactly. Just couldn't see there for a minute."

"Jesus, Paul. You know I hate when you curse like that when you're driving. Makes me think something bad happened."

"Hey, if you catch me on the way to work *without* cursing, that's when you'll know something's definitely rotten in Denmark." He paused to sip his coffee, almost spilling a little on his new collared dress shirt. "So what are you getting into today?"

"Well, I thought about taking Aaron to the park later. You remember Rachel from school? I ran into her at the gym last week. She has a seven-month-old. He's close to Aaron's age, so I thought we could have a little playdate this afternoon."

"Sounds . . . playful."

"It's something to do," she said in her best I'm-not-a-bored-housewife voice. She changed the subject. "So how do you feel this morning? Pretty excited to get to work?"

Paul thought the question sounded suspiciously like a setup. "I guess you could say I'm as excited as anyone wasting away in Atlanta traffic. Why?"

"I just wanted you to know how proud of you I am."

"Oh God. Not this again."

"I'm serious! You worked so hard to get a job in Atlanta. And at Asteria Pharmaceuticals? Do you know how many people they've recruited from Grady? I'm just really, really—"

"Okay, okay," Paul said, gently calling off the congratulatory comments for a minute. "All this praise is gonna go to my head if you're not careful."

"It *should* go to your head, Paul. This is a big achievement for you!"

"Thanks, Michelle. Let's just hope it's enough to hold us over until you start back to work this summer."

For Paul, the new job was a godsend. He never imagined his modest resume would blow up any skirts at Asteria Pharmaceuticals, and his youthful appearance couldn't have helped his case, either. While most of the men at Asteria were upholding the seasonal traditional of cultivating robust facial hair, Paul couldn't grow a beard to save his life.

But regardless of Asteria's reputation for hiring veteran marketers only, Paul was able to get his foot in the door with a junior staff position. Rolling the dice with little more than a business degree, an average GPA and some time in ROTC seemed like a long shot, but Paul was ready to take some chances after his previous career plans had fallen to pieces in less time than it took to say "medically disqualified for military service."

Paul had just wrapped up his second year with the Reserve Officer Training Corp at Georgia State when he learned the downsizing of military personnel had taken an aggressive new turn. The early 21st century had been defined by unpopular wars, starting with the war in Iraq and reaching a tipping point during the War of the Baltics in 2020. With U.S. intervention in Northern Europe at a stalemate, a common theme began to emerge across the international community: putting boots on the ground gave rebel factions an easily identifiable enemy to rally against. The answer? More tech. Fewer troops.

It had been a tough pill for Paul to swallow. Technology had chipped away at the military's need for warm bodies since the late 20th century, making enlistment requirements the strictest they had ever been. Now the United States was being pressured on the global stage to downsize active-duty military even further. For the first time in history, the U.S. military was turning away almost ninety percent of Americans willing to serve their country.

Paul hadn't made the cut.

The Military Medical Standards for Enlistment were crystal clear: "History of recurrent headaches, including, but not limited to, migraines and tension headaches that interfere with normal function in the past three years, or of such severity to require prescription medications, is disqualifying for military service." Every time Paul read the requirements he had secretly hoped one of two things would happen. Either the enlistment ban on severe headaches would change, or his medical records detailing an emergency room admission for a one-time cluster headache would simply disappear.

Still, Paul knew deep down that the standards were there for the good of the country, not personal fulfillment. He had decided it was in his family's best interest to put all his efforts into finding a career that would keep him close to home. His post-collegiate plans might have been dashed, but he had had little room to complain about the position he landed at Asteria. Several of his friends were waking up on Mondays to go to interviews instead of work–something he was reminded of every time he heard a morning show host ranting about a recent jobs report.

Working in the marketing department of a pharmaceutical company wasn't exactly where Paul had envisioned himself ending up after school, but it was a paycheck. A steady job on the home front also made Michelle happy. The prospect of seeing her husband every evening–as opposed to being married to the military–sat well with the interim-stay-at-home mom.

Paul was forcing his way across two lanes of traffic when Michelle asked, "Did you sleep good last night?"

"Let me the fuck over!"

Michelle waited patiently for the commuter-inspired expletives to subside before Paul returned to the conversation. "Sorry, sweetie. It's just these drivers would murder their firstborns just to get a single car length ahead of someone else. I mean, we're all moving slower than sloth shit down here . . ."

"Paul."

"Yes, dear?"

"You didn't answer my question. The sleep. Did you sleep good last night?"

"Yeah . . . Actually, I *did* sleep good last night." Paul thought for a moment as he took his exit. "That's the best sleep I've had in a *really* long time. Why do you ask?"

"I just worry about you, Paul. I know you haven't been getting much sleep lately. You've been so stressed over the new job, paying off your student loans–"

"The new son," Paul said. "Yeah. Pretty sure I've been sleeping in five-minute spells since the little man came on the scene."

"Tell me about it. I told Rachel how Aaron was keeping us both up all night, and you know what she said? '*Well, our little Dylan sleeps like an angel. Sometimes he'll go 10 hours straight before waking up.*' Unbelievable, right?"

"And you're going to have a playdate with this person? I hate her already."

"Well, I was thinking maybe she could give me some pointers."

"We haven't tried the whiskey-in-the-thimble trick yet."

"And I'm not ruling that one out yet, either. Anyway, I'm so glad you're finally getting a little rest."

"Me, too," Paul said. "You have *no* idea."

A sleep-filled night was a rarity for Paul. While coworkers stumbled into work red-eyed and hung over after a night of heavy drinking, Paul's fatigue stemmed from his newborn baby. Most nights Paul and Michelle would paper-rock-scissors to see who would have to get up once little Aaron started calling. Paul was horrible at paper-rock-scissors. Once in a blue moon the kid would sleep through the entire night without a hitch, but most nights meant at least two or three visits to the crib in the other room.

Paul pulled into the parking deck at Asteria Pharmaceuticals, silently thanking the Man Upstairs for the rare and restful night before hopping off the phone with Michelle. Then he thought about the night before. It wasn't just the best night's sleep he'd had in a really long time; it was the best night's sleep of his life.

Paul had never experienced the effects of sleep deprivation before having a baby. Since then, the line between reality and a dream had become little more than a haze. During one episode, he had almost convinced himself he was fully awake, sitting in his car and driving to work with the windows down and the radio blasting. Had traffic been a little heavier, he might have continued believing the illusion well past the clamor of his alarm clock. Another time he pinched his arm so hard during a meeting that it brought blood–a reality check he still wasn't able to explain to the horrified coworker sitting to his left.

Paul sat in his car with the engine off. He knew exactly what he had become: the epitome of the American worker. He was a sleep-deprived family man, gambling with his life every time he got behind the wheel, barreling down one of the busiest interstates in the country while half-asleep to a job he could only describe as, "Meh."

Last night's sleep was refreshing, but likely a fluke. Paul knew it would only be a matter of time before he was driving to work again, dreary eyed and dog-tired after a restless night of tossing and turning and checking on the youngling.

But that sleep last night, thought Paul. *Best I ever had.*

Chapter 3: Coincidence

Alex yawned as he pulled into the rustic, weathered gas station off Highway 20, not far from his early morning destination, a ridgeline overlooking a stretch of rolling green pastures in the foothills of the Appalachian Mountains. He parked his pickup truck and lumbered across the parking lot, eager to get his hands on a tenderloin biscuit, some coffee, and a pack of cigarettes. He glanced to see the sun breaking between the trees just over the horizon, then quickly recoiled his bloodshot eyes away from the light.

It wasn't quite 8 a.m., and already he was regretting going out the night before. He reeked of booze and hadn't showered in over a day. Alex felt a wave of judgment wash over him as he passed an old timer walking into the store. He tilted his head down, hiding a face that had turned a light shade of crimson. He went over the grocery list in his head once more, adding to it a bottle of aspirin in case the headache from the night before decided to come back with a vengeance.

Alex rarely got headaches, drinking or not. He could have easily stayed in bed that morning, but he was a creature of habit, and every day started with a trip to Randall's Store. The rest of his schedule was just as predictable. When he wasn't downing beers with the rest of the good ol' boys after hours, he was working as an assistant manager at a rural farm-supply store, selling overpriced feed and fertilizer to customers too lazy to make the drive into town. Between weekend binge drinking and working the nine-to-five, the young outdoorsman spent what little time he had left either chasing big game or fishing some of the most secluded trout streams in North Georgia.

That didn't mean he was any good at either. Alex's game in the woods was just as humiliating as his game with the opposite sex. Most of his fishing expeditions ended with broken lines and a handful of lures donated to local creeks and streams. His biggest hunting accomplishment had been taking down an impressive twelve-point buck shortly after his 16th birthday. It was far from a record breaker, but enough to excite most outdoorsmen. If only the buck had met his match through the muzzle of Alex's 30-06 instead of the front grill of his Ford F-150.

Over the last six months, however, Alex's luck had changed, and he had a stack of his favorite hunting magazines to prove it. His recent outdoor exploits had turned him into a celebrity of sorts overnight. Nationwide publications, wildlife management agencies, hunting shows and regional news stations hailed him as the up-and-coming hunter of 2021, while an assortment of animal rights groups called for his execution.

Local public opinion was also mixed. Some thought he was a 21st century Davy Crockett, with the half-horse, half-alligator looks to match; others thought he was a fraud. While he had equal shares of fans and dissenters, one thing was certain: there wasn't a soul in town that didn't recognize him. Alex tried to keep a low profile in the convenience store, but Randall quickly called him out.

"Well, if it isn't Grizzly Adams . . . How the hell are ya?" Randall asked.

"Ah, hell," Alex groaned. "I'd be better if I hadn't been suckered into shooting cheap whiskey over at Red's place last night." He walked to the coolers in the back and looked for a high-octane energy drink to carry him through to lunchtime. He opened the transparent cooler door. The red stuff looked good. He grabbed a can and checked out the back label:

NUTRITIONAL FACTS
CAFFEINE: 112 MG
VITAMIN B6: 40 MG
SUGAR: 37 G
VITAMIN B-12: 500 MCG

"500 micrograms B-12." Alex read out to the side. "Percent daily value: 8000 percent . . . 8000 percent?!" *Goddamn, that's got a kick!*

Randall continued to ramble from behind the counter. Alex didn't hear half of what he was saying. The long-winded storeowner was known for his lengthy anecdotes; Alex figured it was probably nothing worth listening to anyway. He walked to the front and set down the 24-ounce can of liquefied neon.

"Know what I mean, man?" Randall said.

"Heard that. I need a bottle of aspirin, and give me a pack of Camels too, if ya don't mind."

"You'll scare 'em off, buddy." Randall three-tapped his finger on the local newspaper by the register. A picture of Alex holding the tines on a record whitetail graced the cover. "Those deer'll smell them smokes a mile away!"

"Yeah, yeah. How 'bout you let me worry about that."

Randall leaned in. "So is that your secret, young fella? You just wake up whenever you take a notion, saunter on down into the woods smelling like warm piss and cigarettes, and wait for God Almighty to send one-uh them big 'uns your way?"

Alex was silent. Randall poked a little more. "Sure you won't be nodding off in your tree stand while every deer in this here county walks on by?"

"That's kinda why I stopped in," Alex said, pointing to his drink.

"Uh huh. Well, I know if I'd been out all night the last thing on my mind would be deer hunting."

"That obvious, huh?"

"I was your age once, too, Alex."

Alex nodded. "Well, some nights it's easier to sleep than others . . ." he stopped talking to search his pockets for his wallet.

"Preaching to the choir," Randall said. "Just hard to believe *anyone* would have the luck you've had without putting a little more effort into getting in the woods on time!"

The clerk was half-joking, but he was right. Most hunters would find it pointless to hit the woods after the dew was gone, since deer were usually active around dawn or dusk. There was one exception, and that was during the rut.

Every hunter knew once the whitetail-mating season set in the bucks became easy targets. Does were under constant pursuit. Lascivious bucks threw caution to the wind. What was usually an intelligent and wily creature descended to the likes of a horny teenager.

But the rut isn't anytime soon in Georgia, thought Randall as he patiently waited on Alex to cough up his money. Randall knew the rut started around Thanksgiving, give or take a few days. Hitting the woods then was the best time to hunt whitetails. Hunting any other time of year was a crapshoot. Maybe you saw something, but most likely–

"Why don't you try reading that thing?" Alex gestured toward the paper. "I can't lose out there, Bubba. I'm the best that ever was!"

Randall wasn't impressed. "That may be, Alex, but you still owe me $9.35."

"Yeah, yeah. Let me go back to my truck. I think I've got a ten in the dash."

"Fine, buddy. Take your time."

Alex left. Randall set his goods to the side and went back to stocking cigarettes on the shelf behind the counter. He fully expected Alex to drive off, just as he had in the past when he didn't have the money to pay for his stuff.

Randall had almost forgotten about the interaction when Alex returned from his truck, cash in hand. He slapped the bill down on the counter, his chin held high.

"Wow. Another cold day in hell. If only you had enough left over for a lottery ticket."

"Just ring it up, smartass," Alex snapped. The clerk forced a grin while Alex played off his distaste for the storeowner's banter.

"Good luck out there," Randall said.

"'preciate it." Alex took his goods and left.

Alex hopped in his pickup and watched the rising sun. He rubbed his eyes and swore off drinking. His head was hurting and his mind was numb. He was tempted to go back home, but his obligation to hit the woods was taking precedence over his current affliction.

I can't go home today. Not after last night.

Randall had every reason to assume Alex had stayed out all night, and Alex wasn't up to correcting him. But the truth was that Alex had called it a night around eleven. He had been at

Red's polishing off a beer when a familiar pain crept in. It began with a ringing in the ears, followed by an excruciating headache he had experienced about a dozen times before. That was when the nausea had set in. He rushed home to take his sleeping pill, hoping he would be out cold before the pain became intolerable. Unfortunately, the medication came up with the beer.

Alex slid his key into the ignition, but he didn't turn it. He sat in silence and stared into the distance, letting his brain take a much-needed breather. He unwrapped the fresh pack of cigarettes and lit one up. He took a slow drag off his first smoke of the day, his eyes fixed on the horizon. He waited for the clarity that came with a sudden jolt of nicotine. Then he thought about last night's dream.

It wasn't a far-fetched dream. No celebrities were involved. No riches were spent. No cars. No monsters. No rotting teeth. No sensations of falling and certainly no sexual fantasies fulfilled (although when those *did* occur, he usually woke up somewhere between first and second base).

He couldn't pinpoint when the dream happened. The headache had caused him to pass out from sheer exhaustion, and what followed was a night of restlessness. He did remember looking at the clock around 2:30 a.m., and then drifting back to sleep thereafter.

Must have happened sometime between then and dawn, he thought.

The dream was lucid, just like the others. He was sitting in his tree stand and watching over a rolling green pasture. He was about to call it quits when he heard the sound of trotting in the distance. He raised his rifle and used his scope to survey the area. A massive figure slowed its gallop and was about to emerge from the foliage across the field . . .

Probably just a coincidence.

Alex's truck was getting cold. He snapped out of his trance and turned the key. The old starter grated and churned before the antique V-8 finally cranked up with a rumble and a roar. He revved the gas and put the shifter into first, easing out of the parking lot and turning west on Highway 20. For a moment, he thought about how ridiculous it was to believe a dream had any real-world implications, and how nice it would be to go back home and get some much-needed shuteye.

But he couldn't afford to take the chance.

Chapter 4: Dangerous Business

Donny Ford fidgeted as he surveyed the grand lobby of the Wyatt Conference Center in Atlanta. It was the morning of February 8th, and the lobby was teeming with fans waiting for the motivational speaker to kick off his latest seminar in the main auditorium. Devotees huddled around coffee stations and vendor booths, hoping Ford would make an appearance and work the crowd before the program got started.

Donny's program, titled *Life Control, Mind Support,* was the talk of every self-help group in the country. By combining centuries-old meditation techniques with the kind of modern-day showmanship his fans craved, Ford had created a package that was custom-fit for his target market. To his followers, he was the light in the darkness. The answer to their prayers. And in many cases, the reason why their checks bounced when it was time to pay the bills.

Donny had always been a talented swindler. From timeshares and weight-loss pills to used cars and kitchen knives, there weren't many things Donny hadn't peddled at one point or another. The man had a knack for getting people to fork over checks, cash, and credit card numbers in exchange for heavily hyped, pre-packaged information that could readily be found by doing a little research online.

Donny watched the crowd from a crack in the auditorium doors. "Look at 'em out there." He turned to his assistant. "What do you think, Marci? Four, five-hundred people here, chomping at the bit to see the show?"

"Sounds about right."

"You think this is gonna pull us out of the hole?"

"It'll help, I'm sure."

"We need to gross at least a hundred grand today. Think there's a hundred thousand out there?"

"You spilled your coffee on you," Marci said. She manifested a napkin and blotted down the front of Donny's Hawaiian shirt. Donny paid no attention, his blue eyes fixed on the walking checkbooks populating the lobby. Donny was an effective public speaker known for his cool demeanor, but today was different. This time there were a multitude of issues weighing on his mind.

He unwrapped a piece of nicotine gum and popped it in his mouth, never taking his eyes off the crowd. For the first time in his life, his nerves were shot.

Doesn't matter, thought Donny. *No excuses. Time to put on the game face.*

He took a deep breath. "Well," he said, "let's go kiss some hands and shake some babies." Marci playfully rolled her eyes as Donny breezed through the double doors, heading into a flurry of fans waiting outside.

Donny was pushing forty, but he still had the energy it took to sell out a show. His followers were willing to fork over a hundred bucks for a few hours of supportive advice and motivational speaking. Over the last decade, he had transformed a floundering act into a multi-million-dollar empire, complete with an exclusive network of websites and affiliates, his own publication company, and recurrent appearances on several morning news programs known for outlandish stories and boisterous guests.

Donny worked the lobby like a seasoned pro. He greeted fans and shook hands and cracked jokes as if his mind were completely at ease. He began to head back toward the auditorium when an assertive young woman approached him from the side, catching him by surprise. The petite inquisitor shoved a microphone in his face and started in.

"Donny Ford? Hi, I'm Maria Moreno with Action News Atlanta. I was wondering if you had a statement you would like to make regarding the alleged suicide of your longtime business partner Bill Stevens?"

Donny ignored the question.

She reached up to place a hand on his shoulder. "Mr. Ford–"

"Don't touch me," he snapped.

"Sorry, Mr. Ford. I wanted to get a statement regarding the death of your business partner Bill Stevens."

"Well, I don't have time for–"

"Is it true that your friend Mr. Stevens was a longtime drug user?"

"I don't know anything about that."

"Some critics think it's strange that Mr. Stevens had recently separated himself from your business–"

"Congratulations, Maria. You've gone from a professional journalist to a common imbecile." He stopped himself and looked around. The crowd was listening intently. He forced a Stepford smile and brushed off the reporter's comment.

"I have to go backstage now. Thanks," Donny said. Maria continued her line of questioning, but Donny didn't stick around to listen. Her voice trailed off as the motivational speaker returned to the auditorium to regain his composure.

Who the fuck does she think she is? Donny was on the verge of a nervous breakdown, and a run-in with a fierce headline chaser had thrown him off his game. The relentless speaking schedule, a murdered colleague, and mounting debt were beginning to take a heavy toll.

The source of Donny's suffocating stress had everything to do with the suspicious death of his business partner Bill Stevens. Stevens had managed Donny's business from the beginning. It was initially a good working relationship. Donny was free to develop his program, trotting the globe in search of new techniques to keep his routine fresh, while Stevens ran the day-to-day operations back home.

Over the last few years, however, the business partnership had strained. Stevens had expected Ford to push the envelope with each presentation, leading to a culture of never-ending one-upmanship from one year to the next. Donny couldn't keep up. Each year, audiences demanded new insights and fresh perspectives, and Stevens was determined to deliver.

Stevens' latest brainchild had been to include Ford's spiritual experiences in his presentations. Stevens had already taken the initiative by overhauling the Donny Ford website, promoting Donny's time spent in the holy regions of the Himalayas some ten years earlier–a sabbatical Ford had wished to keep private. Once Donny's fan base caught wind of his unique knowledge of Tummo meditation, however, Donny had been forced to assimilate it into his latest presentation. He had never forgiven Stevens' deception.

Not long after the *Life Control, Mind Support* tour rolled out in the spring of 2020, Stevens was found dead in a hotel bathroom, lying in a pool of his own blood while he and Donny were both in Las Vegas on unrelated business. The simple fact that they were staying just a few doors down from one another was an unsettling coincidence casting further suspicion on Donny's potential involvement in the murder.

Means, motive and opportunity — Donny satisfied all three. While he hadn't been arrested for the Stevens murder yet, he knew that prosecutors had been putting together an incriminatory case against him for the better part of a year. The lack of a smoking gun didn't matter, either. The circumstantial evidence alone would likely be all a jury needed to take Mr. Ford off the stage for good.

I can't dwell on this now, thought Donny. He was moments away from taking the stage and his nerves were shot. The blaring intro music and the roaring crowd weren't enough to distract him from his racing thoughts backstage. He was trapped in his own mind, desperate to escape the images of inquisitive journalists, a postmortem business partner and a life behind bars.

Come on, Donny. You've got this.

He wiped the sweat from his forehead with the back of his hand, then brought it down to check his watch. It was almost time. Donny stood behind the curtains and waited for the announcer to wrap up the introduction. He adjusted the microphone on his shirt and checked his collar.

"HE'S THE BEST-SELLING AUTHOR OF *LIFE CONTROL, MIND SUPPORT*, AND TODAY HE'S GOING TO SHOW YOU HOW YOU CAN TAKE CONTROL OF YOUR LIFE AND START LIVING THE LIFE YOU'VE ALWAYS DREAMED

OF. PLEASE GIVE A WARM WELCOME TO MR. DONNY FORD!"

Donny emerged from the off-right wing of the stage wearing a million-dollar smile as colorful lights danced and swirled on the stage around him. Artificial smoke billowed from machines at the front of the auditorium. A spotlight cast a long silhouette on the floor behind the motivational speaker. He emphatically greeted audience members, reaching down and doling out high-fives and handshakes at the edge of the stage.

The walking personification of confidence and self-control, no one in the crowd could have ever guessed what a train wreck Donny Ford's mind really was.

Chapter 5:
Your Attendance Is Requested

Paul walked through the parking deck at Asteria Pharmaceuticals, checking his six and watching for the usual threats like speeding sedans and late delivery trucks. Everyone hated the parking deck at Asteria. The company was located downtown, so a certain level of urban mischief was to be expected. Cars were broken into, panhandlers harassed employees . . . even a late-night mugging made headlines in the staff-produced monthly newsletter, prompting the higher-ups to appease concerns by installing substandard security lights in the parking area (personnel lobbied for security cameras, but the C-suite deemed them too expensive). Employees nicknamed the parking deck the Thunder Dome for its post-apocalyptic rush-hour madness, but the complex Paul was walking through was uncharacteristically calm. It was official: The new hire was late.

Paul approached the main-level entrance. Walter, one of Asteria's older security guards, was working the front that morning. Paul waved.

"Morning, Mr. Freeman," Walter said. The security guard didn't know everyone's name at Asteria. Apparently, Paul had made an impression.

"Morning, Walt. What's new with you?" He reached into his pocket and pulled out his I.D. badge.

"You know. Same old, same old. Can't complain."

"I hear ya." Paul fumbled with the I.D. scanner. It wouldn't accept his card. He kept swiping. One noisy beep and a red light, two noisy beeps and a red light . . .

"Fired already, huh," Walter chuckled, knowing the new hires always had trouble with the employee cards. The device finally emitted a pleasant beep of affirmation followed by a solid green light. The door unlocked.

"Looks like I live to see another day," Paul said.

"Have a good day, Mr. Freeman."

"You too, Walt."

The main lobby at the Asteria Pharmaceuticals corporate headquarters was as colossal as the company's profit margins. High ceilings adorning eastward-facing skylights rose forty feet above the main floor. Pillars of light entered from above and slow danced across the marble floors every day until noon. Everything from the warm undertones of the interior paint scheme to the soothing sounds of instrumental jazz playing overhead was designed to inspire tranquility and peace. It was the perfect ambiance for welcoming blue-chip investors and FDA representatives.

Large mahogany doors were on the outer walls to the left, leading to conference rooms, the gym, and the cafeteria. Elevators were placed prominently to the right of the main entrance. A huge octagonal aquarium was the centerpiece of the lobby. Hanging above the aquarium was Asteria's prominent new marketing banner, hot off the press:

Ocula: Rest Easy with Us.

Paul read the banner while briskly making his way through the lobby. *Cheesy*, he thought. He wasn't impressed with the slogan, but it did seem rather fortuitous to see the ad following a rare and restful night of sleep.

Ocula was Asteria Pharmaceuticals' latest wonder drug, capping off two decades of research and development. At first glance, the sleep medication looked like any other, promising sweet dreams and a good night's rest to anyone willing to cough up the money for a hefty copay. But Ocula was in class all its own. It was the first sleep medication to use gene-silencing technology, or antisense, to treat chronic sleep disorders.

Ocula was a revolutionary innovation for 21st century medicine in several ways. The highly publicized clinical trials proved to the world that antisense technology could be delivered through prescription medications to treat common ailments and diseases (even though the clinically successful treatment was still pending FDA approval). Before the Asteria breakthrough, countless pharmaceutical companies had either cut their losses at various stages of research and development, or gone entirely belly up chasing the antisense dream. It seemed Asteria Pharmaceuticals had achieved the impossible, breaking through the glass ceiling and claiming the patent to the most lucrative pharmacological technology of the 21st century.

Antisense had eluded the pharmaceutical industry from the 1980s through the turn of the 21st century. In theory, antisense would apply a gene-targeting drug designed to inhibit a patient's faulty and mutated genes, preventing those flawed genes from causing catastrophic medical problems that were previously deemed incurable. Genetic defects leading to conditions such as Lou Gehrig's disease, cystic fibrosis, muscular dystrophy, Huntington's disease and Hemophilia (to name a few) could all be cured by preventing the genetic defect from replicating itself in other cells within the body. The theory was a promising concept worth pursuing, yet seemed every bit impossible to those who had witnessed years of fruitless labor and billions spent without a glimmer of an operative drug to show for it.

Antisense may have appeared too complex for early 21st century technology, but the theory behind gene silencing was rather simple. First, a doctor would have to pinpoint and diagnose the specific condition a patient was suffering from–a common example would be heart disease. While not all cases of heart disease are linked directly to an inherited set of genes, one common cause of premature deaths related to heart disease was hypercholesterolemia.

This condition caused high levels of cholesterol in individuals from a very early age and, left untreated for decades on end, could result in various health conditions including hypertension, stroke, and cardiac arrest. A simple genetic test could determine whether or not the patient with high blood pressure was suffering from hypercholesterolemia due to a genetic predisposition, in which case antisense therapy could be applied.

When a patient had a genetic predisposition to a disease, it meant that an error in a particular gene was being passed on to other genes. These errors, known as mutations, could be inherited or caused by environmental factors, like a thirty-year smoker forming cancerous lung tissue via the carcinogens that had altered his or her DNA, leading to destructive changes in genetic information. These changes, caused by either rapid cell division or direct changes to the genes themselves, passed on the altered information to other cells through RNA, which acted as a kind of misinformed messenger, using a faulty set of instructions to tell other cells how to build themselves.

This was where antisense would come into play. Antisense drugs would work by keeping the flawed instructions, issued by genes residing in the nucleus of a cell, from making their way out into the body. If a patient was found to have high blood pressure caused by a genetic fubar, the perfect antisense drug could step in and stop the messenger RNA from passing misinformation on to other cells, halting a lethal game of telephone dead in its tracks.

Previous pharmaceutical research teams had been trying to boil the ocean by pursuing antisense technology for treating major ailments like heart disease and cancer; after all, such conditions were the leading causes of death worldwide. The problem was the fact that researching common diseases was rarely profitable for drug companies like Asteria.

Over the course of the last two decades, world governments had moved from private health insurance providers to single-payer systems. Many treatments once regarded as inaccessible to patients were now available as a constitutional right in developed countries across thc globe. If a patient became afflicted with a life-threatening disease, the applicable treatment regimen was likely covered in full by insurance, making life-saving drugs affordable for patients while sending many drug makers into negative territory.

The exceptions were drugs that were blacklisted from government formularies. These lists initially banned medications considered optional or non-life-threatening, such as erectile dysfunction pills and drugs to treat hair loss. Over the last two years, however, insurmountable debt had forced several countries to expand their lists of prohibited coverage to more serious conditions like rheumatoid arthritis and Crohn's disease. These drugs weren't covered by most insurance plans, but that didn't matter. Consumers had to have them, and drug companies loved selling them at premium prices. Asteria understood this, and consequently decided to take a new approach by experimenting with antisense technology in a way that would yield cost-effective results.

It was a smart move. Investors had grown tired of the lack of progress with traditional R&D projects, and were hungry for fresh ideas and lucrative gains. When Asteria put together a proposal that not only promised investors a stake in the most groundbreaking technology of the century–but was also guaranteed to corner the $100 billion sleep industry–funds came pouring in.

The irony of their capitalistic approach wasn't lost on company execs. By appealing to the greed of investors both foreign and domestic, they were able to make astonishing progress on antisense. Once the drug hit a North American market already drooling with anticipation, the company would then have the capital necessary to continue research on the very conditions that had bankrupted industry peers in the first place. The gears had been set in motion; all that was lacking now was FDA approval.

Paul had never given a drug like Ocula much thought; his inherent fear of becoming addicted to prescription meds kept him from considering whatever ostensible benefits a drug like that offered in the first place. He knew plenty of people who started taking sleeping pills to get through a couple of rough nights, only to become hopelessly dependent on them. He wasn't going to make that list.

Paul could trace his aversion toward behind-the-counter drugs to his militaristic upbringing. Prescriptions were taboo in his household. According to Paul's father, pills were for the weak and the dying. The old man would say if Paul couldn't sleep, he should try counting sheep. Sometimes Paul got chamomile tea, but that was only if he was sick. It sounded extreme, but Paul learned from an early age to cope without remedial crutches. He knew that in time his latest bout of sleeplessness would fade away, too. He just needed to ride out the cycle.

There was a large clock above the elevator doors, and Paul couldn't help but notice the time. 8:17 a.m. *Shit.* His office was on the 3rd floor, and already he was dreading the long walk past coworkers tapping fake wristwatches and shaking their heads in dismay. He made it to the elevators just in time to meet a handful of suits waiting on the next lift. The elevator returned from its last run, the doors opened, and everyone entered.

Once inside, Paul marveled at the elevator's interior. Brass handrails. Mahogany trim. Soft golden lighting. There was even a glasses-free 3D television in the corner above the panel of buttons. The money spent per square foot in the elevator alone would rival that of the finest luxury homes.

For the Atlanta headquarters, presentation was everything. The downtown complex was the business end of Asteria Pharmaceuticals, evoking prosperity, success and competency from the inclined-steel rafters to the polished marble floors. The CEO of the company, George Sturgis, had an opulent top floor office that would have made the wealthiest tycoons green with envy.

Paul had never met the man, but the CEO seemed to be everywhere these days. Paul recalled a recent Financial Beat interview; Sturgis was staunchly defending the buyout of a small pharmaceutical company, Gibbs and Griffin. Although Gibbs and Griffin had struggled financially in recent years, they still held valuable assets, including a popular antirheumatic drug developed for the treatment of rheumatoid arthritis.

The fledgling company believed at the time that a Big-Pharma buyout was the best thing for shareholders as well as patients, but once Asteria took ownership of the patent, they immediately jacked the price of the arthritis pill up 500 percent. Ma and Pa were left with an impossible choice: go without the once-affordable medication and suffer, or take out a second mortgage to keep their hands from freezing up.

"Third floor, buddy." Paul felt a nudge from behind as someone broke his trance.

"Oh. Thanks." He squeezed past the suits and through the elevator doors, arriving in the office bullpen.

Paul walked down the main cubical corridor toward his desk on the back row. Chairs swiveled and heads turned as the predictably waggish behavior of his coworkers turned into an informal announcement of his arrival. He finally made it through the gauntlet of playful employees and took a seat at his cluttered desk.

There was a blank envelope sitting on top of his keyboard. He turned on his computer, then leaned back and opened the letter while he waited for the system to boot. He cursed under his breath the moment he laid eyes on the first sentence:

February 8th, 2021
Mr. Freeman,

You are needed in attendance at Donny Ford's seminar, *Life Control, Mind Support*, being held at 10 a.m. at the Wyatt Conference Center, 3405 Shallowford Road in Marietta. This is the last seminar in the area for some time, so it is imperative you make it there for the purpose of market research. Take notes, and pick up a recorder from Sally in her office. Have the recorder and a full report on my desk by end of day.

Regards,

Ryan Tanner
Public Relations Director
Asteria Pharmaceuticals

P.S. Clean up your desk.

"They want to pay me to listen to *this* douchebag?" Paul let the letter drift out of his hand and back into the disarray. Paul had become acquainted with Donny Ford's late-night infomercials while nocturnally channel surfing with a fussy infant named Aaron. Paul could tell right away that Donny was a snake oil salesman preying on the desperate, naive and sleepless; people who were out of work and out of money but would still scrape together every last dime they had just for a shot at a better life.

Paul put his hands behind his head and stared up at the fluorescent ceiling, ruminating on Donny Ford and his so-called miracle programs. Paul knew the kind of cloth Donny was cut from, and it sickened him to watch the speaker's late-night programs knowing that thousands of people were buying into his nonsense.

Donny could sell the endless supply of hot air billowing from his mouth to a balloonist. His ability to induce emotional responses and drive consumers to take action was uncanny. He had used his talents to build a secure future for himself, while doing little for the people forking over their hard-earned cash. His pitches were cliché, bland, and far from magic, but with the right audience, they worked like a charm.

"Are you sick and tired of being sick and tired?" Donny would ask sleepless viewers at home. Donny was always broadcasting from a tropical location and wearing his trademark Hawaiian shirt and khakis. "Living a life of loneliness, sadness, and failure is NOT what God put you on this planet for! There is a *better way to live*, and I'm here to help you find it!" Donny spoke like he was the self-appointed emissary of the Almighty, here to help troubled souls with some of life's most worrisome problems.

What a piece of shit, thought Paul. Paul loathed salespeople who referenced deities in their sales pitch; to him it seemed like a manipulative way of gaining favor with the faithful before draining their bank accounts. But regardless of what he felt about the man's tactics, Paul knew he was going to have to sit through Donny Ford's spiel, so he might as well get over it.

Even so, Paul didn't get why Ryan Tanner, the company's public relations director, was giving him written instructions to attend a quack's latest seminar. The company had a sufficient e-mail and push-notification system, and employees were expected to respond the moment they received correspondence. Of course, the guy could have just called, too.

Guess he really wanted to make sure I got this. Paul rubbed his eyes out of habit. He still couldn't believe he had slept all night; it was a great feeling. Paul reached for his desk phone and dialed #131, Sally's extension. Tanner's secretary promptly answered.

"Good morning, Mr. Freeman. How are you today?"

"I'm fine, Sally. I was told you had a recorder for me?"

"Yes, Mr. Freeman. Mr. Tanner said you would be calling. I've got a voice recorder right here, waiting for you to pick up as soon as possible."

"What's the rush?" Paul asked.

"Well, Mr. Freeman, the seminar is in an hour."

"Shit! That's today?"

"Yes, it's today. Didn't you read the memo?"

Paul looked at the top of the letter, then his calendar. Today was definitely the eighth.

"Damn . . . guess I'd better hurry."

"Yes, sir."

Paul paused, then asked, "Hey, Sally, do you have any idea why Tanner would even want me to attend this thing? Everything I've heard about this Ford guy points to him being an authentic dipshit."

"I completely agree," Sally snickered. "But Mr. Tanner likes to stay up to date with topics involving mind control, intuition . . . things of that nature." She whispered, "I know it sounds crazy, but he claims it helps him get inside his customers' heads."

Paul raised an eyebrow. Surely a major drug company's public relations director wasn't interested in something as absurd as—

"Mind control?" Paul said.

"Yes, it's a little strange," Sally said, "but if you were a man on the verge of losing your job because your superiors thought you were a little too, how can I put this, *eccentric,* wouldn't you want to know a little bit about mind control?"

Paul smirked, detecting Sally's sarcasm. "I guess I would, Sally," he said. "See you in a sec."

Chapter 6:
Mind over Matter

The tumultuous applause shook the foundation of the Wyatt Conference Center in Atlanta. The auditorium was packed. Seats always sold out quickly when Donny went on the road; a sign of his followers' unwavering devotion (or unhealthy obsession). Fans were star-struck at the site of Mr. Ford up close and personal.

Donny bent down along the front of the stage to shake hands before the crowd settled down. Most of the front row was weeping. Donny usually savored the reaction, but this time was different. His mind was distracted with circumstances beyond his control. He told himself now wasn't the time to dwell. He was an expert at going through the motions, and now was the time to act.

Donny greeted one last audience member, graciously nodded, then returned to center stage. The lights dimmed and the intro music faded away. He waited for the audience to quiet down before settling into his spiel. It was a full house, and Donny could already visualize the dollar signs dancing over each audience member's head.

"Thank you. Thank you, everyone," he said. The audience took their seats. "Okay, let's get right to it. I'm glad you could all make it here this morning, because have I got something for everyone that is going to change your lives forever."

A projection screen lowered behind him. The title of the seminar, *Life Support, Mind Control* was on the introductory slide. He clicked over to the next one. It was a photo captioned DZOGCHEN MONASTERY. KHAM, TIBET.

"Has anyone here ever heard of Tibetan monks, or anything about the astounding feats these unique individuals can accomplish by unleashing the power that is harnessed within their own minds?" Blank stares filled the room.

No problem, thought Donny. The question was rhetorical.

"Don't worry, guys. Until recently, I had no idea just how powerful these centuries-old mind-control techniques really were. So how did I discover a new way for you to use your mind to take control of your own life?"

Donny talked with his hands and paced the stage. "Well, it all started ten years ago during a trip halfway around the world, to the region in Asia commonly known as Tibet. Tibet is a land above the clouds; a place of storied mountain lore, where beautiful landscapes and historic holy architecture collide. It's also a place where a man can come closer to God while standing on his own two feet than anywhere else on Earth."

This was the trip Donny abhorred Stevens for revealing. Donny never told Stevens any details about the yearlong expedition, but that didn't stop Stevens from painting the spiritual theme of the Donny Ford website with a broad and fictitious brush. Claiming to have discovered the top-secret practices of Buddhism, and then packaging that knowledge up into a seminar to sell to the masses was in gross violation of everything Donny had learned in Tibet. He was determined to keep what he had learned close to the vest, choosing to take the Stevens Approach by getting creative with the details without revealing too much about his spiritual revelations. The audience, he reasoned, would never know the difference.

"And let me tell you something," Donny said. "This was the one trip that changed my life forever." There was another slide change. The screen behind him showed a panoramic view of Mount Everest. "I bet this place looks familiar. Tibet is the highest region on earth, sharing Mount Everest with Nepal to the south, along with the rest of the awe-inspiring Himalayan Mountains throughout the southwest portion. I'm not sure anyone there would think I was in my right mind if I were to show up in one of my trademark Hawaiian shirts," Donny said. The audience laughed hysterically, proof they could be captivated by the corniest of jokes.

"Ironically enough, by the time my trip was over I would be meditating in one of the highest cities in the world wearing nothing but a Hawaiian shirt, a pair of shorts, and a warm air of confidence. How was this possible? By applying techniques handed down by the Buddhist monks of Tibet for the last seven hundred years.

"This is where things get really exciting. You see, these supportive meditation techniques are some of the most powerful tools our minds can possess. These tools have helped monks defy harsh elements and impossible conditions in sub-zero temperatures for centuries. And not only do these monks survive–*they actually thrive*. Now, you may be wondering what any of this has to do with you, especially since it doesn't get *that* cold here in Atlanta."

The audience begged to differ. Donny graciously caved when he remembered he was speaking to people capable of annihilating local milk and bread inventories the moment a weatherman called for temperatures in the thirties.

"Okay, okay. You've got me on that one. The point is that surviving extreme temperatures is just one way to demonstrate the power behind a method that can improve every aspect of your life. No longer do you have to be a slave to conditions like high blood pressure, depression, anxiety, headaches, obesity, impotence and insecurity. Even more, the gift of this powerful meditation technique is available to *every single person* who is here today. Just imagine having the all the tools necessary to allow your mind to work at its full potential. That, my friends, is how you put control of your life in *your* hands!"

Everyone clapped as Donny stepped to the side of the stage and presented another slide hyping his new program. He was only a few minutes into the presentation, but he was already dying to get it over with.

It was Donny's first seminar following the Bill Stevens murder. It had been almost a year since he looked upon an audience to see the collective faces of admiration staring back at him; now a handful of those faces were casting doubt. Was he innocent, or was he a killer? Did he murder for money, or was something else going on behind the scenes?

Donny could see the inquisitive eyes of a few silent audience members as the rest continued to cheer. It was more than unsettling. He turned away and found solace in the comfort of the projection screen, his eyes happily resting on an inanimate object incapable of passing judgment or distrust. The breather was short-lived, and soon he was back to portraying the resolute leader his faithful fans had come to count on.

The roar of the crowd had long died down when Paul Freeman stumbled in through the main auditorium door with clumsy haste. The hinges creaked and the light shone in. All eyes in the audience turned to Paul, giving a unified look of contempt to the man with the audacity to interrupt a Donny Ford presentation before turning back toward the stage.

"Sorry," Paul said as he quietly shut the door. He squinted as he looked for an empty seat between the dark aisles, but the figures he saw standing along the walls were proof enough that the venue was standing room only.

"Not a seat in the house?" Paul muttered. Once again audience members snapped their heads back toward him, scorching the nonbeliever with fierce eyes and wicked thoughts. Didn't he know this was a sacred place? *The Anointed One, His Holiness, Sir Donny Ford, has graced us with his presence! Put a lid on it, doofus!*

Paul would have apologized again, but the insincerity of such a gesture would have been written all over his face. The onlookers rolled their eyes and slowly turned away. Paul found a vacant space along the wall to the right of the stage and settled in. He took out the voice recorder Tanner had given him and switched it on. Then he braced himself for what could only be the most boring couple of hours of his adult life.

Should've called in sick, he thought. He listened as the man on stage rambled on.

"Okay, everybody!" Donny said. "I would like all of you to follow along with me while we review what's on the screen up here." The title screen, *Life Control, Mind Support*, was accompanied by the program logo, a graphic of an atom with a human brain for a nucleus. Colorful lasers twirled around the stage while inspirational music reverberated through the auditorium.

Donny's programs were always heavy on packaging, scarce on content. It was all lipstick and rouge. He was like a builder who spent all of his money on the exterior features of the home while leaving little for the inside. If only the audience could see what was behind Donny's latest façade.

Paul already knew Donny's modus operandi, and he wasn't impressed with the presentation so far. He tried to daydream his way out of the auditorium, but the strength of Paul's imagination paled in comparison to the resonance of Donny's voice.

Donny pointed his clicker at the screen. More pictures of holy temples.

"Now, you guys and gals have heard me talk before about the importance of perseverance," he said. "Well, when I arrived in Tibet, my first visit was to the capital city of Lhasa. One of the interesting things about Lhasa is that it's home to many, many Buddhist monks. These monks have practiced their religion amidst chaos for over a thousand years.

"You see, throughout the region's history there has been much unrest in Tibet. This unfortunate truth has been well publicized by the likes of western journalists, human rights organizations . . . even a few Hollywood movie studios have profited from stories covering the Himalayan turmoil." Of course, so had Donny, but that was beside thc point.

Donny asked, "Has anyone here heard of the recent Lhasa riots, the Dalai Lama, or the People's Liberation Army?"

The audience deadpanned.

"That's okay. The best thing about my program is that you don't have to be an expert on the region to benefit from my methods. Still, everyone in this audience does need to take a moment to appreciate the resolve of the Tibetan Buddhists, because there's something powerful behind it. These people have persevered in harsh environments; lived through violent regional conflicts; held true the path toward spiritual enlightenment; all by mastering channels long thought inaccessible within their own minds. What's more is that the same practices known to have delivered Tibetan Buddhists from countless tribulations in the past can still be used today by anyone willing to open up their minds and accept the life-changing gift of mind support."

Donny clicked through more slides of subpar Tibetan vacation photos. They were captioned with catchphrases few copywriters would have been proud of:

The STARTLING truth about meditation

This SHOCKING breakthrough in neurology will **leave you speechless!**

You have so much to gain and absolutely NOTHING to lose.

Donny stopped on another temple photo and pocketed the clicker. "In visiting one of the most famous temples in all of Tibet, the seventh-century Jokhang Temple, I was first introduced to Tibetan meditation practices. It was almost a decade ago, but I remember the experience like it was yesterday.

"I was sitting on a bench in Jokhang Square in Lhasa, the capital of Tibet. It was a Saturday afternoon and the square was bustling. Merchants were at their booths selling handmade scarves, jewelry and Tibetan rugs. Traditional monks adorned in long red robes strolled in front of the Jokhang temple. Obnoxious tourists took selfies in front of the centuries-old architecture. Farmers, miners and textile workers biked from the surrounding mountains into the holy epicenter.

"I was taking in the various scenes playing out in the square when a man sat down beside me. He wasted no time pointing out that he knew who I was. Can you believe it? Here I was halfway around the world and I run across a fan just a year after taking my first program on the road . . . I mean, is there *anywhere* I can go to get away from you lovely people?"

The audience chuckled. A few people hollered an enthusiastic, "Nope!"

Donny said, "So I strike up a conversation with this man and find out he's an investor from the United States. He was also a regular visitor to Lhasa, tasked with looking out for his company's copper mines operating across the region. We talked about things to do and places to see in Lhasa, we talked about our families, and then we talked about business. It wasn't long before he asked me about my career, and I answered by letting him know I was in Tibet on a quest for inspiration.

"That's when the businessman mentioned a term I had never heard before: Tummo meditation. Now, keep in mind that I've been a meditation devotee since college, but Tummo was something completely new to me. Naturally, I was curious.

"The man filled me in on the basics of how Tummo is practiced by many Buddhists throughout Tibet; how fundamentalists have kept the method a closely guarded secret for hundreds of years; and how Tummo helps the Himalayan people live at the top of the world without succumbing to a ferociously cold climate. Tummo seemed interesting enough, but it was something he said later that would change my life forever."

Donny stepped to the side as a hologram of a human brain appeared. The oversized brain rose six feet above center stage and rotated slowly. Key areas of the brain were color coded and labeled. As the image turned, these areas were highlighted, with holographic text describing the region. The frontal lobe was first to light up; this was described as the home of the human conscience. Next was the parietal, categorized as the sensory information hub of the brain. Smaller areas of the brain were featured out to the side, including a bullet point covering the hypothalamus, the control center for regulating body temperature, sleep, and circadian rhythms.

Donny stopped the animation. "Consider the hypothalamus," he said. "We all like to think we're in control of our own minds, but does anyone really have control over things like sleeplessness, hunger, or body temperature? For the most part, no. If the average human had the consciousness of mind to control the hypothalamus, there wouldn't be a sleepy, or hungry, or shivering person on the planet. But just because controlling the subconscious areas of the mind seems improbable, it doesn't mean that it's impossible."

Donny took a pensive tone as the audience hung on his every word. "This brings us to what my friend in Tibet revealed to me ten years ago. Tummo meditation opens the door to controlling *every facet* of one's own mind. You just have to know how to use it."

Paul's ears perked up. He had settled into the delirious realm of half-asleep, half-wishing-he-were-dead instead of listening to the talking asshole on stage, but catching the part about controlling the mind brought him back to reality like a slap to the face.

This must be what Ryan is so interested in, he thought.

It was an intriguing topic, no doubt, but why hear about it from a professional pitchman? The whole presentation was weak, at least through Paul's eyes. Worn-out dialogue, suspenseful music, lights, lasers, and a so-called motivational speaker straight off the used-car lot . . . the seminar reeked of late-night-infomercial garbage (although the rotating brain hologram was pretty cool). Most of what Paul had heard that morning was the kind of hyperbole that had made Donny Ford a marketing millionaire–not an authority on mind control.

But then a sensation overwhelmed Paul, one he had never felt before. A gut-wrenching fear had sunk deep into his core, and although he couldn't quite interpret what the feeling meant, he knew exactly what was stirring his emotions. It was the moment he heard Donny say,

"I've learned the most powerful form of mind control in the world. And tonight, guys and gals, I'm going to show you how to harness that power, too."

Chapter 7:
In the Bag

Alex's truck idled down Highway 20 at a snail's pace, leaving a trail of dark exhaust behind it as the carefree hunter drove to his Appalachian hunting spot. Plumes of black smoke billowed out from the tailpipes and masked the road behind him–an unnecessary tailgating-prevention strategy. The morning was cool, and Alex had the rural highway all to himself. He turned up the radio, singing a few verses of his favorite country song with the voice of a chain-smoking angel. He could have cared less about hitting the woods on time.

Late fall and early winter were the best seasons to hunt whitetail. Deer were most active during late-autumn ruts, when cold weather combined with the promise of propagation kept most deer on the move. Early morning was the best time for hunters to catch whitetail deer in the middle of their cool-weather operating pattern.

But it was February in Georgia, and the rut was long gone. So was the morning. Alex looked at the clock as he neared the turnoff to his hunting spot. A quarter to nine. Most hunters aimed to be sitting in their stands a few minutes before daybreak. Alex figured he missed that mark by a few hours, but it didn't have the slightest effect on his enthusiasm. He knew it was going to be a good day.

The dirt road leading to Alex's tree stand was right off the highway. Alex hit his blinker and braced himself for the bump.

There was a slight drop off from the main road, along with a sizeable ditch running right down the middle of the weathered trail. If Alex didn't straddle the trench just right—

"Gawddammit!" A front tire slid off into the muddy channel. He fought the steering wheel and righted the ship, but not before sending his front axle scraping into the rocky edge of the trench. *That's gonna cost me.* He shook his head and cursed the boulders and the mud and the rock-laden road.

Alex drove down the wooded path for almost two miles. The road went through several pine thickets, creating dark tunnels into the backwoods that were a tight squeeze for the antique 4x4. Limbs reached out and screeched down the side of the truck, reminding Alex why he never invested in a paint job. His entrance made plenty of noise, so he parked a couple hundred yards away from his stand, just in case there were any deer within earshot.

He pulled into a small clearing, just large enough to park a vehicle or two. He turned off the truck and rubbed his eyes. The newfound silence was short-lived as a number of crows began cawing in the distance. Alex stepped out to get a better listen. He could see them flocking in the direction of his stand.

Damn. Usually crows only cawed if they spotted a threat, like another hunter lumbering around in the woods somewhere. The loud cackling was a warning siren, alerting other animals nearby that something was amiss. Alex knew the aerial uproar lessened the chances of seeing anything besides a few unruly squirrels. Squirrels would never let a few crows rain on their loud and erratic foraging parades. But most animals, including deer, heeded the caw of the crow.

Eh, Probably nothing. I've still got this.

Alex lit up another smoke, took a nice long drag, and then reached into his truck to grab his rifle and backpack. He locked up his truck and moved toward the front, leaning back on the bumper with his cigarette hanging from his bottom lip. He took out a single bullet from his shirt pocket.

When his buddies hounded him about his hunting tradition, he told them real hunters only needed one shot. He pulled back the bolt on his single shot 30.06 and slid in the cartridge, then pushed the bolt forward and flipped on the safety. He looked down the beaten footpath leading to his tree stand.

That was when Alex saw the first deer of the day. A doe stepped out of the woods onto the trail about fifty yards in front of him, oblivious to the smoking gunman. Alex stood without moving a muscle and watched the whitetail from afar. The doe was lean and gray, just like he remembered. She stopped halfway and looked back into the woods. Alex already knew she was waiting for her two offspring.

The fawns, clumsy and playful as they emerged from the woods, caught up to their mother in the middle of the trail. They danced around their mother's hooves, dodging puddles and frolicking about as they followed her across the trail. Then, as suddenly as they appeared, the three deer were gone, dipping back into the woods on the other side.

They hadn't spotted Alex; he was still as stone. The hunter had experienced this scene before. Every detail from the appearance of the doe to the fawns' choreography had been prerecorded and then played out before him just as predicted. And the scene was far from over.

Just like I saw, thought Alex. *Must be my lucky day.*

He thought it best to give the little family of deer a few minutes to leave before heading out. He had a lot to look forward to, and he didn't want to jeopardize it by interfering with anything leading up to the main event. He took another drag or two off his cigarette and then flicked it into a mud puddle by the truck. The butt hissed when it hit the dirty water, cutting his thoughts short and signaling it was time to go. He flung his rifle across his right shoulder, the backpack across his left, and started toward his outpost at the top of the ridge.

***

The sun was high in the sky by the time Alex settled in for the hunt. He had picked a shady tree to mount his stand on, with plenty of canopy overhead to shield him from the afternoon rays. The cool temperatures were an improvement from the night before, but it wasn't warm enough to keep the chill away. Alex always got cold once he had been motionless in his stand for a while, and this time was no different.

He looked around to make sure he didn't startle any critters nearby–aborting the unspoken hunter's pledge to stay perfectly still–and stretched out his legs to reach a beam of light that was hitting the far edge of the tree-stand platform. His legs caught the warming sunlight from the knees down.

Ah, much better.

Alex groaned as he repositioned himself, sinking into the cloth seat of his stand. It was nice to spend some time enjoying the solitude of the great outdoors. He watched a woodpecker drum on a tree a few yards ahead of him. The bubbling waters of Briar Creek could be heard coming from the bottom of the ridge behind him. The sky was clear and the wind was still.

For a while he was at peace, but as the minutes turned into hours his impatience began to show. He twiddled his thumbs and bounced his knee. He should have seen something by now. He looked down the shooting lane in front of him. Not a deer in sight. He looked left, then right. Nothing but leafless trees and evergreens. He checked his wristwatch. It was already four o'clock.

What the hell is going on?

The thought crossed Alex's mind that maybe he was kidding himself. It wasn't long before other doubts followed. He had picked a horrible place to hang his tree stand; he felt like an idiot for getting in the woods so late; and he knew Randall's smart-ass was probably right about the smokes.

The worst factor had to be the location. Dense woods surrounded him, with the only clear shooting path lying front and center. It stretched out for about thirty yards; anything further meant taking a shot obscured by pine needles and rhododendrons. Couple that with a late start and his chances of seeing a buck were slim. None of Alex's choices made any sense from a hunting perspective, but his conviction remained.

That was because Alex had had a dream he would kill a buck today.

Not that grandiose dreams of big-game success were uncommon among hunters. There wasn't a sportsman alive who didn't have wild fantasies of taking down a massive whitetail or landing a record-breaking bass. But Alex's late-night episodes went far beyond fuzzy premonitions or ambiguous imagery.

The dreams that had occurred over the last several months were unlike anything he had ever experienced before in his life. Vivid. Stirring. Graphic. Gone were the lofty fantasies about lottery winnings and superpowers and hooking up with the high-school crush who ignored Alex for the better part of his life. The scenes filling his head now were less like fanciful dreams and more like genuine memories of events that had already taken place. The kicker was they hadn't.

Alex remembered the night the phenomenon began. Every summer during the first week in July he would make his way into the Blue Ridge Mountains and camp out on the banks of his favorite fishing spots. The pattern was predictable. He would spend the first day fishing the Toccoa River before idling his truck up the road toward Lake Blue Ridge on the second. The last stretch of the annual excursion was dedicated to searching for the elusive native brook trout in the frigid spring-fed waters of Coopers Creek.

The weeklong tradition was a trip Alex used to take with his father every summer. That was before the old man succumbed to a massive heart attack earlier that year. The months that followed were hard on Alex. He was having a hard time letting go of his dad; the two had always been close. He had toyed with the notion of cancelling the summer trip several times, but eventually figured it would be a healthy way to find a little closure while honoring his dad's memory in the process.

Unfortunately, the first trip to the Appalachian trout streams without his father wasn't as peaceful as he had hoped. Alex hadn't slept much since his father died, and forcing himself to take the annual fishing trip alone turned out to be a terrible decision. The first night in the tent was the worst he had felt since the funeral. The cool weather did little to prevent Alex's angst-driven night sweats.

He tossed and turned and kicked his sleeping bag off to the side, desperate to silence the long hours of cogitation. Occasionally a hooting owl or howling coyote would distract him from his train of thought; then it was right back to wallowing in his own misery. It wasn't long before a combination of grief, solitude, and anxiety all led up to the worst headache of Alex's life.

A goddamn migraine? Alex couldn't believe it. He didn't have a history of migraine headaches–or any kind of headaches for that matter–although headaches were known to run in his family. That was how he recognized the symptoms right way. Sensitivity to light, like the beams coming from the lantern in the corner of his tent. Waves of nausea, so intense that he had to leave his tent flap unzipped in case he had to bolt outside to puke. Pain radiating from one side of his head, ringing his ears and forcing an eye shut.

Of all the places to be, he thought. No doctors. No hospitals. No relief in sight. It was just Alex's luck. Over the course of the long night there were at least a dozen times he had convinced himself this was the end; that the migraine was the precursor to a massive stroke that was going to take him out of this world for good. He reckoned there were worse ways to go. By midnight he was completely incapacitated, curled up in the fetal position and begging God for a merciful reprieve. Then the nausea came again.

He mustered the energy to crawl outside and put a little distance between the tent and the impending vomit that was burning in his throat. Rocks and sticks battered his hands and knees, but Alex barely noticed. He was about to start retching once again when a gentle breeze rolled up from the river and cooled his skin. The refreshing sensation slowed his breathing and calmed his nerves. The nausea also subsided to a tolerable level. His head was still pounding, but the present relief was a welcome break from the earlier torment.

He looked up at the stars, bright and twinkling in the clear night sky. He could make out the Milky Way splitting the center of the sky; an impossible observation in light-polluted cities. He sat with his knees in the dirt for the better part of an hour. The dull throbbing between his ears soon wore off as he savored the peaceful tranquility of a quiet southern night.

His head bobbed and his eyes grew heavy. Battling the migraine had been exhausting. He looked to his tent, but it was too far away. It was a nice night, he reasoned. Outside would do. He lay back in the leaves and closed his eyes, drifting off to sleep before he could second-guess his decision.

That night Alex had the most lucid dream of his life. He was fly fishing from the rocky banks of the Toccoa River, in the same spot his dad had showed him the summer before. Below him was the flat-stone peninsula he was casting from, jutting out from the bank and placing him near the center of the river. The point was clear of overhead branches, with few slick spots. A set of rapids flowed fast where the water bottlenecked around the river rock.

That was where Alex would find his fish. He cast his fly into the churning current and watched the bug float atop the water, riding the tiny waves as it floated swiftly away. He let the colorful lure drift downstream until it was almost out of sight. Then he reeled it back in, letting his line roll out in the air behind him before sending the leader back into the frothy rapids.

The dream was as tangible as the stone he stood upon. There was no memory of headaches or puking rallies or deceased fathers. In Alex's mind, he had traded one reality for another: to search for the elusive native brook trout.

The native brook trout was the pinnacle of fly fishing in North Georgia. Many anglers went their entire lives without so much as a tug at the line from the colorful species. Native brook trout, unlike rainbow and brown trout, were the only species indigenous to the Appalachian Mountains.

It wasn't uncommon for the native trout's alien cousins to be periodically stocked in the cool waters, dumped by the Department of Natural Resources at various locations across the state to meet the demands of local anglers. The rainbows and browns were strangers in a foreign land; the tenants of natural selection effectively snubbed by state officials who thought they knew better.

As could be expected, the artificial habitats where rainbow and brown trout were bred did little to prepare them for life in the open water. Stocked trout had no reason to fear suspicious lures or topside shadows. It wasn't uncommon for areas to be fished out a few hours after they had been stocked by the DNR. The newcomer fish didn't know any better, and they always took the bait. No wonder they were so easy to catch.

But the native trout were different. Rare, wily and elusive. A fisherman could spend days chasing mirages of the slippery speck only to go home empty-handed with a story about the clever fish that wouldn't bite. The native brook trout was the old fish in the stream. The one that always got away. Until that day.

Alex almost lost his fishing pole when the trout hit his lure. The line tightened and the rod bent in the direction of the fleeing fish. He gripped the rod with both hands, one firmly planted on the handle while the other worked the reel. He reeled and pulled at the rod in cycles, letting the fish run for short stretches before closing the gap between him and his catch. He carefully stepped off his stony perch and into the frigid waters of the Toccoa, following the prize downstream as he shortened the line.

Must be about ten yards out, maybe less. He reeled a little more. *Line's bulking up now. Almost there.* The fish rose to the surface. Alex marveled at the silhouette of the beast. *Jesus, that fish is huge!* The trout broke top water, breaching the surface and hurling its body into the air just a couple of yards in front of Alex. It warped and flexed and tried to lose the hook, then hit the water and ran again. The trout was easily a record fish.

Alex watched the high-flying spectacle, mouth hung open, clothes soaked up to his collar. He felt two more tugs before the exhausted trout gave in. The valiant fight had drained every ounce of energy from the fish. It was now within Alex's reach, lying dormant at the bottom of the knee-deep water. Alex reached into the water and hoisted up the enormous trout by his bottom lip. The fish didn't protest.

My God, he's heavy!

Alex fought to get the fish clear of the water, dropping his reel to lift the animal to his chest with both hands. The weight of the animal caught Alex off guard. He stumbled backward onto a slippery rock behind him and lost his balance, holding tight to the fish as he fell ass-first into the shallow water.

On any other day he might have been embarrassed, but not today. He looked down on the fish cradled in his arms and laughed himself to tears. The emotional triumph had overwhelmed him. He sat in the creek, oblivious to the frigid waters, awestruck over the prized native brook trout.

That was when his eyes began to deceive him. With each passing moment, the epic catch looked more and more like one of the forest-green hiking boots he had kicked off in his sleep. It didn't take long for Alex to realize he had slept outside all night. He rubbed the sleep from his eyes and gathered his bearings. The tent was a good twenty yards away. He massaged the crick in his neck and stared into the rushing waters, pondering the impossibly lucid experience from the riverbank.

What a dream.

Alex must have sat by the river for half an hour before heading back to his tent. He replayed the fantastic scenario in his head, even calling into question his overnight whereabouts. The dream couldn't have been more real. He still felt the weight of the hulking fish pressed against his chest and resting in his arms.

The scaly flanks of the trout were unforgettable. Deep red dots surrounded by blue halos were unlike any colors he had ever seen. The oranges, blues, and greens sparkled in the bright sunlight and dazzled his eyes. Every detail and every sensation was as palpable as the ground he was sitting on. It was the experience of a lifetime–and it was all in his head.

Alex brushed the leaves off his clothes and walked over to his campsite, dodging a steaming pile of puke along the way. He was eager to pack up his tent and hit the road to Lake Blue Ridge before the putrid smell made him sick all over again. He rolled up his sleeping bag and stuffed the rest of his gear in his backpack, then carried the first load back to the truck.

The 4x4 was parked just off the dirt road leading in, about a hundred feet from the campsite. The rusty hinges creaked as Alex swung the door open and threw his gear in the backseat. Then he searched the glove compartment for a bottle of mouthwash he kept just in case blue lights ever lit up his rearview after a night of heavy drinking. He swished and gargled until his tonsils burned, then wiped his mouth and searched for something else. His pack of cigarettes and lighter were laying on the dash. He took one out and lit it up, looking back toward his campsite on the banks of the Toccoa River.

He thought and puffed, wondering if it was a good idea to go fishing after a night like that. He stared through the morning haze towards the sparkling river waters in the distance. Lake Blue Ridge was an hour away and was full of bass, brim and catfish. He wouldn't find the trout of his dreams there. But the Toccoa was right in front of him. Why not give the river one more day?

He grabbed his rod and reel out of the truck bed and headed downstream toward the rapids he had fished the day before. There was a grassy clearing by the river there. It was a place where a fly fisherman could deliver an excellent presentation without snagging a branch overhead. The rapids moved fast enough to aerate the water, but offered little resistance to anglers wading in the river. It was as good a place as any for Alex to cast a line.

Alex knelt down by his tackle box and found the perfect fly, then tied the fuzzy little bug to his line. He stood up to survey the water. The shallows ended halfway across the river. That was where he would start. He waded out to send his first cast into the rapids. He watched the bug ride tiny waves as it floated downstream at a swift pace, then reeled it back in to dry it off and try again.

He followed the routine for an hour, casting and reeling and watching the shadows of the trees shorten on the water as the day dragged on. Then it happened. A furious hit yanked Alex's line unlike any fish he had ever hooked.

"Holy shit!" he yelled.

The torpedo at the end of the line ran hard and fast, warping Alex's pole just like the trout in his dream. He reeled and pulled without forcing the fish in, knowing that most specks would tire out in a minute, sometimes two. The trick was to keep 'em hooked until they had no fight left.

Ten yards now, maybe less. He reeled a little more.

Line's growing heavy on the reel now. Not much left. The massive shadow appeared below the surface. Déjà vu hit Alex like a ton of bricks.

"You gotta be shittin' me . . ."

Alex closed in on the war-weary fish. He couldn't believe what he was seeing with his own two eyes: a tired, defeated native brook trout, just like the one from his dream. It was at least a nine-pounder, maybe more. Easily a record catch.

That was the first time Alex's dreams came true, and it wouldn't be the last. But while the similarities between Alex's dream and reality couldn't be ignored, there were some notable differences. For starters, Alex wasn't fishing anywhere near the place his father had showed him the year before; that set of rapids was at least ten miles downstream. The scenario played out differently, too. While the high-flying trout put on an incredible show in his dream, the fish he caught the following day stayed below the surface, acting more like a fish and less like an acrobat.

Still, there was no mistaking the end result. Alex caught two fish, one in a dream, the other in reality. And while nuances existed between both experiences, one thing remained the same. The two native brook trout looked identical to one another, down to every bright red dot and shimmering orange scale.

Alex sat in his tree stand and recalled the incredible event. Then he thought about the other dreams. He watched the hours roll by as morning became afternoon, then afternoon turned into evening.

He knew he hadn't picked the best location to hang his stand. He also knew the sun would be setting soon on that cold February day.

But Alex had one of those feelings. And this was the perfect place to be.

Chapter 8: Goosebumps

It was an hour into the Donny Ford seminar when Paul's legs began to ache. He shifted his weight from one leg to another as he stood in the packed auditorium, listening to the loathsome Donny Ford sell another little piece of his soul for a paycheck.

Ford was well into the subject of his presentation - controlling one's mind with Tummo meditation–when Paul's eyes started to wander. He scanned the room and took note of the indoctrinated audience members, then returned to the digital recorder he held in his hand.

Keeping the microphone pointed toward the stage for the better part of an hour was killing his arm. The recorder was heavy for a modern device, and he wondered how old it was. He also blushed every time someone noticed him recording Donny's spiel as if he were a die-hard fan. He most certainly was not.

"So you want to know the secrets held by the Buddhist monks of Tibet for centuries?" Donny rhetorically asked as he paced the stage. "Well, I'm going to show them to you, but first we'll need to know a little more about Tummo meditation. Tummo meditation has been refined through the ages by Tibetan monks and nuns living in one of the harshest regions on planet Earth, the Himalayan Mountains. Sitting on top of the world at five miles above sea level, temperatures can range anywhere from the high 70s at lower elevations to the negative 70s along the highest peaks of world-famous mountains like K2 and Mount

Everest. These extremes can make for some rather harsh living conditions to say the least."

Donny's excitement seemed canned, thought Paul. No doubt an unavoidable side effect of giving the same presentation from one city to the next.

Donny said, "This is where Tummo meditation comes in. Tummo is a form of meditation used by the indigenous people living in these extreme environments to cope with volatile weather patterns and surroundings–particularly the cold, bone-chilling temperatures of the Himalayan region. No down winter coats, no Isotoner gloves, and no fur hats for these amazing individuals. For Tummo practitioners, clothing and accessories are optional. All they need is the power to control their own minds. Once that knowledge is obtained, the rest is just a matter of taking action."

Donny pointed the clicker toward the screen behind him. A slide featuring a line graph filled the projection screen.

"If you'll focus your attention on the screen behind me, I would like to go over a study conducted by Columbia University's Department of Neurology in early 2013. The study, which focused primarily on the neurological activity of individuals claiming to be meditation experts from the across the Himalayan range, was orchestrated to answer a simple question: Can human beings control the physiological functions of their bodies? Such functions include controlling one's heart rhythm, blood pressure, and body temperature. Put another way, can our own homeostasis be adjusted at will by making a conscious effort?"

Blank stares filled the chairs of the packed auditorium once again, but Paul found the dialogue intriguing, much to his own surprise. He turned his head to get a better listen.

"Believe me, folks," Donny said, wagging his finger at the crowd, "I was just as lost as some of you when I first started looking into this. But once I dove headfirst into how our subconscious mind works, it all started to make perfect sense. You see, the researchers at Columbia knew the subconscious mind came with an administrative password the average person didn't have access to. That's why controlling physiological functions would essentially mean learning how to hack the human mind.

"Anyone ever try to open a computer file only to get a message telling you access is denied? Well that's how a lot of our body functions work. When we're awake, there are countless tasks we perform that are considered conscious acts, like using our hands to play an instrument, our mouths to chew our food, or our legs and feet to run at the gym. These are all activities we can willfully participate in, using our conscious mind in conjunction with our body's own motor functions.

"But there are many, many things our bodies are doing behind the scenes that we typically don't have control over, at least on a conscious level. Such actions include our stomachs releasing digestive enzymes every time we eat a meal; our adrenal glands secreting hormones in response to stressful situations; or our skin's ability to help regulate internal temperature through sweating. Many of the functions I mentioned relate to the human body's homeostasis, which is the body's ability to maintain an even keel on the inside, even when the environment on the outside is changing."

"Take the cold weather," Donny explained. "It can get pretty chilly this time of year in Atlanta, right? I want you all to take a moment to think about what your body was doing on the way from your cars to the front doors of the conference center. I know most of you probably had a good 10-minute walk just to get inside the building, and I bet *none* of you were considering what your body was doing on the inside to get you here without completely freezing your butts off.

"The moment you stepped out of your heated vehicles and into the cold winter air, your bodies immediately reacted to the surrounding environment on a subconscious level. The hairs on your arms stood at attention. Goosebumps quickly covered your skin. You started to shiver and, if you got cold enough, your fingers and toes went a little numb before you entered the warm and welcoming grand lobby."

Donny paused for a split second to admire how well the presentation was going. No longer was he sweating profusely with forced enthusiasm. In the midst of a crucial presentation, he had found his natural rhythm again.

"So the big question is, why did your bodies do this? The simple answer is because the cold weather outside activated subconscious processes inside your bodies. Reactions beyond human control such as hair-raising goosebumps are actually responses left over from evolution. Goosebumps warm hairy mammals by expanding the area each hair covers above the skin, thickening their coats and providing more space for insulation. This worked wonders for prehistoric hominins, but does little for today's relatively hairless Homo sapiens.

"Shivering, however, does help modern-day humans stay warm. Shivering is the rapid-fire response of our bodies to frigid temperatures. When we become chilled, our brains tell our muscles to twitch at a quick and repetitive rate to generate heat from the accelerated muscle use. Shivering is a reflex, not unlike blinking when something comes close to your eye, and can actually help your body fight off a chill–as long as it doesn't get *too* cold outside."

Donny lowered his pitch. "This is where our friends in the Himalayas ran into problems. Even though shivering is the body's way of tricking itself into warming up, it does very little to help individuals in extremely cold environments. Our bodies are very fragile, and without an effective way to keep them close to 98.6 degrees Fahrenheit, they begin to slowly shut down and die. This left the people of the Himalayas with two choices. Either abandon the region altogether, or develop a way to adapt to the punishing weather conditions.

"Enter Tummo meditation. Tummo is the practice of taking uncontrollable bodily functions, like thermoregulation, and willfully controlling them. This technique essentially gives practitioners administrative access to the once-forbidden files within their own minds, allowing them to increase their heart rates, raise their blood pressure and adjust various nervous system responses to warm their bodies on demand.

"Now, the people of the Himalayas have been doing this for centuries to stay warm. But what if you could harness the ability to control your subconscious mind in a way that would give you the power to take your life back once and for all? What if you could use that power to strengthen your relationships, focus on new projects, set ambitious goals and achieve everything in life you've ever dreamed of?"

Paul waited for the call to action. The music got louder and another slide appeared on the projection screen behind Donny. On it was a picture of the motivational speaker with his arms crossed, wearing a million-dollar smile and touting the slogan of his new and unreasonably priced program titled, *Life Control, Mind Support.*

Predictable, thought Paul. The entire charade reminded him of a real-estate mogul who used to sell DVDs revealing the little-known secrets of buying real estate for pennies on the dollar. Both salesmen were simply putting a clever package on information that was readily available to the general public. People could research meditation practices just as easily as they could short sales and foreclosures–no checkbook required.

A new slide was on the screen hyping the "Unbelievably Low Price of $795." Paul would have mimicked some of the audience members who were blinking hard to verify they weren't seeing things, but he already knew how guys like Ford operated: introduce a set of pain points everyone can relate to, back them up with favorable data and research, and then establish one's self as the only person in the world who could solve the problem(s). Most of these time-tested scams went something like this:

"Are you sick and tired of being sick and tired?"

That sounds just like me!

"One university study showed that 78 percent of the population is tired at least three days a week."

Wow. That's a lot of people.

"Wouldn't you like to wake up feeling refreshed and rejuvenated, ready to tackle the day with a renewed thirst for life?"

Of course, I would!

"We have the solution you're looking for. Act NOW before this offer expires!"

Goodness, I better get my checkbook.

Paul couldn't stand being in the presence of such duplicitous trash. His late grandmother Leigh Anne had fallen victim to a prominent television evangelist back in the 1990s, and watching his poor grandmother die bankrupt and broken had left a noticeable scar. Over the course of five years, Leigh Anne willfully drained every last penny of her retirement savings in the hopes of purchasing good favor with the Lord, an act encouraged by a young multimillionaire television emissary named Jonas Perch.

Reverend Perch was blessed with the power of persuasion, and he didn't limit himself to retirees with healthy pensions, either. From bedridden octogenarians to the working poor, Perch was able to convince followers from all walks of life to donate everything they had–no matter how dire their financial situations might have been–directly to his megachurch.

The challenge he posed with every pitch made it hard for some to deny his logic. If your faith is strong enough, Perch would goad, prove it by making a donation. Perch called this planting seeds of faith. If you *really* have faith, the Lord is going to take care of you financially, why be hesitant to tithe? Go on ahead now; plant that seed and watch your heavenly fortunes grow.

Of course, Paul never saw anything wrong with the able-bodied giving one-tenth of their income to their favorite religious organization. But what the so-called reverend was doing was quite different. For Jonas Perch, anything less than everything wasn't good enough.

Leigh Anne ran across Jonas Perch's Power Hour of Prayer while channel surfing late one night. The religious program aired on the East Coast at midnight–an ironic timeslot for viewers familiar with John 3:19. Unfortunately, Leigh Anne never made the connection.

It was no coincidence that Jonas's favorite time to solicit sanctimonious praise kept him hidden from a large segment of the general public. He didn't have the capacity to stand up to the kind of public scrutiny a daytime orator was subjected to, but the generally afflicted audience drawn to his late-night pitch did little to expose his deeds.

The anointed Reverend Perch would persuade people like Leigh Anne to "take a step out in faith by giving to the Lord," which was just a clever way of asking the pious for a check. In return for their donations, Mr. Perch would promise everlasting peace, answered prayers and liberation from the troubles and strife of this world.

If liberation meant his congregation would have their promises fulfilled the moment they left this world, then his message was actually spot on. But until that day came, Perch was intent on making sure his pockets were lined and his jet was ready for takeoff the moment he took a notion to hit up some seedy prostitutes on the outskirts of Las Vegas.

Paul watched his grandmother drive herself to bankruptcy, and he couldn't stand to listen to another Jonas Perch sucker people desperate for answers out of their hard-earned money any longer. He set the recorder on the ledge behind him and left the auditorium. He was thirsty anyway, and a leisurely stroll to the nearest water fountain seemed like a more logical solution than paying someone $795 to teach him how to convince himself water wasn't the answer.

Chapter 9:
It's Curtains for You, Donny!

If Donny Ford had lived in the 19th century, he would have made a handsome living as a traveling snake oil salesman, roaming through the American West in search of credulous settlers desperate for the answers to the hardships and troubles they faced.

In those days, promoting dubious products like liniments, oils and potions was only a matter of talking a big game and putting in the time on the road. These salesmen moved from town to town, drawing crowds and touting the latest cure-all medications guaranteed to alleviate any ailments inherent to life in the Old West. For most melancholic townsfolk, the feigned excitement of a traveling apothecary was all it took to convince them to cough up their nickels and cents.

Snake oil salesmen had their presentations down to an exact science. Their wagons were rolling billboards, with every square inch dedicated to promotional hype and propaganda. Their potion bottles, containers and vials intrigued audiences with impressive copy that promised absolute cures for the most common aches and ailments.

While one-man operations did exist, the truly savvy salesmen would put a plant or two in the crowd. These accomplices would go along with the act, transforming from feverous farmers to healthy product advocates after guzzling down whatever potion the salesmen were hawking that day.

Donny might have skated by on a clever pitch and a smile in the good ol' days, but selling dubious products to the masses in the 2020s took a more concerted effort. No longer were people disconnected from civilization by mountain chains and unsettled prairies. Information that used to take days or weeks to obtain was now available through digital devices at the drop of a hat.

A simple query into the validity of a new product through a person's smart watch or voice-command device could verify the truth or falsehood behind any new offering in a matter of seconds. The Digital Age had created a world of connectivity where individuals around the globe were more informed, educated and enlightened–circumstances that made it very difficult for people like Donny to sell their goods and services.

Donny knew the material at the heart of his latest program offered little to no value for most people with an Internet connection. But appealing to curiosity? Now that was something he could work with. If there was one thing Donny was sure of, it was that no matter how far humanity progressed toward rational thinking, claiming to have solved any one of life's great mysteries would always pique the curiosity of poor souls who were desperately seeking answers.

Paul washed his hands and listened to Donny's voice echoing through the intercom outside the men's bathroom. "Does this guy ever shut the fuck up?" he muttered, prompting a look of shock from the man at the sink beside him.

In Paul's eyes, Donny's message was already spent. As he commenced the slow walk back toward the auditorium, Paul couldn't help but wonder why his new boss would want him to attend such a stupid seminar in the first place.

Ryan Tanner wasn't someone Paul knew a lot about, but he had picked up on the rumors floating around Asteria over the last several weeks. As public relations director for the multi-billion-dollar drug company, Tanner was in charge of cultivating positive interactions between the Big-Pharma behemoth and the general public. The position meant Tanner was responsible for managing media contacts and press releases, overseeing online publications and Internet forums, heading up sponsored events, and doing everything else necessary to ensure the company's upcoming release of its latest miracle drug Ocula was well received by the general public.

Lately, however, Tanner had been suffering from a professional identity crisis. While his job description failed to mention anything about mind control techniques, neurological disorders, biochemistry or psychic phenomenon, Tanner had taken an exceptional interest in such topics, devoting countless hours at work to his new hobby, with little explanation given to his subordinates. His superiors, on the other hand, knew exactly where their budget spend was going. This made the long-time PR director's devotion to pseudoscience and the occult the perfect fodder for bored office staff and part-time conspiracy theorists.

Of course, one could just chalk Tanner's behavior up to thinking outside the box. Perhaps his interest in Ford's mind-over-matter message was actually an investigative look into the validity of mind control techniques that could potentially land Asteria some new customers down the road. Still not the best use of the company coffers, thought Paul, but who was he to question their spending?

As Paul got closer to the double doors of the auditorium, he heard a loud disruption coming from within. It was the sound of a rambunctious crowd shouting at the stage, with jeers and inquiries and insults directed toward the star of the show. Paul swung the auditorium doors open and stepped inside.

"Don't you think you should answer the question?"

"What were you doing that night in Vegas?"

"Did you murder Bill Stevens?"

"We all have a right to know, asshole!"

The scene was chaotic. Donny Ford fought to maintain an even keel on stage, but every time he started to address one question, he was cut off by another. The audience had turned rabid, stirred up by the apparent ringers for the media who had infiltrated the seminar. Donny had used the same tactic to provide social proof for his programs before. The irony was not lost on him.

"Okay, okay, everybody. Just calm down for a minute," Donny tried to explain, but the crowd wasn't having it.

"Why should we listen to you?"

"Just tell us the truth!"

"Answer the question! Did you murder Bill Stevens or not?"

For the first time in his life, Donny was at a loss for words–at least on the outside. On the inside, he couldn't stop thinking about Maria Moreno, the journalist from Action News Atlanta who had caught him off-guard earlier that day.

That wicked bitch.

Donny looked out on the crowd. The angry and frustrated voices culminated into one large and tumultuous roar, growing louder and louder as the ringing in Donny's ears dwarfed every other sound in the room. His eyes sank down in dismay as he rubbed his brow. Nothing he could do or say would bring the crowd back to his side.

Donny took the clip off his microphone, tossed it to the ground and walked toward the curtains. An ascending chorus of boos set the tone for his march backstage. Normally such a vicious sendoff would have sent Donny into the grips of depression, but the ringing in his ears had quickly grown so loud that he couldn't focus on anything else. The aching at the front of his head was getting worse by the second. The pain spread over his face and past his temples, wrapping his entire crown with a sickening sting that was quickly becoming too much to bear.

"Marci! Marci!" Donny yelled. His assistant rounded the corner and met Donny in the hall.

"What's wrong, Don?"

"My head," Donny said. "I need something. Motrin. Pills. Anything."

"I'll round something up right now. I am *so* sorry, Don." She left the room.

What a disaster, thought Donny. What began as a hopeful comeback post-Stevens had morphed into a trial by mob, likely set in motion by his fans over at the local newsroom. *Sons of bitches. Every last one of them.* His anger exacerbated the pain, and it didn't take long for a full-blown migraine to set in.

Donny moaned. "Goddamnit, not this. Not now."

He sat on a folding chair backstage, his head resting in his hands. His blood pressure was through the roof. Beads of sweat streamed down his brow and through his fingers, dripping onto the floor. He raised his thumb and finger to rub his eyes, but the fierce burning of salt and sweat quickly jerked his hand back.

Then the nausea came. The first wave hit him before he had time to react. He leaned forward and vomited all over the floor in front of him, not a single care given to where he was or who may have been watching.

Fuck. This is not good. Donny had felt this way once before, on the night of a business trip to Las Vegas the previous year. It was the last time he saw Bill Stevens alive.

Donny rocked in the chair and tried to calm his nerves, but it was pointless. He knew exactly what was coming next.

Relief. The pain, the sweats, the vomiting . . . as quickly as they had appeared on the scene, they vanished like thieves in the night. Relief should have been a good thing, but Donny was not happy. In fact, Donny had never been more afraid in his life. That's because he knew what had happened last time.

But none of that mattered now. Before Donny could worry any longer, his eyes rolled back into their sockets and his body went limp. He fell out of his chair and hit the floor face-first. The once-influential salesman had reached a new low, lying next to a puddle of his own puke while the boos of his one-time fans echoed in the distance.

Chapter 10: The Hacker's Device

Paul couldn't believe what he was seeing. He stood in the noisy auditorium, the crowd still reeling from the drastic turn of events Donny Ford's latest presentation had taken. Most of the loyal audience members sat speechless in their seats, with a few dissenters already leaving. Gossip circles had started to form. Some defended their fearless leader; others chastised his alleged behavior. Regardless of their current positions, none of them could have predicted the unexpected usurping of the once-revered speaker that morning.

Karma's a bitch, thought Paul. In his eyes, Donny's downfall was a long time coming. People like Ford were leeches on society, and judging by the turmoil in the auditorium, it looked like several of his former supporters had finally plucked the parasite from their thin skins.

As for Paul, he just wanted to grab his boss's voice recorder and get back to Asteria before the rest of Donny's flock stampeded toward the door. He squeezed down the aisles and made his way to the ledge where he had left the device. He didn't see the recorder. Paul's fears were realized as he drew closer to where he was standing.

"You've got to be kidding me," Paul said.

He stood on his tiptoes to see if the recorder had been knocked behind the ledge. There was a soda can or two, but no device. He frantically looked down the wall where he was standing. More trash. He dropped to his hands and knees to peer under the row of chairs in front of him. Paul wondered who would steal such a bulky piece of crap. Didn't everyone have a voice recorder on their cellphones these days?

Paul was about to give up when he caught a glimpse of something rectangular under one of the seats several rows down. He chased down the lead, kneeling in a flurry of candy wrappers and program flyers.

It was the recorder.

Paul breathed a huge sigh of relief. "Thank God," he said. Someone must have knocked it off the ledge during the mayhem. There was no telling what would have happened had he gone back to Asteria without the recorder, but he was sure it would have involved a pink slip.

The new guy gets his first out-of-office assignment and comes back empty handed? Not a good way to build a rapport with the higher-ups.

Paul sized up the damage. The battery compartment latch on the back was broken, putting the internal workings of the instrument in plain view. He looked closer and noticed there were no battery slots. Instead, a tiny blue pipeline formed a perimeter around the buzzing internal components. Paul thought it looked like one of those new liquid-cooling systems he had read about in an article about smart phones. The rest of the space was occupied by a printed circuit board, complete with capacitors, resistors, three chips, and a massive central processor.

It was apparent the device was more than a voice recorder, and if that were the case, there had to be another way to activate its hidden function. Paul inspected the device from top to bottom. On the side below the volume controls was a sliding tab covering a small, square button. It didn't appear to be pressed in;

Paul thought it must have clicked off when the device fell. He pushed the button back into place.

Paul immediately regretted the decision. Piercing sound waves shot deep into his ears like tiny needles hemming the linings of his eardrums. Waves of nausea twisted his stomach and rose to his throat. The high-frequency squeal made it impossible for Paul to hear anything else in the auditorium, but no one standing around him seemed to be affected.

Paul pressed the button beneath the tab and the screeching stopped. He stuck a finger in his ear and shook out the ringing. It was a strange revelation, because the faux recorder hadn't made a sound prior to it taking a nasty hit. He figured the now-busted case had been doing a pretty good job of hiding whatever the machine was originally designed for. A covert device hidden in a fully functional voice recorder. Some real cloak-and-dagger shit. And Paul had just broken it.

Paul checked his watch. It was 11:17 a.m. The seminar was supposed to run through 12, break for lunch, and then wrap up by 2 p.m. The way Paul saw it, he had plenty of time to stop by a hardware store, pick up some supplies to fix the broken tab, and have everything ready for Tanner by the time he came calling later that afternoon. It was as good a plan as any. He stuffed the recorder and latch in his pocket and left.

***

Paul emptied the bag full of supplies on his desk: a tube of super glue, a pocket-sized vial of black auto-body touchup paint, Ryan Tanner's enigmatic electronic device, and the busted latch that went with it. He had stopped by an auto parts store on his way back from the seminar to pick up a few essentials that, with a little luck, would cover up his clumsy tracks.

Paul was apprehensive about the whole ordeal. The Donny Ford seminar was his first big assignment, and he had blown it. It didn't matter that the seminar was cut short by several hours, because Paul had also busted the one piece of equipment Tanner had entrusted him with. What's more was that the potentially career-ending accident led to another puzzling matter altogether.

First, there was the obvious question of why Ryan Tanner, a PR guy for a nationwide pharmaceutical company, would be the slightest bit interested in a person like Donny Ford. If Tanner were a true believer in Ford's programs, then Tanner's interest in the brand would make sense. But if Tanner's interest was strictly personal, did it make sense for him to ask the new guy to go to a seminar on the clock and record it for him?

Actually, it kind of does, Paul thought as he got to work on the device. Organizations like Asteria Pharmaceuticals had a tendency to adopt lax rules for the most productive members of upper management. Lenient morning policies; lunchtime cocktail hours; afternoon golf outings masquerading as business meetings . . . it was all part of the game at Asteria. As long as senior salesmen closed clients and promotional teams provided consistent returns, the C-suite was willing to look the other way. Asteria cared about one thing, and one thing only: results. Nothing else seemed to matter.

Still, Paul couldn't ignore the strange request. The boardroom might have been used to company expenses like tennis matches and Braves tickets, but Tanner's behavior must have stuck out a mile. Paul had previously chalked up the gossip surrounding Tanner to colorful elaborations about a strange PR man prompted by residual office boredom. He could hear the cross-cubicle whispers now.

"Psst. Hey, Pete. Don't tell anyone, but someone told me Tanner used to hack people up for the CIA."

"Like, on computers?"

"No, not a hacker. He literally hacked–people–up. Like, with a saw."

"*Jesus* . . . I knew something was up with that guy. Did you see him this morning with that book on the principles of neurological surgery? What the *fuck* does he need that for?!"

"I don't know, man. Maybe when he's hacking 'em up he starts headfirst. But word is he still does some covert shit for the CIA. That's why he's gone all the time."

The rumor mill never stopped churning. But after covering his first assignment for Tanner, Paul was starting to think the absurd stories about Tanner's obsession with mind control actually made some sense.

Then there was the device Paul was trying to put back together. What exactly did he have his hands on? The secrecy behind the covert recorder gave him the creeps. Why lie and tell him it was just a voice recorder? What was it really supposed to accomplish at the seminar? And why were his ears still ringing from the intolerable squeal it produced the moment he pressed the covert button on the side of the case?

Maybe I'm just paranoid, thought Paul. He dismissed the questions for now as his tidy little repair came together. He had already superglued the jaded latch back into place and was waiting for it to cure. If he could get it back to like-new condition, hopefully the man upstairs would understand the damage to the device was an honest mistake.

Suddenly the desk phone rang. Paul hastily answered.

"Hello?"

"Hi, Paul. How'd everything go this morning?"

It was Tanner.

"Ah, perfect, sir. Just great. I really enjoyed the presentation, really interesting–"

"Enough bullshit, Paul. Did you record everything?"

Damn. Paul hadn't been back thirty minutes, and Ryan already wanted his toy back? What a disaster. Kiss that flashy new job goodbye. Didn't even make it to the six-month evaluation. Conflict at home would surely follow. It wouldn't matter what the reason for the firing was, either. In this economy, excuses didn't really get you anywhere.

"Paul?" Tanner was impatient.

"Yessir, I've got it. I recorded everything."

"Good. I need it. Get up here right now. You've got five minutes." Tanner hung up the phone.

Paul sighed. "Well, fuck."

Chapter 11: Bluffing

Paul opened the door to Ryan Tanner's office. "You asked to see me, sir?"

Tanner waved Paul in, then continued barking into his phone. A reporter on the other end of the line was the unsuspecting subject of today's wrath. Paul took a seat in one of the uncomfortable leather chairs facing Tanner's desk and waited for Tanner to wrap up the call.

To Paul, Ryan Tanner's office was a paradox. He looked around the room, finding it hard to distinguish between the Director of Public Relation's workplace and a college dorm. Clutter was everywhere. Books were stacked haphazardly on each corner of his desk. Papers were strewn across the floor. Burger wrappers and soda cans overflowed from the trashcan. Even the man's $1,200 suit was disheveled. It was obvious Tanner had been living out of his office.

Paul skimmed the frames on the walls. A mixture of press releases, magazine covers, and newspaper clippings showcased the biggest stories Tanner had pushed through to the media. Pretty normal for a PR guy. What wasn't normal, however, were the books on mind control.

Paul focused on the precarious stack of texts sitting at the edge of Tanner's desk. *Believing In Your Brain*, *Mind Over Matter*, *Clinical Neurology*, *Why We Dream* . . . not exactly required reading for people who talk to the media every day.

Tanner's eyes caught Paul meticulously going over the book titles sitting on his desk. Tanner wrapped up his call by politely telling the young man on the other end of the line to go fuck himself, then he slammed the phone down on the receiver. His demeanor changed on a dime.

"Paul!" Tanner said. "How's everything going today?"

"Fine, sir. I was going to say, this is the first time I've been–"

"Did you bring what I asked for?"

Paul reached in his pocket for the fake voice recorder Tanner wanted back. The moment of truth was upon him. He slid the device across Tanner's desk as if he were playing high-stakes poker, trying to pass a pair of twos off for a full house.

Tanner glanced down at the device, then back up at Paul, calling his bluff. His stern appearance did little to conceal his agitation.

"This thing looks like shit."

So much for that, thought Paul.

"What did you do, drop this thing in the fucking parking lot on your way to the seminar this morning? Then kick it around a little? Then kick it around a little more with that geriatric security guard out front, what's his name?"

"Walter."

"Yeah, Walter. You and Walter think it would be funny to have a fucking soccer match with my recorder this morning, Paul?"

Tanner had officially blown his top, probably for the umpteenth time that day. All Paul could do was sit there and take it; he knew he had screwed the pooch on this one. But Tanner's behavior was revealing. Paul had busted the latch on an alleged dinky voice recorder, and Tanner was reacting like he had backed into his Mercedes.

And what was so important about that stupid seminar anyway? If Tanner was so interested in Donny Ford's discourse, why didn't he just buy Ford's latest book and add it to the already-impressive stack of pseudoscientific shit that was currently sitting on his desk? What was so important about getting that morning's presentation on tape?

It didn't matter, Paul decided. He was given an assignment and he had dropped the ball. At least he still had a couple of empty storage boxes stacked beside his cubicle. Those would come in handy soon enough.

Tanner continued to murmur obscenities while he looked over the device. He turned it over to the back and glared at Paul's handiwork. His consternation quickly turned to curiosity.

"Whose shoddy craftsmanship is this?" Tanner asked.

"Sir, I'm really sorry. I was trying to fix your recorder. I know it looks bad, but–"

Tanner popped the plastic off with ease, and once again the device began emitting a high-pitched frequency Paul couldn't bear. Tanner sat still and watched as Paul cringed and contorted, covering his ears and gnashing his teeth.

Tanner asked, "Is everything okay?" but Paul couldn't hear a word.

The reaction got Tanner's attention. He could hear the noise, too, but it was subtle and innocuous. Nothing that would warrant a response as exaggerated as Paul's.

Tanner leaned back in his chair. He looked down at the device, then up at Paul, and then he smiled.

Chapter 12: Answers at Asteria

What had started off as a tumultuous morning was turning into a fortuitous day, at least in the eyes of Ryan Tanner. His battered device continued to emit debilitating ultrasonic sounds only Paul could hear. It was like playing with a dog whistle, and Paul was the pet. The victim held tight to his ears, begging his tormentor to stop.

"WILL YOU PLEASE TURN THAT OFF?!" Paul yelled.

Tanner obliged. He pressed the small button on the bottom of the device. In an instant, the noise vanished, and Paul was left with hissing ears and a splitting headache.

"What in the *hell* is that thing?" Paul asked.

"This little thing? Oh, I'm sure you've got plenty of questions about it."

Tanner stood up and walked around his desk. "Tell me, Paul. What's it like? The noise filling every fold and fissure of all that gray matter between those ears of yours. Can you tell me what it's like?" Paul could hear Tanner, but Tanner's voice sounded like he was talking underwater.

Tanner asked, "Is it like standing next to a freight train barreling down the tracks; the wheels grinding against the solid-steel rails; feeling the energy radiating from thousands of tons of cold metal speeding by you; the sound of such immense power so palpable that you feel like your head is going to explode? Is that what it's like?"

Tanner grabbed the back of Paul's chair and shook it.

"What the hell!"

"Calm down, Paul. I'm just fucking with you." Tanner paced the room. "I know you don't feel well. Let me guess. You're nauseous? Head's pounding? Feeling a little irritated? *Really* irritated?"

Paul shook his head in agreement, but he didn't utter a word. His green complexion gave Tanner the sense the poor boy was going to puke at any moment.

"Try not to make a mess on my floor, Paul. It'll pass. All of it will pass. What you're experiencing is just a temporary side effect of the device you recently had an encounter with."

Paul's eyes searched for answers before looking down at the mystery device Tanner was carrying in his right hand.

"I'm sure by now you've figured out this isn't just a voice recorder," Tanner said. He pointed the device at Paul. "If I really gave a damn about that blowhard Donny Ford, or what he had to say about anything–*which I don't*–I would have just picked up his rants online."

"Then what is it?" Paul asked.

"Tell me, Paul. Do you think I'm oblivious to the water-cooler gossip that's been spreading like a BSL-4 virus in this building?"

"What do you mean?"

"Oh, come on, Paul! You know exactly what I'm talking about! The stories about Tanner searching for ways to control minds while losing his own in the process; Tanner's quest for enlightenment through motivational seminars and conspiracy newsletter subscriptions; Tanner's mind-reading poker-wizard retirement plan . . . you haven't heard any of this?"

"Well, maybe a little–"

"Of course you've heard it. If you hadn't, I'd think you were out of work for the last six months."

"Sir, I just started–"

"The truth is," Tanner said, "like the best rumors, they're not completely unfounded. Take for instance the concern over my recent interest in the realm of mind control. It's absolutely true. Sure, I've been a little obsessed with the topic for some time now, but not without reason." He walked behind Paul and locked the door.

Tanner continued, "I'd never really given much thought into claims of psychic phenomena until a few months ago. Mind reading, telepathy, mediums, spirit guides . . . I always called bullshit on stories like that. And to some extent, I still do. Ninety-nine percent of those cases are nothing more than cheap parlor tricks that have been around for centuries. Believe me, tricking people into believing something you want them to believe is one thing I *do* know something about. But these so-called psychics who claim to have a window into some mystical world no one else has access to?" Tanner said derisively, "Please. I have yet to see a single shred of scientific evidence that would even begin to explain such a phenomenon. Now, does that mean everyone claiming to have psychic powers is a complete fraud? Not entirely, because what they lack in magical powers, they more than make up for with their powers of persuasion."

Paul was starting to feel a little better. His headache had become almost nonexistent in the few minutes since Tanner had deactivated the device. Still, the short-lived experience had drained his energy. Fatigued, he weighed in on Tanner's rant.

"So you used to think this was all nonsense, but now you don't?" Paul asked.

Tanner snorted. "Well, now, Paul, I don't want you to get the wrong idea here. If a gypsy claims you're being haunted by evil spirits and she can make them go away for a small fee, by all means, check your back pocket to make sure you've still got your wallet and then get the hell outta there, because you're talking to a scammer. But is mind control even a possibility? And if it *is* a possibility, can't it also be synthesized, or better yet, monetized?"

Tanner leaned back in his chair, locking his fingers together on his chest. "Like I said before, I used to think all of this was little more than fodder for sci-fi novels and late-night television. But that was before our little company here started receiving some interesting clinical-trial feedback."

"Wait," Paul said. "Asteria Pharmaceuticals received feedback about mind control during clinical trials? Trials involving which product?"

Tanner looked at the door and checked the lock. Then he answered, "It was a small percentage of users involved in the Ocula trials. Apparently, the sleep medication had some unintended side effects."

Paul was speechless.

Tanner shook a finger. "And it's worth mentioning that the observations actually had little to do with the common understanding of mind control. You know, none of that hand-waving and mind-trickery shit you see in the movies."

"That's kind of what I was thinking," Paul said. "So what exactly were the findings?"

Tanner leaned forward. "A very small percentage of respondents told us that after being on the medication for varying lengths of time, their *dreams* started to come true."

Chapter 13:
Far from a Sugar Pill

Paul was already halfway to the door when he decided to turn around and give Tanner one last piece of his mind.

"I don't know what your angle is, Tanner. But if you expect me to buy into this bullshit, you've got the wrong guy. What–somebody tell you I haven't slept in days? You and all your cohorts get together and decide to mess with the new guy? Drug my coffee? I never played this frat boy shit in college, and no job's worth putting up with it now."

Tanner asked calmly, "Are you done?"

Paul shook his head in stubborn affirmation. "Yeah. I think I'm done."

He already knew he was out of a job, but *damn* did it feel good to tell the man where to stick it. The sense of calm that came after blowing off such a tremendous amount of steam far outweighed any apprehensions he had about being loosed back into the wilds of unemployment.

Paul turned again to leave. "Don't worry," he said, "I'll have my office cleaned out by 5 o'clock today. I've still got plenty of boxes."

"Sit down, Paul."

Paul looked back at Tanner, puzzled by the command.

"I said sit down. We're not through talking yet."

No way Tanner could pull off such a joke without cracking at this point. Even the most experienced prankster would have called the whole thing off the moment his victim exploded in a rant of frustration before tossing his career out the window. It was clear the PR man wasn't kidding.

Paul walked back to the chair in front of Tanner's desk and slowly took a seat, suddenly finding it hard to discern between anger and embarrassment. He gripped the armrests and braced for the ass chewing of the century. "What could we possibly have to talk about?" he asked.

"The program, of course."

"The program . . ."

"Maybe I'm getting ahead of myself," Tanner said. "Let's try and walk it back for a moment. You were skeptical about the dreamers in the Ocula program? The ones who said the sleeping pill made their dreams come true?"

Paul nodded.

"Right, well. Can't blame you there. You'll have to forgive my candor. I've never had to explain this kind of phenomena to a program outsider. Naturally, you're skeptical." Tanner pulled a pack of cigarettes from his desk drawer and lit one up. "I know you're well aware of the rigorous clinical trials pharmaceutical companies are required to conduct before obtaining FDA approval. Well, Ocula was no different. Asteria has spent the last five years and over $400 million developing this sleep medication, and that doesn't include the R&D involved in antisense therapy, either. All in all, I'd say the first product to come out of Asteria's genetic-modification line has cost the company well over a billion dollars. That's a modest estimate."

Paul wasn't impressed. "Expensive R&D. That's no surprise."

There was a steely edge to Tanner's voice. "I don't know if I can emphasize this enough, Paul, but the future of this entire company was riding on the success of this new product. It's true Asteria has had a long-established relationship with the FDA. But that doesn't necessarily mean clinical-trial failures are guaranteed FDA approval. An average one out of every hundred drugs makes it through the crucible through traditional channels, and much of our capital had been tied up in research and development. Under normal circumstances we'd cut the FDA a check and move on, but this time was different, and pay-to-play wasn't an option.

"Still, it was a calculated risk. It was also a risk the board of directors thought worthy of taking almost two decades ago when the notion of antisense therapy was first brought to the table. You have to remember, antisense isn't some new innovation. Everyone who's been in the drug business long enough can rattle off a half-dozen companies that have lost their asses chasing after the gene-silencing therapy."

"I remember hearing about Heathero Pharmaceuticals going belly-up a couple of years ago," Paul said.

"That's right. Problem was, the Heathero people were idealists," Tanner said. "Trying to cure the world's worst diseases without any consideration for the bottom line. Two bad quarters and that was all she wrote." Tanner talked and puffed away. "I don't know if you're a poker player or not, Paul, but let's just say the pot odds for Asteria were looking good at the time. Especially after the company devised a way to develop the most innovative drug treatment program of the 21st century, while at the same time cornering a section of the market the so-called gene jockeys at companies like Heathero weren't even considering."

"You're talking about sleeping pills?"

"*Genetically enhanced* sleeping pills," Tanner said. "So the CDC estimates around ten million Americans are on prescription sleeping medication; certainly no small number. Now, combine that with Americans who don't have a prescription for sleeping pills, but still can't get the shuteye they need on their own. I'm talking about insomniacs who rely on over-the-counter treatments found in cold remedies and cough syrups. You know, stuff like diphenhydramine, doxylamine . . . even melatonin pills have grown popular with people who are reluctant to see a doctor, but are just fine with grabbing something off the shelf at the local grocery store. Our current estimates have the total number of Americans suffering from various types of sleep disorders around forty million–and that's a conservative guess."

Paul gazed up and remembered something a coworker had told him. "Pete Williams mentioned the investor proposal for Ocula; said he helped draft it some years back. He also said raising money for Ocula was easier than shooting fish in a bucket."

"It's fish in a barrel."

"I know," Paul said. "But this is Pete Williams we're talking about here."

"Yeah. Pete's not the sharpest knife in the drawer, but he's right. Raising money for Ocula was the easy part; it was always the clinical trials that had us worried. How familiar are you with the FDA's clinical trial process?"

"Not too familiar, really."

"I see." Tanner snuffed out his smoke. "Phase One is the primary safety and profiling stage of FDA approval, and consists of anywhere from twenty to one hundred volunteers. The first stage taking place after primary clinical research can be a real nail-biter. It also sets the tone for phases two and three. Lucky for us, Ocula passed Phase One with flying colors, proving to be a safe treatment while only exhibiting mild side effects that were common to all medications, like nausea, upset stomach . . . things of that nature.

"So Ocula wasn't lethal, but we weren't out of the woods yet. Phase Two was all about the efficacy of the drug being tested. This phase involved several hundred volunteers, and was designed to put our Big-Pharma promises to the test. Did the drug do what the company said it was going to? Was it an effective medication and did it treat the symptoms it was designed to treat? If the answer was no, the drug was essentially labeled a sugar pill and disapproved."

Tanner couldn't hide his excitement. "The amazing thing about Ocula was the fact that it did *everything* it was designed to do. Tell me, Paul, do you know exactly what Ocula was originally designed to do?"

Paul shrugged. "I heard something in the office about perfect sleep cycles, but never thought that much about–"

"Ha! Perfection doesn't do Ocula justice, Paul. Our medication inhibits the primary gene identified with restless sleep cycles and insomnia, and effectively turns it off. The result is an untarnished internal sleep mechanism that is free to engage in a perfect eight-hour sleep cycle. Ocula proves to the world that we are no longer bound by restraints of a cruel and indifferent genetic lottery. What we've done here is the medicinal breakthrough of the 21st century."

Tanner took out another smoke and offered one to Paul. He declined, and Tanner lit up again. "That brings us to Phase Three," Tanner said. "The final phase of clinical trials. More people, broader demographics, and more scenarios, like mixing Ocula with other medications to test for possible side effects. During phase three, we monitored *exactly* two thousand individuals for adverse reactions to Ocula, and found that only twelve volunteers–0.006 percent to be exact–suffered from a single side effect of the drug: the onset of migraine headaches."

Nothing about the numbers shocked Paul. He already knew most drugs came with a whirlwind of side effects, some of which were contradictory to the conditions they were designed to treat. Ibuprofen might cause headaches, antacids could cause heartburn, antidepressants might worsen depression . . . for every single drug on the market, there were at least half a dozen possible side effects listed on the back of the bottle. To Paul, it sounded like Ocula had passed the clinical trials with flying colors.

"You believed the headaches were part of a larger problem with the drug?" Paul asked.

"Most certainly," Tanner said. "We always stay in touch with all of the clinical-trial participants until the FDA has approved a drug. If a problem's reported, we want to know about it long before the Feds do. Turns out there were twelve participants who muddied the waters of the otherwise-perfect Ocula trials, and we wanted to know why. So we asked ourselves: Why were these patients reporting debilitating migraines, when 1,988 people using Ocula had a positive response? They had no documented history of chronic or recurring headaches, and then BAM! These people were rushing to emergency rooms, picking up painkillers at their local pharmacies–"

"Wait. You were *following* them?"

"Of course! Why wouldn't we? One of the requirements of participation in the clinical trials was to check in with progress reports once a month for the next 36 months. Thing is, it only took about two months for all twelve to drop off the radar. No returned phone calls, no emails, nothing." Tanner's eyebrows snapped up. "Our fault, really. Sending them packing with enough Ocula to last a year. Anyway, we had to find out more about the twelve outliers, so naturally, we followed them."

Paul's chest tightened as a sense of foreboding sank in. That same feeling of dread he had when Donny Ford stated his intention to teach the world about mind control was starting to crawl all over him once again. The hairs on the back of his neck stood high and firm. His skin tingled as he resisted the urge to squirm in his seat. He looked past Tanner in a haze, his breaths growing short and shallow as he realized he was sitting in the presence of a very bad man.

But Paul couldn't let Tanner know that. He snapped out of the trance and tried to hide his apprehension. Reticently, he asked, "The reports of headaches. Did those coincide with the dreams?"

"Well, now, those are details we'll get to later," Tanner said, glaring at Paul. "But first, we're going to take a little trip."

Paul went with his first instinct. *Run.*

Paul threw his chair behind him and made a run for the door. The effort was useless. He hadn't made it three steps before his head began to swim and his vision blurred. Then the pain came. He looked back at Tanner, who was speaking in garbled tones as his body drifted quickly out of consciousness.

"This device usually just works on our outliers," Tanner said.

Paul's body hit the floor. Tanner walked over, marveling at the effect the device was having on the new hire. He nudged Paul with his foot. His subordinate was out cold.

"But for some reason," Tanner said, "it works on you, too."

Chapter 14: Bienvenido a la Jungla

First there was nothing. Everything was black. Pitch black. No sights, no sounds, no smell, no fear. Nothing. That's where Paul was. In that eternal void, where time and cognizance ceased to exist.

Until a sound. A loud, dull, whirling sound, like a heavy blade cutting through the air in steady tempo, growing louder by the second. It was overwhelming, but Paul embraced it, because at least it was something.

Then came a feeling. Shaking. Unstable. The shuddering wasn't caused by nerves or fear or drugs; it was where Paul was sitting. His seat trembled as the heavy blades chopped overhead, louder and closer with each passing second.

Paul tried bringing one hand up to rub his eyes, but was surprised to find it was firmly duct-taped to the other. He looked out a small window to his side. A thick jungle canopy was a few hundred feet below. They were moving fast and low, the constant changes in altitude feeling less like a helicopter ride and more like a cheap rollercoaster, the kind kids made up stories about flying off the tracks, where mass devastation and carnage ensued. Paul was feeling sick all over again.

"We'll be landing in just a few minutes, Mr. Tanner," the pilot said over the intercom.

Great, thought Paul. I'm in a helicopter with that asshole. Paul's memories came flooding back as the helicopter flew to an unknown destination. He peered around the leather seat in front of him. Tanner was sitting up front, a couple of seats up from where he was in the back of the chopper.

It was a nice chopper, too. Wood-grain trim around the windows and tray tables, bucket seats on the port side, long leather couch on starboard . . . this kind of luxury didn't come cheap. If they had cut back on the opulence, Paul supposed, they could have built a helicopter that flew a little smoother.

Tanner looked back, noticing Paul was awake. "Ah, Mr. Freeman! How nice of you to finally join us! Did you sleep well?"

"What do you think?"

Tanner ignored the quip. "I know you've still got a lot of questions, but don't worry. We'll arrive at the facility soon."

"What facility?"

Tanner pointed out the starboard window. "There."

Paul squinted through the bright sunlight outside to see a small clearing in the jungle. As the chopper closed in, Paul could make out a single-level building. The windowless concrete structure was built into a steadily sloping hill, with the side furthest from the entrance completely underground, almost like a bunker.

He didn't see a single road leading in or out, no visible power lines, and no antennas or satellite dishes covering the exposed portion of the building's flat roof. What he did see, however, was a large chain-link fence separating the development from the surrounding jungle, topped with barbed wire and running the perimeter of the clearing.

There was no helipad, either. As the helicopter made its descent into the middle of the field about fifty yards in front of the facility, Paul saw a large steel door at the building's entrance swing open. Out marched half a dozen guards sporting AR-15s, tactical gear and flak jackets. These weren't the penny-loafer-wearing security guards back at Asteria. The sentinels met the helicopter as the engine shut off and the rotors slowed. Tanner stood up and stretched before addressing Paul.

"Ready to go?"

Paul looked out the window toward the guards and had a brief glimpse into his childhood. He remembered how his career-military father taught his kids to be fearless; to suck up the pain; that crying was for little girls and real men weren't afraid of shit. He desperately wanted to act like he didn't fear for his life, but rattled nerves and a shaking voice were making it hard for him to play the part.

"Tanner . . . Can I call my wife first? Just once. It'll be a quick call. I don't know how long I've been out, but–"

"Two days. Well, two days and change."

"Okay, well, my kid . . . is there any way–"

"'fraid not, Freeman. At least not for now. Look, I know I could've probably gone about this a little differently, but it's not as ominous as it looks. We just need to run some tests for a few days. That's it. If we wanted to kill you . . ." Tanner smirked, then motioned toward the door. "Come on. Let's go for a walk."

Tanner led Paul down the helicopter steps and past the armed guards, who quickly fell in line behind them. They walked on a path of matted grass toward the front of the facility in the hot, humid middle of nowhere.

Paul couldn't be sure, but he had every reason to believe they were in Costa Rica. Tanner was known to take off for days at a time without letting any of the junior staff know where he was going, but rumor had it Costa Rica was the destination. (Chatty Pete Williams could always be counted on for the latest office gossip, whether anyone wanted to hear it or not). Judging by

Tanner's raccoon-eyed sunburns, as well as his tendency to interject Spanglish into every conversation following such trips, the notion of him visiting one of America's long-standing trade partners to the south made perfect sense.

There was something else, too. When Paul woke up on the helicopter, he swore he picked up a whiff of sulfur. Normally he would have ignored the pungent odor, but the stench reminded him of his honeymoon on the southern Atlantic coast.

The smell had nothing to do with sour nuptials. Coastal sediment and algae blooms were known to release the briny aroma on the coast. Most days it was barely noticeable, but the week of Paul and Michelle's honeymoon was exceptional. Even the tap water reeked of sulfur. Michelle could hardly take a shower without turning green, and went so far as to beg Paul to buy a few cases of bottled water for her to wash her hair with. Paul obliged, but continued to have his fun by spiking her cocktails with freshly prepared sulfuric ice cubes over the course of the trip.

Paul remembered asking the front desk clerk why the smell of sulfur covered the hotel grounds like a warm and rancid blanket. The clerk filled him in, and then told him it could have been a lot worse; they could have honeymooned in Hawaii. The clerk said the fog of volcanic farts rising from Hawaii Volcanoes National Park was enough to ruin even the strongest of marriages.

Paul knew Costa Rica had its fair share of volcanic activity, and judging by the strong scent he had picked up during the helicopter ride, he knew he could be near an active volcano. Paul scanned the terrain and decided the theory checked out. Too mountainous for the Everglades, too green for Mexico.

Tanner approached the steel-clad door first. He looked up at a security camera and gave a two-fingered wave. The buzzer sounded, and the automatic door swung open. Once inside, Paul wondered what kind of hellhole Tanner was leading him into.

The smell of mildew in the basement-like interior was overwhelming. Puddles filled low spots on the concrete floor. Water-stained ceiling tiles hung from the rafters; a few of them were missing. Rats dashed in and out of the fluorescent light that outlined a set of double doors in the back. They scurried behind old desks and dusty office chairs as Paul and his abductors marched toward the light.

They walked through the doors and into a small lobby, home to a single elevator. Tanner pulled out a security card and swiped it through the reader. An automated voice said, "Hello, Mr. Tanner," and the elevator doors opened.

"After you," Tanner said, directing Paul inside. Tanner and two guards followed him in, leaving the other four to catch the next lift.

The ride down was a fast one. The lights flickered as the elevator shook and shot toward its subterranean destination. It must have taken thirty seconds to reach the bottom–an eternity for a nonstop trip.

How far underground are we? Thirty stories? No way it's thirty, Paul reasoned. *Wasn't there a calculation for these things? Maybe it's a floor every two seconds or something?*

Even at a floor every five seconds–which seemed rather conservative, given the pace of the ride–that would have put him at sixty feet below the surface; far from anyone or anything able to help him now.

The elevator came to a screeching halt and the doors opened onto an unblemished and sanitary scene. Everything that was topside had been a cleverly constructed veil designed to cover up Tanner's state-of-the-art research facility located deep beneath the surface of the Costa Rican jungle.

Tanner flanked Paul on the left. The guards took the right. They walked down a brightly lit corridor with rooms on both sides. To the left, tempered glass separated the hall from a large pharmaceutical analysis laboratory. White coats were scattered throughout, some carrying clipboards while others manned workstations, analyzing data and peering through microscopes. Lab techs weren't the only ones who were busy, either. Paul spotted at least half a dozen workstations staffed by articulated robotic arms. The robots whistled and whirled as they organized lab samples and cataloged vacuum tubes, moving and sorting in symphonic fashion.

There wasn't much to see on the right side of the hallway, just a line of windowless doors, each one marked with a bold number at the top.

"Pretty amazing, isn't it?" Tanner said, pointing out the lab side of the complex. "The work that gets done here is light years ahead of any type of research back in the states, for reasons probably simpler than you think."

"No regulation."

"See? I knew you were smart. Too many barriers exist back in the U.S.; too much bureaucratic red tape to hack through. Here we can test, analyze, and improve at a reasonable pace without sacrificing years to market that are wasted on federally mandated waiting periods and procedural delays. Basically, Paul, we can do what we want."

"And what is that, exactly?"

Tanner stopped at the end of the hall. He reached in his pocket and pulled out his security card. He turned to a windowless door on the right marked "11", swiped his card and stepped to the side.

"Your new quarters, Mr. Freeman."

At first, Paul didn't budge. One of the armed guards used the butt of his AR-15 to give him a convincing nudge from behind.

"Don't worry, Paul," Tanner said. "This is temporary. We just need to run a few tests. You'll be back in the States in no time."

Paul reluctantly moved forward, his eyes fixed on Tanner before turning his attention to the room. He stepped in, and Tanner closed the door behind him. Paul looked around. There was a fold-down cot attached to the wall. He sat down, put his head in his hands and sighed. Things weren't looking good, he thought, but he wasn't dead yet.

At least that was something.

Chapter 15: Side Effects

The cell was small, about eight feet by eight feet, complete with a toilet, a bed and a sink. The LED lights shining down from the clear ceiling panel turned the white walls aqua blue, and were bright enough to keep Paul from getting any meaningful rest. The ceiling was high–at least twelve feet. Cold air fell from the register next to the light panel, keeping the small cell a comfortable 68 degrees. Given the circumstances, the AC was a nice touch.

Paul was exhausted. He sat on the bed and fantasized about catching a little shuteye. *No way that's happening*. Who knew if he would even wake up? Besides, Tanner was going to come back any minute to run his so-called "tests." If there was any way out of the cell, he reasoned, he had better find it fast.

Paul went around the room, inspecting every nook and cranny for weak points. He checked for plumbing around the toilet only to find there was none; the traditional porcelain throne had been replaced with a commode that looked more like an oversized jellybean, molded into the back corner of the cell and free of any moving internal parts he could use to hatch his escape. The bed was memory foam–no springs. The sink had motion-sensor water activation, with an automatic shutoff feature that kicked on when someone tried to clog the drain and flood the cell. Paul knew this, because he tried.

The eight-by-eight cell was also strategic in size. Too small to pick up any momentum toward the door, too big to climb the inside walls like a little kid would scale a doorframe. Paul was stuck, and no matter how hard he tried to hatch his escape, each epiphany ended in disappointment.

He decided instead to focus his attention on why he was there. He paced from one wall to the next, going over the events of the last two days with careful scrutiny. Everything seemed to be fine on Monday when Tanner asked Paul to go to the Donny Ford seminar. Tanner had even trusted him with a top-secret device; that was until Paul found out it was more than just a voice recorder.

Tanner wanted the device at the seminar, but why? Paul recalled how the device held some strange power over him on two separate occasions: when his makeshift repair job failed, and when Tanner activated something on the device that knocked Paul unconscious.

Paul knew the device wasn't a voice recorder, but it had to be recording *something*. He wondered if Donny Ford was one of the twelve clinical-trial outliers Tanner had spoken of. It would make sense, given Tanner's fixation on a person he should otherwise have had nothing to do with. There was definitely something peculiar about Tanner, but he wasn't the type of guy to obsess over a motivational speaker like some lonely middle-aged cat lady, either.

And what was Tanner's role in all of this to begin with? He was just the public relations guy at Asteria. He didn't sit on the board of directors, he wasn't involved in research and development, and regardless of how a particular drug did or did not perform, he was still guaranteed a check at the end of the month. Right?

Paul couldn't put the pieces together, but had the metal corner of the fold-down cot failed to stop him from pacing the small room, he might have been able to walk out a solution. The sound of his shin hitting the sharp edge followed by a series of incensed epithets made for a clamorous racket inside the holding cell.

Paul was nearing his breaking point. He was sitting on the bed and nursing his bleeding shin when he heard a voice coming from the air vent above. He stopped cursing long enough to listen.

"Is someone there?"

It was a woman.

"Hey, yeah . . . someone's here. Who's this?"

"Claire. Claire Connor." Her voice echoed from the other side. "Everything okay over there?"

"I've been better," Paul said. He pressed a wad of toilet paper to the cut on his shin and thought, *at least they're not complete sadists.*

"Right there with you," Claire said. "Are you over there in eleven? I'm over here in twelve. The last room on the end."

"Yeah. I think I'm in eleven," Paul said. He looked up at the vent. "Do you have any idea why we're in here? How can I even hear you?"

Claire chuckled. "Government spending. That's the rational explanation. My best guess is they paid the lowest bidder to install the heating and air system for this place. Looks like we're sharing an air duct."

"Have you heard from anyone in the other cells?"

"No. You're the first person I've talked to in weeks."

Just us two, thought Paul. That led to even more questions. Who were the other cells for? Were he and Claire the first ones to be abducted by Tanner? The last?

Paul decided to stick with the basics. "Did you know we're in Costa Rica?"

"Yeah. One of the guards let it slip a while back," Claire said. "So you got a name over there, or should I just call you eleven?"

"I think Paul Freeman sounds better."

"Much better. Any idea why you're here?"

Paul went over the list. "Well, I know I was kidnapped in Atlanta two days ago; now I'm in the jungle. I know a guy named Rick Tanner is one of the kidnappers. And I know I'm sitting in a secret research facility where we seem to be the guinea pigs, which means I *also* know that we're pretty much fucked."

"Rick Tanner," Claire repeated. "Sounds familiar, but I can't place him."

"He's the media jockey for Asteria Pharmaceuticals," Paul said. "I've worked with him once or twice over the last several weeks, but something tells me the PR position isn't his day job."

"Believe me, if the guy's involved in this thing, that job is just a cover for something a *helluva* lot bigger."

Paul agreed. "Do you know why we're here?"

"You wouldn't believe me if I told you."

"Try me."

Claire knew the truth was hard to swallow. She considered her response while Paul patiently waited, then she asked, "Have you ever had a dream come true?"

"Sure. I guess," Paul casually answered. "I mean, really, who hasn't? There was this one time I actually won a trip to the

Grand Canyon in junior high; that was pretty awesome. Then there was the backseat of Katie McCall's SUV my sophomore year of high school. She was on the gymnastics team and she could do this thing with her–"

"No. Gross. Just . . . no. That's not what I'm talking about, Paul. I'm talking about laying your head down at night, falling asleep, having a dream, and then waking up to find out it came true; that it was reality. You dreamed it, and then it happened. That's what I'm saying. Has *that* ever happened to you?"

"You're joking, right?"

Claire sighed. "Didn't I say you wouldn't believe me?"

Paul's hopes of having a sensible cellmate were dashed in an instant. Either Claire's captors had driven her to the brink of insanity, or she was a basket case from the start. *Dreams coming true?* The assertion was almost unworthy of a response. Still, it wasn't like Paul was going anywhere. He decided he might as well play along.

"So what you are saying is, the tests Tanner mentioned are to determine whether or not we can make dreams come true?"

"No, Paul. *They already know* we can make dreams come true. Remember that god-awful device they use? The one that effectively drives a stake through your head using nothing more than your own neural emissions?"

Paul knew the device well. It was the one Tanner sent him to the Donny Ford seminar with. It was also the one that put him on his ass in Tanner's office.

"How could I forget something like that?" he said. "You also mentioned 'neural emissions'? What does that even mean?"

"The technology is reflexive," Claire said. "Not only does the device detect the kind of electromagnetic energy that's emitted from these so-called dreamers, it can also return the energy to its source."

Paul wasn't buying it. "The device could have easily been a sonic weapon, Claire. Those things have been around for years. Doesn't mean it detects anything. I mean, come on, do you really think people like you and me are going to dream up a sports car and then VOILA! We wake up the next morning and it's parked in the driveway?"

"I know it sounds insane, trust me. I'm a journalist and a born skeptic, so don't think I'm trying to sell you a fairy tale. There's a scientific basis for all this; you just have to hear me out. Have you ever heard of electromagnetic radiation?"

Paul rolled his eyes. "Nope. Enlighten me."

"Electromagnetic radiation is all around us. It moves through the air without been seen or heard, that is, unless you've got a device that detects electromagnetic radiation, like a radio. Radio waves are a form of electromagnetic radiation all of us are familiar with, but there's another type of radiation we don't hear too much about. *Brain waves*."

Paul could feel the reference to a certain paraplegic professor coming any minute.

Claire said, "Brain waves are the byproduct of thousands of neurons firing at once. These waves are emitted from our minds in the same way radio waves are broadcast from a tower, only at much lower frequencies. Any higher and your favorite morning talk show would likely be interrupted by the guy in the next car contemplating whether or not he had time to pick up a coffee without being late for work."

Paul's shin had stopped bleeding. He tossed the bloody paper into the porcelain jellybean, and then lay on the cot, putting his hands behind his head.

"Let me guess: these quote-unquote *dreamers* produce this radiation at a much higher rate?"

"Sort of," Claire said. "But only in certain situations. Specifically, when we're sleeping, and even then it doesn't always happen. Several elements have to come together in order for our dreams to influence reality. For starters, the test subjects can't just be asleep; they have to specifically be in the middle of an REM sleep state. REM, or rapid eye movement, is typically characterized by the high level of brain activity sleepers experience without being fully awake. This leads to lucid dreams, vivid imagery . . . It's like being fully awake when you're actually in the deepest kind of sleep there is, short of being in a coma."

"I've had vivid dreams before, Claire, and I've never changed the world with them."

"Fair enough," Claire said. "Even after experiencing a flawless REM sleep cycle before waking, the typical human being isn't going to emit enough electromagnetic radiation to influence anything outside of their own minds. That's where Ocula comes in."

Paul's focus on the vent sharpened. Claire had his full attention.

"Ocula . . . the sleeping pill?"

"The one and only. We covered this one pretty heavily in the press. It was the first medication to use antisense technology to treat individuals with a genetic predisposition for insomnia, creating the perfect eight-hour sleep cycle. Weight, height, metabolism, tolerance . . . none of those issues mattered anymore. If you happened to be carrying a gene linked to sleeplessness, Ocula would address that gene and nothing else, picking off a single, specific genetic trait out of a crowd of millions. Of course, creating the perfect sleeping pill would only be the beginning for antisense gene therapy."

"I haven't worked at Asteria long," Paul said, "but word around the campfire is that Asteria bet everything on antisense technology. Theoretically, antisense would mean that genetic mutations found within the body's colossal set of biological instructions could be corrected by simply taking a pill. Precision genetic treatments would be the new norm. Patient personalization would be the medicinal buzzword of the 21st century. Specific problem genes would be silenced, while untargeted genes remained unharmed. It's promising technology, and the efficacy seems to have been proven with Ocula, with minimal side effects. Not a bad gamble, if you ask me."

"*Minimal* side effects?"

"The headaches? In a dozen or so people? I'd say minimal's a fair assessment."

Claire was offended. "The headaches are the tip of the iceberg, Paul. I took Ocula for almost a year. I thought signing up to participate in Phase Three of the clinical trials would kill two birds with one stone, giving me an inside scoop on a developing story while finding a cure for my insomnia in the process. Crazy, I know, but I would've done anything, tried anything, to get some sleep.

"You wanted to talk about efficacy? Well, Ocula worked like a charm. The first night I took it I was hooked. Chased the pill with a glass of water from the comfort of my bed at 10 p.m. just like my program manager recommended. By 10:05, it was lights out. No tossing, no turning. Just pure, continuous sleep. When I woke up, I immediately checked the clock on my nightstand. It was 6:05 a.m. A flawless eight-hour sleep cycle. I hadn't slept that long in years."

Paul heard Claire stop to take a sip of water from her sink. Then she continued. "For the first few weeks, Ocula gave me a new lease on life. The doses we were given during the clinical trials had a short half-life, so I had to take it every night at bedtime. Still, it was a total miracle drug. That was until the headaches started. Surely you can relate to that."

"Headaches, I can relate to," Paul said. "But here's a newsflash, Claire. I never took the drug! Even if Ocula could amplify something within our own minds, I shouldn't be here, because I wasn't part of the clinical trials. I hadn't even heard of Ocula until a few weeks ago."

"Then what the hell do you know about side effects?"

"Nothing! But there's one thing I *do* know, and that's the fact that everything you're saying is completely insane."

"Like I said–"

"I know, I know," Paul said. "I wouldn't believe you."

Claire's narrative was hard to believe, but she explained it in a way that made everything seem plausible. *No doubt she's a journalist*, thought Paul. That part had to be true. She could spin a yarn, but then again so could a writer for a supermarket tabloid about alien abductions, batboys and Nostradamus predictions. Being a great storyteller didn't mean she was trustworthy.

But what about the facility itself? Top secret. Secluded. Out of the country. The location easily set investors back tens of millions of dollars, maybe more. There were at least two-dozen employees working within the facility, and those were just the ones Paul saw on his short trip from the helicopter to the underground labs.

Paul couldn't ignore the obvious. Everything had to add up to something important being developed here. People didn't spend millions of dollars on fairy tales unless it involved a magic kingdom somewhere, and the Costa Rican jungle wasn't exactly a place where childhood dreams came true.

Paul was lying on the bed and staring at the ceiling when a thought occurred to him. "Hey, Claire. How do you know all this stuff, anyway? About Ocula and the drugs and the side effects and everything?"

"They told me," Claire's voice trailed off. "During one of my sessions."

"Sessions?"

"Yep. Testing sessions. A guy named Doyle is the moderator. He holds them up top in a makeshift chamber. Rock walls and bugs and humidity and all the worst that the jungle has to offer. Doyle talks his head off during the sessions. Probably thinks I won't remember, but I always do, sooner or later. Anyway, you'll find out soon enough what the sessions are all about. Or maybe not, who knows. If you didn't take the drug, I'm not really sure what they'd want with you."

Paul propped up on his elbows. "But even if he thought you wouldn't remember, why would he risk it? There's so much at stake here; why would he tell you every detail about the program? I mean, the device, the drug, the tests . . . it sounds like he told you everything."

"Ha!" Claire said. "That's the easiest question you've asked me yet." Her voice was sobering.

"Because he is going to kill us, Paul."

Chapter 16: Flight of the Deer Hunter

Alex sat in his stand and watched the shadows of the tall Georgia pines stretch out across the forest floor as the sun began its slow descent on the horizon. Since midmorning he had called a gently swaying oak his home, impatiently waiting for his dream buck to come strolling through the woods. Only this time, things weren't playing out the way they had in the past.

Maybe I just showed up late, Alex thought. When he first came to the realization that his big-game dreams were working their way into reality, the prospect of screwing the whole thing up had kept the young hunter on his toes. To Alex, the phenomenon had always seemed too good to be true, and it was only a matter of time before the gift vanished as quickly as it appeared.

In those days, he could always tell when a promising dream was about to transpire by the awful headaches he would get the night before. He didn't sleep good on those nights, but that didn't matter. In the beginning, every dream turned him into a kid on Christmas morning. He practically leapt out of bed on mornings following one of his lucid dreams, stepping into his coveralls before running out the door, grabbing his rifle, his bag, and some junk food along the way. He would be in his stand long before first light, eager to see the day's events transpire in the same way they had on his pillow the night before.

Things weren't like that anymore. He had grown comfortable, perhaps even lazy, with his arcane ability. These days he was lucky to hit the woods by 11 a.m.–a time when most hunters were thinking about heading back into town to grab some lunch at the local diner.

With each successful hunt, Alex moved further away from the doctrine he had set out for himself long before he ever thought about taking a sleeping pill: *Dreams don't come true unless you make them happen.* Alex had become a slacker, cocksure and carefree. And now he was paying for it.

He turned his wrist to check his watch: 5:45 p.m. It wouldn't be long before the sun was resting below the horizon, calling an end to the day's hunt and to Alex's grand ambitions. He turned to spit, shaking his head and bitching to the trees.

For the first time in a long time, Alex remembered what it felt like to go home empty-handed. *This is bullshit. Why didn't things happen like before?* The dream was still explicit in his mind. He could even count the points on the buck's head. Sixteen, to be exact, perfectly symmetrical with a good two-foot spread between the inside tines. Easily a 230-inch score. Would have been a new state record for sure.

Alex recalled the scenario play by play. He was sitting in his stand, not a shadow in sight. Must have been noon, maybe one o'clock at the latest. He looked down the ridge and focused on a game trail running east to west about forty yards in front of his stand. The buck lopped in from the east, alternating between a head-down search for scents and a head-raised perimeter check. He stopped in the middle of the path directly in front of Alex and looked toward the hunter. He tilted his head, inspecting the unusual object in the tree.

By the time the buck realized something was amiss, it was too late. Alex pulled the trigger, sending the synthetic-tipped bullet directly behind the buck's front shoulder, clipping his heart and forcing him to the ground. He let out one final bleat before exhaling a bloody mist onto the frosty leaves, dying within seconds of meeting the hunter in the tree.

Alex was overjoyed. A sixteen-point buck, and a *monster* at that! This would surely be one for the record books. But his heart racing beneath the bed sheets kept him from enjoying the thrill of the kill. Just as it always did before, he was quickly sucked out of his dream and back into reality. He found himself lying in bed, his sweaty palms still clinging to an imaginary rifle.

And he was tired. Dog tired. That was the problem with the so-called "perfect" sleeping medication. If Alex didn't dream, he woke up feeling like a million bucks, fully rested and ready to tackle the day. If he had an episode, however, he woke up groggy and tired, just as he had before signing up for the Ocula trials in the first place. Normally he would have hit the snooze button and rolled back over on mornings like that. But every mind-numbing headache had led to a nocturnal revelation that was making all of Alex's dreams come true. That was usually enough to get his ass out of bed.

Alex thought about his final dream while watching the last slivers of sunlight outline the ridge ahead. The timing was poetic. After all the trophies, the magazines, the TV spots and headlines, the sun was setting on his supernatural talent.

"Well, shit," he said. "Fun while it lasted." He tied a rope to his rifle and lowered it down before making his descent. Then he put on his backpack and faced the tree so he could work his self-climbing tree stand. He lowered each section a foot at a time, descending slow and steady to avoid an accidental slide down the tree. He was about six feet from the ground when a noise stopped him in his tracks.

It was a footstep.

Not just any footstep, like an erratic squirrel barreling through the leaves or a bird prancing down a fallen log. The footstep Alex heard was large and calculated. Was the record whitetail buck making a late appearance?

Better late than never, Alex thought. There was just one problem. He was frozen on the tree. He peered down to see his rifle lying broadside in the leaves below. How could he possibly get to his gun without scaring off whatever was approaching in the woods downrange?

He couldn't make a move, and he knew it. He stood still and helpless while he faced the tree, examining what he could see out of the corners of his eyes, desperately searching for the source of the single, calculated step.

Then there was another.

Two steps, moving slowly up the hill toward Alex's stand, only this step was a good thirty seconds from the last. *Is this buck really being that careful; that slow to move?* The caution would make sense if Alex had been spotted. He couldn't be sure, but he felt like he was being watched.

Alex worked up the courage to turn his head. He looked down the shooting lane where–according to his dream–the trophy buck should have been about forty yards in front of him. Instead, the silhouette of a man stood halfway down the ridge, completely still now that Alex had turned. The dusky setting made it hard for Alex to see the man's face, but he could make out a body: tall, broad shoulders, wearing a trench coat . . .

. . . and holding a handgun.

The man stood and waited. Alex stared back, his eyes locked on the shadowy figure before him, afraid to break the trance the ominous stalker held over him like a snake honing in on its prey. Alex knew if he made a move it could mean an unhappy ending to the woodland standoff. Lights out for the ol' farm boy. He also knew the man was there for a reason, and he wasn't going away.

Alex remained steady as a rock, only moving his eyes to sneak a peek down at his weapon, then back up at the figure. He calculated the risk. He was unarmed and had little time to act.

It was now or never. Alex leapt from the stand toward the rifle. The man raised his weapon and fired toward Alex, the shots hitting all around the hunter's firearm. The bullets kicked up dirt and leaves, with one splitting the gunstock in two. Alex quickly drew his hand back and pivoted behind the oak tree his stand was on. The gun was no use.

He would have to make a run for it.

He took off up the ridge, trying to keep the thick Georgia oak between him and his assailant. His feet slid on the leaves as he ran up the hill behind his stand, using his hands in steep places to aid his hurried escape. If he could make it to the top of the ridge just a few yards away, it would be all downhill from there.

Keep moving. Don't stop. Don't look back. Alex could feel every square inch of skin on his back tingling with awful anticipation. As he cleared the peak of the hill, he couldn't shake the thought that any second now a bullet was going to lodge in his back.

He scanned the landscape below. There was no time to double back to his truck; that would mean running close to the man with the gun. But Alex did know he could haul ass down the opposite side of the ridge and make it to Briar Creek, a deep-water stream that ran right into County Road 108. If he could make it to the road, he could flag somebody down and get help from there.

Another shot rang out. Alex flinched as the bullet hit the tree right next to him, spraying bark and grime into the hunter's face. He checked his ear to make sure it was still attached, and then he took off down the steep hill. He struggled to stay afoot, grabbing at saplings to steady the run down, dodging boulders and stumps on the decline toward Briar Creek at the bottom of the ridge.

He slowed near the bottom of the hill as it leveled out into an ancient creek bed twenty yards away from the creek itself. He looked back toward the mountain of mud and roots and shrubs he had just cleared. Two shadows stood at the top.

You've gotta be fuckin' kidding me, he thought. The two men started down the hill, carefully navigating their way toward the hunter's position.

Only one way out.

Alex got a running start and leapt from the edge of the creek and into the fast-moving water, creating a splash that drew further attention from the two men. As he surfaced, he heard shots ring out from a distance, then watched upstream as bullets pierced the top of the water like hard-thrown pebbles. The trackers eventually reached the creek bank, but they were too late. The frigid waters had already carried Alex far away.

The young hunter appeared to be in the clear, if he could stave off hypothermia long enough to make it to help. The current was moving fast, rolling hard from a heavy storm that had blown through the night before. County Road 108 was only a half mile or so away. He looked back again, checking his six as he floated downstream. Not a shadow in sight.

***

County Road 108 was paved, but desolate. It was dark now, with few signs of life on the secluded route. The porch lights of rural homes were scattered throughout the surrounding mountains like fireflies in the distance. A stretch of the road narrowed at the small bridge crossing Briar Creek, a place where meeting a semi-truck meant squeezing by with a little faith and a steady hand at the wheel.

That was the bridge Alex arose from. He scrambled up from the creek, muddy and wet. He clung to his arms, shivering and shaking as he walked north on 108, straddling the white line and praying for a car to come along soon. It had been dark now for almost an hour, and although the mild heat radiating off the asphalt was like a warm blanket compared to the icy stream, it wouldn't be enough to keep Alex from going into hypothermic shock.

Alex walked for half a mile before he heard the purr of a motor in the distance. *Oh thank God.* A car was heading his way. The headlight beams broke rapidly over the paved horizon. Alex trotted toward the light, still hugging his arms as he ran toward the approaching vehicle.

"Hey! Help me!" he yelled. He loosed his arms to wave down the car. The car was a hundred yards out and closing the gap fast. The driver must have seen Alex by now, but the hunter didn't want to take any chances.

"Over here! Stop! I need help!"

The car kept coming.

"Hey!" Alex yelled. The car wasn't stopping. Alex lowered his arms and his eyes widened.

The car was veering right toward him.

Alex tried to lunge off the road, but it was too late. The car accelerated at full speed, swerving enough to cover the shoulder of the road and nailing the hunter on the right-hand side. His body flew over the sedan like a rag doll, landing on the asphalt behind the vehicle as it sped away into the night.

Alex lay on his side, his body a tangled mess of flesh and broken bones. His face pressed on the asphalt, taking in the fleeting warmth left over from the afternoon sun. He saw red, but it wasn't the taillights speeding away. This red was oozing out around him, pooling in front of his eyes as if a faucet had been turned on at the top of his head.

There was so much blood now. He wouldn't be making it home, but that didn't matter anymore. His vision began to fade and he closed his eyes, his thoughts leading nowhere as blood continued to pour from his head.

At least now he was finally warm.

Chapter 17:
The Good Ol' Days

"Okay, boys. Let's go over this just one more time," Frank Freeman said as he wiped down the hood of his red Mustang, towel-drying his prized possession in the driveway while his two sons bickered over a video game. He motioned toward the house.

"You two are supposed to be taking turns in there, and instead of trying to get along you come running to tattle on one another?"

The boys were silent.

"Tell you what," Frank said, tossing the towel in the garage. "No more video games today. Instead, I think we'll take a little trip up to the farmhouse, maybe do a little scoutin' for deer. Season's coming up soon, anyway. It'd do you boys some good to get out."

"Ah, come on, Da–" Paul started, but his father wasn't having it.

"Listen, Paul. You two are lucky I'm not threating to give all your games away."

Frank looked to Alex. "Any complaints from you?"

"Nah, Dad. I *love* scouting for deer. I'd rather be doing that than playing video games anyway." Alex gave Paul a shit-eating grin. Paul couldn't handle it.

"Oh, shut the fuck up, Alex!" Paul's eyes swelled with fear the moment the words left his juvenile lips. He couldn't believe he had dropped his first F-bomb, and in front of his clean-cut military father no less.

Frank looked down at his son and stifled his anger. He took a deep breath, and then he looked at Alex. "Go inside, son. I need to have a talk with your brother."

Alex strutted back in the house, turning around halfway to cast a derisive sneer toward Paul once more. Frank leaned back on his ride and crossed his arms.

"You know we don't speak that way in this house, son. So where did you hear that word?"

"I dunno," Paul looked down, sinking his hands into his pockets and kicking an acorn down the driveway. "I guess I heard it at school. I mean, the kids in middle school all say stuff like that. I never heard it 'til we moved here, but everybody going to Oak Grove says stuff like that, sometimes even worse stuff."

Frank got down on one knee, holding his boy's shoulders to look him square in the eye. "Son, we *don't* say words like that in this house. Doesn't matter who says what out there in the world. In this home, we don't curse. You understand me?"

Paul nodded his head.

"Even more," Frank continued, "you've got a brother in there who looks up to you. Anything you say and do, he's going to follow suit, right down to the letter. You just can't talk like that, and you can't let those boys at Oak Grove influence you. You've got to be bigger than that."

"But he gets away with everything, Dad! We were inside and he wasn't taking turns. I even let him die three times before I came outside to tell you. He just kept on playing, laughing about it the whole time, saying the whole time if I hit him then he'd run tell you." Paul was flustered and red-faced, pleading his case.

"Doesn't matter," said Frank. "You can't let yourself get frustrated like this, Paul. It doesn't help anything. If it happens again, just come tell me. I'll believe you. But don't let your anger get the better of you like that again. Okay?"

Paul nodded once more. Frank stood up and returned to his Mustang. "I'm going to move the car, and then you're going to help me load up the truck."

"But–"

"No buts, Paul. We're going to the farm today, and you two had better get along." He would have asked if Paul understood a third time, but he felt things were finally starting to sink into his oldest son's stubborn twelve-year-old brain. "Now run inside and get your brother."

Paul turned to go inside when Frank called out once more. "And Paul? Just remember, you get one get-out-of-jail-free card with that kind of language. One. If I *ever* hear you say anything like that again, I'm getting the belt."

Paul didn't have a clue why, sitting in a cell in a Costa Rican basement and staring at the ceiling, his mind would go back to a memory that occurred some fifteen years ago. He could remember the argument with Alex like it was yesterday, as well as the following pep talk he received from his stern father.

He had thought about that day before, but it wasn't because it was the first time he dropped the F-bomb in front of the old man. Nor was it because it was one of the few times his father had taken disciplinary action without the use of his trusty go-to leather belt, stuffed in the back of the closet and reserved for special occasions.

The memory didn't stick with Paul because it was the first weekend in their new home, either. Frank had decided to move what was left of the family into a new house just outside of their old school district after their mother had succumbed to cancer the year before.

Paul always figured the farmhouse (as his father called it) bore too many memories for the old man to bear, but they still rode up to the property from time to time. His father never went inside the longstanding home; instead, they would work the pastures surrounding the house, planting food plots and clearing the brush while getting ready for deer season.

Frank didn't talk much when they went to the farm, but he felt just getting the kids outside was better than sitting at home and dwelling on the past. He had to learn real quick how to take on the role of both parents with a couple of Irish twins. Maybe that's why he had gone so easy on Paul in the driveway that day.

The fall afternoon had symbolized so many things for the Freemans, a kind of crossroads in the life of a middle-class southern family shattered by the loss of a beautiful woman. But it wasn't his father's patience Paul remembered most about that day, nor was it the feeling his mother was there in spirit, the cool autumn breeze that had kept tempers from flaring beyond absolute control. Unfortunately, what Paul remembered most about that day was the look on Alex's face.

That shit-eating grin. Such a pompous expression, as if Alex knew he had outplayed his slightly older brother. Although the two boys grew out of most of their childish behavior, Alex would always retain a sense of arrogance about him that Paul could never relate to. Paul was usually quiet and reserved, unless he had hit his boiling point. When that occurred, the gloves were off. F-bombs were dropped with extreme prejudice. And it almost always ended with the old man's trusty leather belt.

Alex, on the other hand, was loud and boisterous. Any attention was good attention. All eyes had to be on him, all of the time. They were only thirteen months apart, but the two couldn't have been any more different. Paul was ying; Alex was yang. Extrovert versus introvert. And for the extent of their adolescent years, they were stuck together.

Paul's teenage ambition turned to getting out of the small town as soon as possible so he could carve out a niche for himself, and college was supposed to be just the place to do that. He applied to several in-state schools that were close enough to home in case his father needed help, but also far enough away so he could reinvent himself without the persuasions of past acquaintances getting in the way.

Alex, however, was content to live his entire life in his hometown.

Nothing wrong with that, Paul thought as he turned to his side, the cot creaking loudly in his holding cell. *Big job in the big city. Look where that got me.*

Paul remembered the last conversation he had with his father, just before Frank succumbed to a massive heart attack. The elder Freeman would call to check in on Paul from time to time. Frank would talk a little about the weather; complain a lot about the Braves; and always asked Paul about his headaches, while pointing out that Alex never got them.

Frank had always been closer to Alex, and Paul was okay with that. So it surprised Paul when his father called to tell him that he wanted to leave the old farmhouse to him when he died. Paul always avoided such conversations, but he promised to consider his father's wishes at a later date. *What's the rush?* He remembered telling the old man.

Frank Freeman was dead within the week.

Paul wasn't sure why, but the recollection of his father prying about his headaches triggered something. He sat up in bed and spoke through the makeshift intercom in the ceiling.

"You awake over there, Claire?"

"Sure am," Claire replied from the adjoining cell. "Haven't been able to sleep worth a damn since I got here. Imagine that."

Paul sat with his back against the wall. "Tell me more about the headaches you get. How do they come on?"

"Fast . . . like a clap of thunder." Claire reminisced about her last episode. "I can't imagine anything worse than those headaches; it's like having a wooden stake hammered into your head during the worst hangover of your life. I used to think they came out of nowhere, until I started keeping a headache journal with me to document every occurrence. When the headaches would kick in I would write down what I had eaten that day, what I drank, where I was, what the daily high and low temperatures were, barometric pressure . . . Any details I could think of would go into my journal."

"Were you able to make heads or tails from any of it?"

"Sure," Claire said. "After a while I noticed a pattern of stress correlating with some pretty nasty headaches. I would notice things in my journal pointing out sleep deprivation coupled with rigorous work demands. I remember getting an absolutely debilitating migraine last fall covering the rebel uprising in Ukraine. Our entire crew went weeks without significant sleep, which led to a headache that almost made the top-five list in my journal. *Almost.*"

"And the top five?"

"Those had nothing to do with stress," Claire continued. "That was the scariest part. Most of the headaches could be controlled by reducing stressful situations, avoiding too much caffeine, diet, exercise . . . things of that nature. But the worst of the headaches, the mind-numbing episodes that should have sent my body into a state of shock, those occurrences were brought on by the weather. Specifically, rapid drops in barometric pressure."

"Weird. The air pressure drops, triggering a migraine?"

"Exactly. I had a neurologist friend offer a pretty reasonable explanation for it. Apparently, migraine sufferers are typically well adapted to their surrounding environments, as long as changes don't occur suddenly. These adaptations include the pressure exerted on our bodies per the atmosphere.

"When air pressure is relatively high, the blood vessels surrounding our brains and intracranial muscle tissue are compressed and, therefore, avoid unnecessary contact with those tissues. However, when barometric pressure drops at an accelerated rate, our bodies don't have time to adjust to the changes, causing our own blood vessels to dilate and swell. When this happens, swollen blood vessels press against sensitive nerve endings inside our heads, inducing the pain associated with migraine headaches."

"Sounds familiar," Paul said. He remembered his last migraine attack, before his son was born. North Georgia was known for hosting springtime tornadoes, and Paul had marked the last devastating occasion with a migraine he would never forget. He recalled the weatherman reporting the events.

"An area of low pressure has given way to a rotating supercell storm moving east from Birmingham at 35 MPH. Expect heavy rain, hail, and lighting. If you are in the storm's path, seek shelter immediately."

Paul wasn't about to leave his bed for the basement. He sent Michelle downstairs after the warning sirens sounded, refusing to join her below. Instead, he clung to his tiny trashcan while the wind howled and the hail commenced, dry heaving into the night while a part of him fantasized about being whisked away by the impending tornado. At least then he would be free of the pain he was in.

"Didn't you say you suffered from headaches? Migraines, specifically?" Claire asked.

"Every kind you can imagine," Paul said. "Migraine headaches, tension headaches . . . even a cluster headache that put me in the hospital for a few days. I thought I was having a stroke. Temporarily lost my vision in my right eye during that one. My wife Michelle was terrified; she'd never seen anything like it."

"But your headaches weren't the result of the medication," Claire pondered. "Kinda makes you wonder why you're here, doesn't it?"

Paul didn't have time to answer. There was a shuffle of feet at the door. Paul heard the heavy bolts of the door retract into the walls, the clanging metal resonating through the cell and down the hall. Then the door opened.

"Mr. Freeman!" Tanner said, smiling as if he were greeting an old friend. "Are you ready to begin?"

Chapter 18:
Crystal Balls and Tarot Cards

The trip from the holding cell to the elevator would have been a short walk under normal circumstances. The room Paul had called home during his brief stay was the second-to-last cell at the end of an all-white corridor, brightly lit with the only visible seams surrounding the cell doors and the windows facing the lab. The corridor was spotless, much like the cleanrooms Paul remembered touring on a college field trip to the CDC. He imagined any evidence of wrongdoing in the underground facility would be tidied up within the hour.

Tanner led Paul down the corridor while two guards brought up the rear.

"Where are we going?" Paul asked.

Tanner pointed to the ceiling. "Heading up to run a few tests at ground level. I hope you don't mind."

The stonewall chamber. Claire said I'd know about it soon enough.

Tanner noticed Paul's silence. He stopped halfway down the hall and turned toward the lab, crossing his hands behind his back while he spoke. "Come to the window, Paul," Tanner said. "I want to talk to you before we begin."

Paul walked up to Tanner while the guards stayed back. The overpowering smell of cigarette smoke coming from Tanner's jacket made Paul's nose crinkle. He tried to hide his reaction, but it didn't matter; Tanner's eyes were on the lab.

"I know you've got a lot of questions," Tanner said. "I would expect no less from someone who's been whisked away from his normal life and held against his will."

"Does that mean I can call my wife?" Paul asked.

"No. I'm afraid not. Not yet, anyway." Tanner nodded toward the lab. "Do you have any idea what's going on in there, Paul? It's miraculous, really. Some of the world's most brilliant pharmaceutical scientists working day in and day out to synthesize a product that is already changing the world as we know it. Bigger than anything Oppenheimer ever did, and far less destructive . . . in the right hands, of course."

"You're talking about Ocula."

"Yes, specifically the effects induced by the sleeping medication on a limited number of individuals. The effects haven't gone unnoticed. It's even possible other countries could be on to what we're working with here. We're talking global implications, Paul. That's why our mission here is necessary. The research, the funding, the experiments, the surveillance . . . everything we do here is about securing our homeland. Our country. Our way of life."

"The surveillance–"

"Yes. I already told you about the twelve outliers. Remember?"

"The ones with the headaches," Paul said.

"Precisely. The outliers were the only clinical trial participates to experience any documented side effects. Migraine headaches, to be exact. A few of the headache sufferers were also the only patients out of two thousand volunteers to claim their dreams were precursors to impossible experiences during the waking hours. Naturally, Asteria wanted to explore this more, but soon after the clinical trials ended, the outliers fell off the radar.

So, we tracked them down and had them put under surveillance. That's when things got really interesting."

Tanner put his hand on Paul's shoulder. "Paul. You *really* need to believe me when I tell you this. Those outliers have the ability to change the world around them through the power of their own dreams."

Paul scrutinized the remark, analyzing his captor's face and searching for tells. Tanner glared back, waiting for a sign Paul was with him so far. If Tanner was lying, Paul concluded, the man had one hell of a poker face.

"Even if Ocula was causing the outliers to have lucid dreams," Paul said, "how can you assume those dreams have an impact on the physical world? What they're dreaming about is going on in their own minds. No outside connection. No scientifically plausible way to change the world. I mean you're talking about mind control, telekinesis . . . hasn't the government already spent countless taxpayer dollars researching this shit? You're basically telling me mind control exists, or at least some form of it. And you're crazy if you expect me to believe that."

Tanner dismissed the charge. "Surely you've witnessed mind control before, Paul," he said, turning back toward the lab. "Not in some mystical sense, which is unfortunately the place most mind-control conversations end up. Consider psychics for a moment. Now, I've never believed psychics have a window into another dimension. But these people are powerful nonetheless, because they have another ability that is often overlooked: the ability to control minds . . . just not in the sense most of us picture when we think of mind control.

"When people buy into palm readings and aura sightings, they believe psychic readers are using a supernatural gift to access information. What these people don't realize is that *they* are the ones providing the psychics with everything they need to make so-called clairvoyant predictions. Without any input from the customers sitting across the table, psychics wouldn't have the information necessary to create a believable story."

"Takes two to tango," Paul said.

"Exactly. And providing information isn't limited to verbal communication, either. Think about a woman who asks a psychic reader to tell her the significance of a necklace. The woman gives the necklace to the psychic, then goes silent. Doesn't tell the psychic a thing. How then is the psychic able to recall the necklace's origin, approximate age, familial history and significance, all from an ornamental piece of metal without utilizing some type of extra-sensory perception or magical prowess? What explanation could there be besides supernatural talents or ESP?"

"Maybe the psychic is just a really good liar."

"You're not far off," Tanner explained. "The psychic developed a legitimate story by listening to the thousands of 'tells' the woman revealed. Her choice of clothing, her hairstyle, her mannerisms, her approximate age . . . every piece of data gathered about the subject is bundled up with colorful generalizations before being used to churn out an elaborate story about a mysterious necklace. The age of the necklace makes the inference that it's a family heirloom a safe bet. If the woman is older, alluding to the pain and suffering that can be felt through the necklace is also an easy prediction. What grown adult hasn't experienced pain and suffering over the course of a lifetime?"

"Makes sense," Paul said.

"Psychics take a miniscule amount of information, polish it up and feed it back to their clients. And the clients let that information fuse with what they already know, or something they are looking for, to create a final product that makes psychic powers seem real. Their talent is believable because they're essentially controlling the minds of their clients with a form of garrulous brainwashing that takes little more than a colorful imagination and a keen eye for detail. Are they tapping into mystical powers long passed down to those lucky enough to have a direct link to some spiritual realm on the other side? No."

Paul scratched the back of his head. "I'm with you on the whole demystification of psychics, but what you're describing is plain old trickery. It has nothing to do with physically controlling the outside world with one's own mind. Or dreams."

"You're missing the point," Tanner said. His arms were crossed in front of him now, his index finger sending Morse code up his sleeve. Paul could tell he was jonesing for a cigarette. "Psychics use influence to control minds, and minds run on neural connections. Think of it like a low-grade electrical broadcast. Recalling last night's game? Neurons fire. Thinking about sex? Neurons fire. Every thought, every image means a never-ending stream of brain waves, which is a form of electromagnetic radiation. So what would happen if our outliers could influence the brain waves of others by emitting focused electromagnetic radiation? No crystal balls. No tarot cards."

"I'm listening," Paul said.

"I was working the press circuit, doing the PR thing while parading around with Donna Edwards, a satisfied client and participant in the Ocula trials. Donna was singing our praises, crediting Ocula with giving her the first restful night's sleep she'd had since a terrible auto accident left her permanently blind some five years back.

"Donna suffered from a condition known as non-24. Non-24 occurs when people suffering from total blindness can't perceive light of any kind, disrupting their circadian rhythm and causing insomnia. It hit Donna hard, causing more than a few sleepless nights. In her own words, she had become a zombie, drifting through life in a drowsy fog of exhaustion. Certainly no way to live."

"Fortunately," Tanner said, "Ocula was an immediate cure. Following the clinical trials, Donna was more than willing to stump for Asteria Pharmaceuticals during a few media events. I remember the first press conference we held in the grand lobby of Asteria like it was yesterday. The lobby was packed, lights were glaring, speakers were booming, cameras were flashing . . .

That was until some kind of electrical pulse destroyed half the devices in the building. Fluorescent light tubes shattered overhead. Glass rained down on the crowd. Everyone panicked. Cameras malfunctioned, verified by the confused looks of photographers in the audience. The overhead speakers squealed so loudly that people bolted for the doors, covering their ears and climbing over one another to get outside."

"What do you think it was?" Paul asked.

"I know what it was now. Then? Not a clue. But something stuck with me that day. It was Donna's headache. She had complained about having a tremendous headache before we took the stage the day of our first in-house presser. I didn't think much of it at the time, nor any time after. Until the next press conference. Same situation, same circumstances, same result.

"In fact," Tanner said, "every time Donna got in front of those bright lights and big cameras, she'd have an episode. Her head would kick in, she'd run to the bathroom to puke her guts out, and then all hell would break loose. It happened so much over the next few weeks that anyone paying attention could've figured out the correlation. That's when we starting looking closely at the remaining eleven participants who'd complained about the medication giving them headaches they'd never had before."

Paul looked confused. "I still don't see the connection between Donna and what happened in the lobby."

"We soon discovered the damage to the lobby equipment was caused by a series of electromagnetic pulses," Tanner said. "These EMPs destroyed cameras, lights, and other electronic devices within a fifty-yard radius. While our team of internal investigators was expecting to find an electromagnetic bomb placed by industry rivals at the center of the radius, or the source of an electrical surge caused by a nearby storm or substation malfunction, we came up with nothing. No bombs. No surges. All we found was poor Mrs. Edwards, unconscious in the back stall of the ladies' room and at the center of a surge of electromagnetic radiation so powerful it put our entire department–and several pissy members of the press–out of commission for a week."

Paul asked, "You believe the electromagnetic radiation emitted from her brain caused the disruption in the lobby?"

"Absolutely."

"And you think these pulses are magnified during sleep cycles, when people are dreaming?"

Tanner emphatically agreed. "And further," he said, "they aren't limited to destroying electronics. In fact, our research has found that the likelihood of damaging EMPs being emitted from someone like Mrs. Edwards increases when neural activity is less focused."

"Less focused?"

"Yes. Like being zoned out. Oblivious to the world. Without focus neurological activity, the consequences of these emissions can be unpredictable. But lucid dreams, on the other hand, provide all the visual and auditory focus one needs to interrupt electromagnetic activity within the brains of other organisms nearby. We already know that the typical human brain already emits low levels of electromagnetic radiation to function. We also know that external frequencies of electromagnetic waves can interfere with normal brain function. Our outliers have the ability to affect the neural function of organisms within close proximity–even influence–the thoughts of surrounding organisms, simply by dreaming."

"So that's where mind control comes in," Paul said. He watched the lab techs through the glass, working tirelessly on what seemed to be the revelation of the 21st century. "And you keep saying organisms. What do you mean? Like dreaming your dog would stop humping your father-in-law's leg every time he came over to visit?"

"Sort of," Tanner replied. "The electromagnetic activity has been found to affect organisms other than humans. That could include dogs, but the pulses generally influence organisms based on the focused instructions coming from the source. In other words, it all depends on what a Ocula outlier is dreaming. If one of them dreamed about their dog learning to shake or roll over or sit, and the dog was in close proximity when the dream occurred, then technically, yes, a dog might be influenced to obey. But we still have a lot to learn in that department. We've been experimenting with a variety of species, including mice, fish, deer."

Deer. Like trophy whitetail. Alex's recent fame immediately came to mind. Tanner was leading the conversation too close to home. Paul's fears were quickly realized.

"Tell me, Paul. When's the last time you spoke with your brother, Alex?"

Paul's mouth twitched. "What's Alex got to do with any of this?"

"Now, Paul. Try not to get too upset." Tanner gestured for the guards to move up. "Your brother volunteered to be a part of the clinical trials. You'll have to keep that in mind as we move along." Tanner walked toward the elevator while Paul lagged behind. The two guards fell in line behind Paul and pushed him along.

"If anything's happened to Al–"

"Spare me the threats, Mr. Freeman. I've been more than kind to you since you arrived at our facility. I've told you the facts, filled you in . . . I could have easily cranked your room up to a hundred and ten degrees, but I chose to keep you comfortable." He turned to the captive. "I would hate for your stay to become *uncomfortable*."

Paul pressed. "Tell me Alex is okay. Where is he? Is he being held here, too?" He craned back, looking toward the holding cells.

"No," Tanner said. "But he should be. God, I wanted him here with you! The insights we would've gained from those experiments . . . Of course, the claims he made during the clinical trials were, to say the least, *colorful*. But knowing what we know now? Can you imagine?

"Thing is, we lost your brother right after the trials. No social media. No cellphone. He probably would have been gone for good were not for his fifteen minutes of fame. A few magazine covers and a boastful local news interview later and we were back on his trail. Another Ocula outlier using his newfound powers for personal gain, dreaming up things he could never attain on his own. I don't think I have to explain the danger here."

"So where is he?"

Tanner sighed as he stood at the elevator door. "Unfortunately, we had to dispatch your brother. He was becoming too loud, too popular. There was no way we could have disappeared him to this facility without someone taking notice, so we tried to stage a hunting accident. It was going to be quick. Painless."

No. It can't be true. Paul's fists were tight and shaking. He had lost his mother, his father, and now his only brother? The two siblings couldn't have been more different, but Paul still cared for Alex. The thought of being the last of the Freemans rattled him to the core.

Tanner chortled, "But wouldn't you know? The poor guy leapt in front of one of our cars, making it look like just another hit-and-run. Can you believe it?" He checked his watch. "Anyway, let's hurry along now. We don't want to be late for our appointment with Mr. Doyle."

Paul's eyes were blazing fire. He couldn't think–only react. He drove his elbow into the face of the guard behind him on his right, busting the sentinel's nose and sending him tumbling back. He turned left to take a swing when he felt a powerful blow to the back of his skull.

It was the butt of an AR-15.

The other guard sent Paul to the floor with an assault that was seamless and swift. Paul lay there, unconscious and bleeding, a touch of red on the once-spotless surface of the all-white corridor. The altercation was over in a matter of seconds.

That's when the dream began.

Chapter 19:
First Time for Everything

Paul sat up in bed, the morning sun projecting long yellow rectangles on the floor between the footboard and the dresser where Michelle was standing. Her head tilted sideways while she brushed her long, flowing hair. She watched Paul in the mirror.

"You've always liked it long, haven't you?"

"What can I say. I married you for your hair."

She smiled back. "You would still love me if I cut it off though, right?"

"Of course, sweetie. Just not as much."

She turned to throw her brush at him. "You asshole!" She pounced him on the bed, grabbing a pillow and playfully smothering the comedian. The early morning wrestling session began hastily, but soon slowed to gentle intimacies. Michelle threw her pillow to the side and began to kiss down Paul's neck, the sensation of her soft lips sending sparks through her husband's body. He was almost lost in the moment when a thought interrupted.

"Do you think Aaron's awake?" He glanced at the baby monitor.

"I don't hear anything," she whispered in his ear. "We've got time."

It was the perfect Sunday morning. The sunlight warmed the room, and birds could be heard just outside the window, filling the air with the first song of the day.

They settled back into one another, their bodies entangled as Paul embraced his wife in the beginning throes of passion, one hand running down Michelle's side, another losing itself in her long and silky hair. His fingernails gently traced from the side of her neck to the back of her head, letting her hair glide between his fingers as he ran his hand from roots to ends.

But something wasn't right. Paul slowed, lying on top of Michelle, startled by the sensation he felt in the palm of his hand. He pulled his hand from Michelle's hair to find it draped in cobwebs, the sticky mess stretching from his fingers to the ends of Michelle's sandy blonde locks.

"Michelle," Paul gasped. She looked into his horrified eyes, passion still burning in hers.

"Don't stop, Paul. Please, don't stop."

"Michelle, something's wrong."

"Nothing's wrong, Paul. Just don't stop."

Paul sat up in bed and analyzed his wife. A look of confusion swept her face while the rest of the room underwent a dramatic change. Picture frames, wall art and all the little cracks in the sheetrock melted into a smooth, aqua-blue-colored wall. The bedroom window spun clockwise to the ceiling, the yellow sunlight now artificial as the window morphed into an LED panel. It was a place Paul had only recently become acquainted with: his holding cell.

Michelle sat by Paul on the cot, her hair restored and the cobwebs nowhere in sight. She was wearing the same nightgown Paul had just taken off her. She asked, "Is this the place you told me about?"

"Yes," Paul replied. "I tried calling you, but they wouldn't let me. I didn't think I'd ever see you or Aaron again. I just knew they were going to kill me."

"Who was going to kill you, Paul?"

"The men from Asteria. Tanner. Doyle. The guards."

"Your boss, Tanner?"

"Yes. Well, one of them."

"Did you turn in the assignment Tanner asked for?"

"The assignment?"

"Yes," Michelle said. "It was due yesterday. You turned it in, didn't you?"

Paul began to sweat profusely, beads of water rolling down his face. His skin was blushing red. His hair was soaked and dripping like a soggy mop. He took the bottom of his shirt and wiped his forehead. "I had forgotten all about that," he said. "That's going to get me fired for sure."

"You'd better tell someone quickly," Michelle said. "Maybe he won't be so mad about it after all."

"Who should I tell?"

Michelle pointed to the cell door. "Why don't you start with them?"

The door opened, and in walked an armed guard. Then another. And another. Suddenly the walls of Paul's cell began to expand, growing from a small holding cell to a room the size of a hangar, large enough to house over a hundred guards. They stood at attention, lined up in rows, twelve wide by twelve deep. They looked forward and into the distance. None of them spoke.

Paul recognized some of the faces in the crowd, but the two standing directly in front of him stood out like sore thumbs. They were the guards from the corridor.

"I hate those fucking guys," Paul said.

Michelle singled them out. “Those two?”

“Yeah. Those two. They’re the guys who locked me up here.” Paul stood up and walked over to the men. They stood fast and expressionless, as resolute as the Queen’s Royal Guards. “This one here knocked me out cold,” Paul said, rubbing the bulging knot on the back of his head. Michelle got up to examine Paul’s wound. She tilted his head down so she could see.

“Hmm . . . doesn’t look so bad to me, Paul.” She kissed his head. “I think it’ll heal up just fine.”

“That’s not the point,” Paul said. “I wish all these guys would eat a bullet already so we can go home.” Paul thought he saw movement on the floor toward the back of the crowd. The guards were wearing black combat boots, but this was a bright blur of Kelly green, filling the spaces between the rows. Paul squinted and the scene sharpened. The guards remained perfectly still. The movement wasn’t their feet.

Oh my God, Paul thought. *Snakes.*

They slithered toward Paul and Michelle, still at a distance but rapidly approaching. The once-pristine holding-cell floor was becoming filled with legless reptiles, moving and hissing and closing in on Paul and his wife.

“We’ve got to get out of here,” Paul said. He took Michelle by the arm and turned to the door. It was wide open, but two guards were blocking it–the guards from the corridor.

“Just fucking die already!” Paul yelled.

The guards faced one another. Suddenly their steely, hardened expressions turned into looks of alarm and action. Both guards went for their weapons, drawing their service pistols from their holsters and bringing the muzzles to one another’s foreheads. Then they pulled the triggers.

Paul's ears were ringing. Two shots went off at once, the violent act followed by two bodies slumping to the floor. Blood spatter covered the walls behind the last place the guards stood. The two lifeless corpses lay at Paul's feet, the shocked inmate forced to scoot his feet back to avoid the swift-flowing blood that poured from their heads.

More shots followed. Paul instinctively grabbed Michelle to shield her from the blasts. Round after round, small weapons fire filled the room, accompanied by the jingle of shell casings and the thuds of bodies hitting the floor. Snakes hissed and struck as the guards fell on top of them. Soon a sea of slithering green and seeping red covered the bodies. Michelle began to scream.

Paul held her tight as he looked down at one of the dead guards lying on the floor. Something about him had changed. He was still wearing his combat boots and tactical fatigues and weapons and clips . . . everything was the same, except for his face. Something was familiar. Paul looked closer.

Jesus Christ. It's me. The dead eyes were milky and glazed, but every other feature was identical to Paul. Paul's fears compounded when he looked back at the faces of the other guards in the cell. They were all Paul's duplicates, dead or dying, with snakes framing their mortified faces.

"Is this it, Paul?" Michelle asked as she closed her eyes, clinging to her husband. Paul had been in some precarious situations before, but nothing put the fear of God in him like hearing his wife panic. Paul's heart was beating out of his chest. Terror had stricken a heavy blow. He wanted to cry, but he found himself unable to catch his breath. With each passing second, breathing grew more and more difficult. Soon he couldn't inhale at all. He fell to his knees, grabbing his throat and fighting for air.

"I . . . can't . . . breathe . . ."

Paul gasped loudly as his face lifted off the cold linoleum floor. He sat upright, still dazed as his mind quickly left the terrifying world of guards and snakes and returned back to the reality of the underground corridor. He touched the back of his head; the knot was still there, covered in the same iron crust that was on the floor in front of him.

Oh, thank God. Paul never thought he would be happy to be back in the facility, but the nightmare was proof positive that it could have been a lot worse. He stared at the floor and rubbed the knot on his head. Then he looked up the corridor. That was when he saw them.

Lying just a few feet away were the two guards blocking the door in his dream. Paul got up to take a closer look. He noticed one of the guards was lying face down. Paul knelt down to turn his head; it was cold to the touch. He could see the bloody nose he had given the guard just seconds before he was knocked unconscious, along with a fresh bullet wound to the forehead.

Impossible.

Paul pivoted to the other guard lying on the floor and examined the body. *The same wound to the forehead.* This was not a dream.

He jumped to his feet, looking down each end of the hall. No one in sight. He turned his attention to the lab. A solid white door was the only entrance from the hallway. Paul jiggled the handle. Locked. He noticed one of the large panes of glass had been shattered by a stray bullet. Cracks spidered out from the hole in the center.

Paul scanned the lab through the tempered glass for signs of life. The machines buzzed and the robots continued to work, carrying on as if nothing had happened. *But something did happen*, thought Paul. And it was something he could never begin to explain.

But maybe one of the lab technicians could.

Paul noticed him right away, shaking and cowering behind a desk on the far end of the lab. Paul took the service pistol from the dead guard's hand and used it to break through the weakened glass, clearing the pieces from the edges of the window frame before stepping through to the other side. He pointed the gun at the trembling man as he approached.

"Don't shoot! Don't shoot!" the tech covered his face.

"What the hell happened here?"

"Please, don't shoot me. Please, don't shoot–"

"Hey, hey, *hey!* Just calm down, I'm lowering my gun, see?"

The technician looked through his weathered fingers and watched Paul lower his weapon. He adjusted his black-rimmed glasses, and then cupped his elbows with his hands, rocking back and forth. Paul addressed him again.

"Tell me what happened *now*. What happened to the guards?"

The tech's voice was shaking. "They shot each other. They all shot each other."

Paul looked back at the two bodies lying in the hallway. "What do you mean, all?"

The tech explained. "I saw your scuffle with the guards in the hallway. The one guard clocked you pretty good. Then they stood around for a minute or two while Tanner barked at them. He was cussing up a storm when the two guards jumped away from one another like they had just seen a ghost. They started yelling 'Freeze!' and 'Stop!' with their guns drawn at each other. Then they both started shooting. Tanner just stood there. He was in shock. He looked down at the guards–you were lying there, too–then back up at us in the lab. That was when he took off."

The tech's hand quivered as he pointed up to a split-screen television mounted on the wall. "We watched Tanner ride the elevator back up to ground level. That was when we saw the rest of the bodies. Every one of the armed guards, lying dead all over the compound. The perimeter, the upper level, down here . . . bodies were everywhere, and they're still not moving. Tanner had to step over a half-dozen just to get out the front door. Apparently, the helicopter pilots were okay, too, because they all took off together just before you woke up."

Paul stuck the gun in his belt and helped the man to his feet. "Where are the rest of the technicians?" He looked around the room. Empty.

"No idea," the tech said. "I went and hid in the corner when the shooting started. They may have made it topside, but I watched the helicopter take off, and they weren't on it. Maybe they are running around the jungle, trying to find help." He took his glasses off and cleaned them with his shirt. "They won't find anyone. We're too deep in the Costa Rican jungle, halfway between Pueblo Nuevo and Poás Volcano National Park. At least ten clicks from anything walking upright, and those are just farmers and ranchers scattered across the countryside. Tanner's people picked this place for a reason."

Paul looked for the exit. "I'm willing to bet those same people are going to be checking back in on this place real soon, and I don't want to be here when they do. Do you have an access card to the elevator?"

"Of course."

"Good. We'll need to get topside as soon as possible. But first I need to check the holding cells to see if they've got anyone else locked up here." Paul already had in mind to double back for Claire, but he couldn't shake the feeling that Tanner was lying about Alex not being there, too.

Paul went back into the hallway, with the scruffy technician following a few steps behind. He moved past the guards, stepping over one of the bodies to get to the first cell on the right. All of the cell doors had been opened. He peered into the first cell. No one there. He walked on to the next cell, paying no attention to the technician.

Suddenly Paul heard a loud click behind him. It was the hammer of a gun, cocked back and ready to fire. He turned to look.

"Sorry, Mr. Freeman," the technician said. "I can't let you leave. Too great a liability. I'm afraid this is as far as you go."

"Who are you?" Paul asked.

"No one, really. But around here I'm known as Mr. Doyle. Just an old company man trying to protect the world from people like you."

"People like me?" Paul said. "*You* kidnapped *me*, remember? I haven't done anything to anyone."

"That's right. You haven't–yet. And we're going to keep it that way." Doyle kept the gun trained on Paul. "The tests we've conducted here have uncovered a power greater than anyone could have ever imagined, hidden inside the brains of a miniscule percentage of the population. This power would have remained locked away for eons, were it not for the key that Asteria Pharmaceuticals created."

"You're talking about Ocula," Paul huffed, tired of explaining himself. "I already told Tanner, I've never even taken the drug!"

Doyle scoffed. "Look around you, Paul, and explain to me the mess you're in." He kicked the body of one of the guards. "You're going to tell me you had nothing to do with this?"

"It's impossible. All of this . . . impossible."

"Nothing in this world is impossible, Mr. Freeman. There is only what we know, and what we have yet to discover. When Tanner first came to me for help, I thought Ocula was a product we could contain while strengthening our position in the world. That's why I agreed to follow him to this God-forsaken hellhole.

"'Weaponization for the greater good.' That's what Tanner told me. Ocula gives individuals with a specific genetic sequence the power to change the world around them using the images they project during REM sleep cycles. If we could harness Ocula's power, and then enhance it, we would be able to use them to change the world however we saw fit."

"You keep saying *we*."

Doyle smirked. "Didn't know Tanner was a company man before taking the Asteria job, did you? You know, for a guy that's supposed to be an asset to the program, you're not too quick on the uptake."

Paul gave Doyle his best eat-shit-and-die look.

Doyle continued, "The CIA had a vested interested in the program. Tanner's prior work with Central Intelligence involved studying the plausibility of using illicit substances to influence national elections south of the border in an effort to strengthen U.S. national security. Ever hear of the Venezuelan election conspiracy of 2018?"

Paul knew the story well. Every worldwide media outlet had covered the Venezuelan conspiracy at one point or another over the last three years. Following the controversial election of right-wing demagogue Alonso Padilla, left-wing factions had accused the right of tampering with voting procedures in the national elections. Some critics even went so far as to allege the United States had a hand in setting up a western-sympathizing leader, but no credible evidence was ever brought forward.

"But the whistleblowers were on to something," Doyle said. "The United States feared a Venezuelan credit default, as did conservative-leaning Venezuelans who were seeking a government resolution to pay down the debt. A lot of western interests were riding on that election, so when the CIA saw an opportunity to establish a friend to the south, we took it."

"By rigging the election?"

"By swaying voter sentiment toward our choice for office," Doyle said. "Countless peer-reviewed journals have theorized that liberally minded individuals have different brains structures than people who identify as conservative. These differences are marked by physiological and neurological traits that can be identified and measured.

"Take the anterior cingulate cortex, for example. This portion of the brain is remarkably larger in liberals, who demonstrate more tolerance for uncertainty. A larger right amygdala, on the other hand, has been linked to conservatives, whose sensitivity toward fear and threats is more pronounced than their political opponents.

Doyle's mouth curved into a smile. "That was where we came in. Studies had shown that trace amounts of cocaine could increase brain function in the amygdala portion of the brain, while limiting activity in the anterior cingulate cortex. In theory, this would create a voter with neurological traits that leaned conservative. By interjecting the readily available narcotic into the Venezuelan water supply of the most left-leaning districts in the country, the CIA hypothesized that the heated 2018

Venezuelan elections could be influenced in a manner favorable to the interests of the United States."

Paul pursed his lips in reflection. "But conservatives didn't win that election. I remember seeing it on television. All of the right-wing pundits were worried the election spelled the end to U.S.-Venezuelan diplomatic relations."

Doyle agreed. "You're right. It was a huge blow to our theory. Who would've thought people still had the ability to think for themselves? Luckily, our research continued. That's the beautiful thing about working for the government, Paul. The private sector demands results, while we're free to try and spend and try again."

"And kidnap and murder and–"

"Like I was saying," Doyle interrupted. "Tanner left the public sector for greener pastures soon after, but we kept our back channels open, hoping our connections would one day pay us back for all of the shit we put up with from the federal government. That's why we can't let someone like you screw up our little venture–"

"A venture I should have nothing to do with!" Paul yelled. "Because, once again, I *haven't* taken the drug!"

"Everyone needs a key to get into locked away places, Paul. This is science, not sorcery. You've taken the drug. I'm certain of it." Doyle steadied the gun, aiming at Paul's head. "Now, I'm sorry to say we've been here long enough, and I have to go. Sorry, Paul. I was really looking forward to working with you."

Paul couldn't bear to watch. He closed his eyes tight and waited, wincing as he anticipated the shot. It would be loud. Hopefully it would be quick, too.

A single shot rang out. A loud cracking sound filled the corridor, echoing to the end before fading away. Paul felt the disturbance in the air, but he didn't feel anything else. He hesitantly opened one eye and looked forward. Doyle was standing there, bleeding, holding his hands to his stomach. He moaned. Blood dripped from the corner of his mouth. He looked at Paul, confused. Then he fell to his knees.

Claire was standing behind him, the barrel of the 9mm she was holding still smoking.

"He always did talk too much," Claire said. She walked up to Doyle and put her knee in his back, nudging him over. His face hit the linoleum. He exhaled a final, exasperated breath, and then Doyle was dead.

Claire asked Paul, "You okay?"

"Yeah, I'm okay. What about you?"

"Really?" Claire said. She looked down at Doyle, then back at Paul.

"I see your point," Paul said, finally putting a heart-shaped face on the woman in the vent.

It was only seconds into the informal introduction, and Paul could already tell Claire's tenacity was as fiery as her hair. She wasted no time making their escape, kneeling down by one of the guards to rifle through his pockets. She pulled out a security card, then grabbed Doyle's pistol and handed it to Paul.

"I think you're gonna need this," Claire said.

Paul took the gun and looked down the hall. All of the cell doors were wide open. "Is there anyone else here?"

"No. I already checked. It's just you and me." Claire tucked her gun away. "Listen, if we're gonna survive this thing, then we're going to have to stick together. Agreed?"

Paul looked at the three dead bodies on the floor. “Agreed. Now let’s get the fuck out of here.”

***

The elevator ride back up to ground level was surreal. Neither Claire nor Paul thought they would ever make it out of the facility alive. Claire looked over at her former partner-in-captivity. “Can you fly a helicopter?” she asked.

“No, but it wouldn’t matter anyway. Doyle said he watched Tanner take off in the chopper right after the guards started shooting each other.”

“That’s a pisser.”

“Tell me about it. Did you ever hear anyone mention another way out?”

Claire shook her head. “Unfortunately, no one ever discussed the details of their commute here.”

The elevator slowed to a halt before reaching the top. A chime sounded and the doors opened. They were back at ground level. Rodents scurried away from the elevator light. “I never thought I’d be so happy to see rats in all of my life,” Claire said.

“Or dead people.” Paul saw two dead bodies lying in the corner of the small elevator lobby. Then he looked past the open double doors toward the main entrance. “That’s six so far.”

“I’m sure there’s more outside,” Claire said. “I’ve seen trained soldiers turn on one another like this before.”

Paul was curious. Claire explained, “In my dreams, during one of Doyle’s sessions. But I wasn’t on the synthesized drug when this happened. As a matter of fact, I wasn’t even dreaming. I was wide awake when the cell door swung open, right before the shooting started.”

Paul hadn't remembered his dream until Claire brought up the subject. At that very moment, every memory came rushing back like water through a floodgate. Michelle. The bedroom. The shootings. Everything that had happened to the guards in his dream happened in real life. There were at least a dozen bodies to prove it.

Paul had caused this.

Chapter 20: Why Can't We Be Friends?

Maria Moreno. What a bitch.

It was the first thought to cross Donny Ford's mind as he woke up in a hotel suite in Atlanta. The details of his dream were fading fast, but he knew he had dreamt about the reporter nonetheless. A thin column of light shone through a gap in the blackout curtains, hitting Donny square in the face and prompting a heavy groan.

"I'm so sorry, Don," Marci said, hurrying to the window. "I've tried to keep it as dark as possible in here. Quiet, too. I took the liberty of booking the adjoining rooms, just to make sure no one would disturb you. I hope you don't mind."

Donny sat up and rubbed his temples. "How long was I out?" he asked.

"You passed out backstage Monday after the incident. We were going to run you to the emergency room—"

"How long, Marci?"

Solemnly, she replied, "It's Thursday morning."

"You're joking." Donny remembered the backstage episode. It felt like it had happened fifteen minutes ago. Now Marci was telling him he had been asleep in a hotel for the last three days, with no recollection of the time in between. Except for an image of Maria Moreno, fresh on his mind.

"It's no joke. You've been in and out this entire time. We were very worried about you."

Donny looked around the room. “Definitely not the E.R. Looks like you respected my wishes,” he said. Marci came and sat on the end of the bed.

“Yes, of course, Don. Although it wasn’t easy,” Marci said. “The Wyatt staff almost made the choice for us. Luckily I was able to get your personal physician on the phone. Dr. Yates put all worries to rest. He assured everyone you were just having a stress-induced episode. No one there was going to argue with that.

“We waited for the doctor to arrive, and then we had you transported here as discretely as possible. The press was starting to gather outside the Wyatt, so we decided to rent a moving van to smuggle you across the street. We threw a drop cloth over you and wheeled you out the back door. No one batted an eye.”

Donny couldn’t help but smile. “You’re so clever, Marci. That’s always been one of my favorite things about you.”

Marci leaned in. “Don. Hun. If you don’t mind me asking. Why are you so adamant about staying away from the hospitals? What would we have done if you had stopped breathing? Or, God forbid, had a heart attack?”

“It wasn’t a heart attack, was it?”

“Well, no,” Marci said. “But what if–”

“LOOK!” Donny yelled. “I already told you I didn’t want to talk about it. I have my reasons and that should be enough.” He regretted the outburst the moment it left his lips. He looked into Marci’s eyes. They always gleamed with sympathy, even when he was being an asshole. He shrank away and stared at the floor.

“I’m sorry, Marci. I didn’t mean to lash out like that. But I can’t go to the hospital. I just . . . I just–”

"You don't have to explain, Don. I didn't mean to upset you. I just worry about you, that's all." She rubbed his leg over the covers. "You've been through so much this week, and you need your rest. I'll leave you alone for a while, let you have some time to yourself." She stood up and walked to the door. "I'll be in the next room if you need me. Room 710." She laid her room key on the end table next to the door.

"Marci?" Donny asked, just as she was about to leave. "Dr. Yates has a number for me. Do you mind getting it?"

"Sure thing," Marci replied. She left. Donny sat up in bed, staring at the blank television screen across the room. He heard the occasional chorus of door slamming and hotel-cart rattling, but for the most part it was quiet. Peaceful. Nothing like the melee at the Wyatt Conference Center a few days earlier.

Donny shook his head in disbelief every time he thought about the headaches. He had never experienced such debilitating pain before participating in the clinical trials for a sleeping medication. Two years earlier a friend had told him about the study. A drug company was looking for volunteers for clinical trials. This drug was going to revolutionize the way medicine was practiced and the company was specifically looking for volunteers with sleep disorders. Now Donny was lying in a hotel room, recovering from the second migraine of his life. The man had little doubt. Ocula had to be the culprit.

Donny couldn't imagine how people lived with migraines, but of course, they did. He had read somewhere that over forty million people suffered from migraine headaches–and that was just in the United States. Now he was one of them. Light sensitivity, vomiting, dizziness, visual disturbances, numbness . . . all symptoms Donny wouldn't have wished on his worst enemies. Except for maybe Maria Moreno, that shit-stirring hack from Action News Atlanta.

But even with the most atrocious, freakiest symptoms migraines had to offer, Donny's headaches didn't hold a candle to the phenomenon that seemed to follow. *The dreams.* While painless in nature, the dreams had tormented Donny ever since Bill Stevens had been murdered the year before.

Donny stared into the ceiling, recalling the dream that preceded the death of his long-time business partner. Donny had always assumed it was the heated argument with Stevens on the night of his murder that led to the first migraine of his life. Not knowing what to do, Donny went to his hotel room, took a few airplane bottles from the minibar, and chased down a handful of ibuprofen. He crashed on the bed, grabbing a pillow to cover his face with before grumbling himself to sleep. Apparently, the cocktail of NSAIDs and liquor had done the trick.

That was when the dream started.

It was a continuation of the argument they had had hours earlier, right in the middle of Stevens' hotel room. In the beginning, it was hard for Donny to distinguish Round Two from reality. Stevens and Ford were wearing the same clothes and arguing about the same business strategy they had fought over for years.

At first, the shouting match was largely one-sided. Stevens was in Ford's face, chastising him for wanting to scuttle the new plans for the Donny Ford brand. Stevens grew even angrier when Ford reminded Stevens whose name was on the marquee.

In reality, Donny didn't back down, even placing a hand on Stevens' chest and warning him to back off. The dream, however, took a timid turn. Instead of giving Stevens a solid shove, a piece of his mind, and the middle finger, Donny just stood there and took the abuse.

Stevens screamed at Ford with every denigrating sound bite he could think of. "You're a *HACK*! A con artist! A *goddamn* loser!"

Donny kept his head down. He wouldn't look Stevens in the eyes.

The antagonist went on. "Your wife left you because she knows what a phony you are. She didn't even want to have your kids. Who the fuck could blame her?"

Ford clenched his fists, white-knuckled and shaking at his side. He still wouldn't look up. Stevens said, "What are you gonna do, pussy?"

Finally, Donny raised his head. He felt something in his hand. Stevens was smirking. "Nothing. You're not going to do a thing, because you're a *fucking pu–*"

Donny snapped. He drove the ice pick into Stevens' left eye, pushing it all the way down to the wooden handle. Stevens screamed as Donny beat the contents of his eye socket like a cook whipping an egg in a mixing bowl. It wasn't long before Donny's arm tired. He left the ice pick in its new socket, then pushed Stevens back to let him assess the damage.

Horror glinted from the only eye Stevens had left. He grabbed the handle of the ice pick with both hands and slowly pulled it out of his skull. A purée of sclera and brain matter oozed from a hollowed eye socket. The screams were deafening.

The bloody pick lay in Stevens' hands. His only eye filled with tears, but Donny wasn't fazed. He swiped the pick from Stevens and shoved it into his remaining eye in one fluid motion. There was no hesitation. Stevens shrieked in pain. "No, no, *NO*!"

Stevens' feeble attempts to fight off his attacker were in vain. Donny worked the ice pick just like before, then pulled it out and let his friend's body collapse onto the floor. Stevens hit with a loud thud, and then the room was quiet again.

That was until Donny felt the presence of a spectator to his left.

"Whoa. That was wicked, man."

A bartender. He was formally dressed and holding his hand out. He stood in front of a fully lit bar, with reflections of lights and club rats dancing across the mirrored glass behind him. "Can I have my ice pick back now? These drinks aren't gonna serve themselves." Donny nodded, then looked down at the bloody pick. He handed it over.

"Thanks, buddy," the bartender said. He shook his finger at Stevens' dead body. "You know, I heard the way that guy was talking to you. Can't say I blame you for fuckin' him up real good like that."

Donny looked at his friend, lifeless and mutilated. Clubbers danced around him and ignored the body as if he were just some drunk who had passed out on the dance floor. Then Donny looked back at the bartender. He held a bloody finger to his lips.

The bartender said, "Don't worry, bro. I won't tell."

That was the moment Donny awoke from his first post-migraine nightmare. The hotel bed he had been lying in was drenched with sweat. If he hadn't known any better, he would have thought he had pissed himself in the night. He looked at the clock. It was only 4:15 a.m., but the pandemonium coming from the hall outside sounded more like checkout time. He rolled out of bed, still fully dressed from the night before. He grabbed a towel from the bathroom to pat his face off with before stepping out into the hall.

The hotel was a madhouse. EMTs, firefighters and police officers were scrambling in both directions down the hallway. Some were pushing people out of the way and forcing them to step back behind the crime-scene tape, while others lifted the tape and led investigators in hats and overcoats to the scene of the crime in the hotel room a few doors down. All of them were there for Bill Stevens.

Donny tried waving down a couple of firefighters passing by, but the first responders didn't have time to chat. He stood on his tippy toes, trying to see what was happening outside the room down the hall. He spotted a civilian who was forced from the scene, apparently getting in the wrong person's way. The man was storming off when Donny got his attention.

"Excuse me, sir! Do you know what's going on here?"

The man turned back. "Yeah, some guy decided to go all hara-kiri in his room last night. Didn't exactly fall on his sword, though. One of the reporters said he gored his own eyeballs out with–"

Jesus Christ.

"–a ballpoint pen." The man cocked his head. "Hey, pal. You okay?"

Donny was horrified. "D-Did you get a name?"

"No, but the guy was in 1213. Pretty disturbing scene. You can see where the blood ran under the door and into the hall when you walk past on the way to the elevators. If you need to leave, I'd take the stairs."

The man left. Others rushed by while Donny stood in the doorway. The color had left his face. For the first time in his life, the professional speaker was speechless.

1213. Bill's room. He couldn't believe it. Had he somehow been the reason behind Bill's murder? Was he sleepwalking that night? A thought came to him, abrupt and sharp. *I'm still wearing last night's clothes.*

He quickly dipped back into his room, slamming the door shut and whirling into the bathroom. He frantically checked himself in the mirror, starting with his face before moving all the way down to his shoes. Not a speck of blood to be found. He evaluated his hands, turning them palm up, then back over. Spotless.

He breathed a sigh of relief, then sat down on the edge of the tub. His hands were over his mouth. None of this seemed real. The quiet hum of the air conditioner serenaded the hotel room, but it wasn't enough to drown out the bedlam still taking place outside his door. Bill Stevens was dead, just a few doors down from a disgruntled business partner. And while the murder weapon in Donny's dream wasn't a ballpoint pen, Bill's actions–stabbing both of his eyes out before bleeding to death in his hotel room–were either the mother of all coincidences, or a direct result of the dream he had had the night before.

Donny stared into the black television screen, ruminating on his first horrifying headache and the nightmare that followed. Then he considered the recent migraine attack; it was only the second episode he had ever experienced. If his impossible suspicions about the first episode were true–that somehow he dreamed up the real-life murder of Bill Stevens–then something would have happened to Maria Moreno, too.

Donny decided to investigate the theory from the comfort of his king-size bed. He flipped on the television and searched for the cable news network. It was Moreno and company from Action News Atlanta who had launched the assault on his motivational seminar two days earlier. If anything happened to her, especially if she was working that day, odds were the cable news giant would be the first to report it.

But the more Donny scrolled, the dumber he felt. *What am I doing?* He thought. *Dreaming up murders?* He chuckled over the lunacy of it all. He was about to give up the search when he saw the red-letter news ticker scrolling across the bottom of the screen:

OUR OWN MARIA MORENO WAS INVOLVED IN AN EARLY MORNING ACCIDENT * SHE HAS BEEN ADMITTED TO ST CATHERINE'S REGIONAL HOSPITAL AND IS LISTED IN CRITICAL CONDITION * FAMILY IS REQUESTING PRAYERS AT THIS TIME

Impossible. Donny jumped out of bed halfway through the first sentence, snatching his pants off the floor and hurrying to get dressed as he continued reading the slow-scrolling ticker. Each word revealed itself at an agonizing pace. Ford shouted at the screen to hurry it along, but there was one word he got hung up on. *Accident.*

Deceitful, he thought as he buttoned his shirt. When reporters mentioned early morning accidents, they were usually talking about car wrecks. The assumption rang especially true in Atlanta, where going an entire day without an interstate collision was about as frequent as a major-league pennant win. The problem with labeling Moreno's condition an early-morning accident was that eating an entire bottle of ibuprofen was quite deliberate, and rarely–if ever–an accident.

That's exactly what Maria Moreno had done that morning, just before breakfast. Ford didn't have to see it broadcast live on television to know it. He finally remembered his dream, and he knew exactly what had happened.

Chapter 21:
¿Habla Inglés?

The sun was blazing hot, beaming down on Paul and Claire through the thick, humid Costa Rican air. Heat rays rose from the tall grass and rippled the mountains on the horizon. They searched for signs of civilization outside the compound, but nothing pointed to a way out. It was all jungle in every direction.

The compound on a hill was now eerily quiet, except for the occasional toucanet flying overhead and croaking at the trespassers. It hadn't been long since Paul's persuasive dream cycle had convinced the surrounding guards to commit mass suicide, but already the stench from the bodies was beginning to rise in the hot subtropical sun. A whiff of death caught Paul by surprise. He looked to Claire.

"Correct me if I'm wrong, but isn't Costa Rica known for its big, meat-eating cats?"

"Among other things," Claire said. "Don't worry. Jaguars are endangered here."

"Yeah. So are we."

Claire searched the perimeter. "I wonder how those lab techs got out in such a hurry?"

"Well, we know they didn't fly out," Paul said. "I didn't see any roads leading out on the way here, but there's no way they employed all that staff here without some kind of contingency plan."

"You're right," Claire said. "They must have transportation close to the facility."

"I would if I were running the place." Paul scanned the fence and noticed a gap at the far corner closest to the jungle canopy. "There."

They started out across the field, wading through the tall grass toward the opening in the fence. As they got closer, they realized the gap was actually a gate, hanging wide open and leading to a small footpath on the other side. "Keep your eyes out," Claire said. Paul nodded as they continued their trudge through the weeds. He was about to take another step, foot raised, when he quickly jumped back.

"Snake!" he yelled, eliciting a what-the-fuck-did-I-just-say look from Claire. "Sorry," he said. "I just hate those fucking things."

Her attention turned back toward the trail, but Paul's eyes were locked on the snake. He was like a hypnotized little field mouse, caught in the gaze of a formidable predator. He caught a glimpse of the bright green serpent as it slithered away, the reptile likely just as startled as he was. The color, the size, even the shape of its head looked exactly like the snakes from his dream. Paul was stunned by the revelation, but he decided to keep the information to himself.

"Let's keep moving," he said in his best tough-guy voice. Claire was already way ahead of him.

They walked through the fence and out of the sun, shaded by the dark jungle canopy that lay ahead. The footpath was clear now. It meandered through the forest, choked with roots and winding through the trees as far as the eye could see. Claire looked down and noticed several sets of footprints leading the way out.

"I don't see any combat boots," she said. "That's probably a good thing."

"A very good thing," Paul said. He knelt down. "This one is tiny, maybe a size eight or so?"

"Champs. Women's. Nine and a half. Kinda big for a girl, but this tech's a girl, nonetheless."

Paul looked up, impressed. "Holy shit. How did you know all that?"

Claire pointed. "It says so, right there in the footprint. The trick is to read the words backwards." She continued down the path, leaving Paul kneeling in the dirt. He dusted off his knees and followed close behind, scouring the dense surrounding jungle for any clues he could find.

They had walked along the path for almost a mile before Claire stopped dead in her tracks. She held up her hand as if to quiet Paul as he approached. She cut her eyes down the path, kneeling and pointing toward a small utility shed at the bottom of the hill. The shed appeared to be about twenty feet across, equipped with a dropdown garage door on the trailside and a standard exterior door on the other. The garage door was open, and the two could barely see the front end of an old Jeep resting in the shadows.

Paul whispered, "The contingency plan." Claire nodded. They knelt for a moment to listen. They could hear a commotion coming from inside the garage. It sounded like someone dumping a box full of tools out onto the concrete floor, followed by a plethora of Spanish curse words.

Claire's eyes panned the landscape around the garage. "How many do you think there are?" she said.

Paul was quiet for a moment, focusing on the noise. "I just hear the one. I think he's talking to himself. What do you think?"

"I think we have to make a move," Claire said. "Everyone in the facility is either long gone or on their way. That Jeep's not going to stay there forever."

Paul agreed, and the two slowly made their way down the hill, using the beaten path to silence their footsteps while sticking close to the trees. They crept at a snail's pace, coming within twenty feet of the garage door. They watched as a short man in a lab coat emerged, a screwdriver and wire cutters in one hand, a hammer in the other. They quietly drew their weapons, then counted down, *three . . . two . . . one . . .*

"FREEZE!" Claire said.

The tech dropped the tools and put his hands up. "Don't shoot!"

To Paul, something about this was all too familiar. It was the same introduction he had made to Mr. Doyle not long before the man tried to kill him. Paul gripped the 9mm tighter and considered getting past the deceptive formalities by shooting the man in his bound-to-be-lying face. After all, the man was working in a top-secret spook house in the middle of the jungle, in a lab directly across the hall from a dozen human holding cells. No way any person could plead ignorance to what was going on there. His hands had blood on them, and Paul was fresh out of sympathy.

"Give us one reason why we shouldn't shoot you now," Paul said. The man was speechless. "Speak English? Habla Inglés?" Paul took a step closer. "You better start talking *real* fast." The man looked to Claire in desperation. She was unmoved.

The tech said to Paul, "Yes. I speak English." He motioned toward the Jeep. "I can start the car. Get you two out of here." Forgetting his position, the man bent over to pick up his tools.

"Hands up!" Paul said.

"Lo siento, sorry," he retracted. "It's just . . . it's what I was doing when you two showed up. Trying to get the car started. We had three Jeeps here for emergencies. The other two were missing when I got here. I'm sure some of the other guys beat me to it. The keys are usually hanging on a board in the garage, but I couldn't find the keys to this one. Guess the others didn't bother to look any harder, either."

Paul whispered to Claire, "Do you know how to hotwire a car?" She shook her head no. Paul turned his attention to the technician. "Okay, here's what we're going to do. You're going to hotwire the Jeep for us, and then you're going to thank us for not killing you. Then we're going to leave."

The tech nodded. "Okay, okay. Fair enough. I can hotwire the Jeep for you, and you can leave me out here if that's what you want. But how are you going to find your way out?"

Paul shrugged. "Follow the trail."

The tech disagreed. "I've been on the Jeep trails many times. There are at least half a dozen splits between here and the nearest town, and none of them are marked. You won't make it out of here without someone who knows the way." He looked left, then right. "And it looks like I'm the only one around who can get you back into town."

Claire looked to Paul. "He makes some good points."

Paul sighed. "Yeah, you're right." He glared at the tech. "Okay, we'll take you with us. But if you try anything, it's lights out. Got it?"

"Got it." He turned his palms upward. "Can I pick up my tools now?"

"Sure. Of course," Paul said. "Let's get this thing started so we can get out of here."

Paul and Claire walked up to the jeep, never taking their guns off the new acquaintance. They watched closely as the tech opened the driver-side door, squeezed under the steering wheel, and lay face up in the floorboard. Paul noticed the man's nametag stitched onto his lab coat above the left breast pocket. "R. Ramirez," Paul said. "What's the R stand for?"

"Roberto," he answered, never looking up. Roberto was concentrating on the jeep's steering column. He had already taken the plastic housing off, and was thumbing through a bundle of wires in search of the ones leading to the battery and starter.

"Tell me, Roberto: where'd you learn how to hotwire a car?"

"I grew up in San José. Many of my friends were questionable characters to say the least. Some were pickpockets, some were conmen. I was the car thief. I never actually stole a car to make any money–I just took them for joyrides every now and then. One night I got caught by a policeman who knew my parents. He made them vow to ship me away from the bad neighborhood influences, or he would send me to jail. That's why I went to college in Miami."

Claire asked, "Really, which one?"

"University of Miami. I majored in molecular biology there before going to work for a small pharmaceutical research firm in Orlando. That job only lasted about a year before the company was gobbled up by Asteria Pharmaceuticals. Asteria had no interest in keeping any of our staff; they only wanted our research and intellectual property. Those who weren't willing to come work in the Costa Rica facility were laid off."

Paul watched Roberto isolate two wires, casting the rest of the bundle to the side. "Is that when you met Tanner and Doyle?" he asked.

"Yes. They offered me and a few others positions at the research facility in Costa Rica. They said we would have the chance to carry on groundbreaking research that would have been impossible in Orlando. I also saw it as an opportunity to return to my home country. Of course," he said matter-of-factly, "it doesn't really matter what country you're in when you're not allowed to leave the facility."

Claire was fuming. "Impossible in Orlando? What, like kidnapping and torturing American citizens against their will?"

Roberto held up a hand. "Please understand, the laboratory staff had no idea humans were being tested until days after we were flown in. By that time, backing out was too late. We were heavily guarded 24/7. We lived at the compound. They even installed special lighting in the cafeteria so lab workers wouldn't grow sick from Vitamin D deficiencies. Most of us were held against our will, just like you."

Claire scoffed. "Bullshit. Your research was based on analyzing the effects of a synthetic drug on the human genome, and you didn't think humans would be involved?"

"Like I said, we had no idea what we were getting into before we arrived."

Paul and Claire had every reason to be skeptical, but at least they knew Roberto was telling the truth about his questionable teenage hobby. He took the two exposed wires and flicked them together, creating a flash of sparks followed by the rumble of a 4.0-liter engine firing on all cylinders. The tension among the three quickly dissipated.

"Yes!" Paul said. Roberto pumped his fist, relieved.

Claire hopped in the passenger side. She leaned over to Roberto–who was still lying in the floorboard–and motioned with her gun. “In the backseat.”

Roberto complied.

***

Paul hadn’t driven stick in years, but working the clutch between first and second gear quickly came back to him. The jeep rolled through puddles and navigated the steep jungle terrain without a hitch, so long as Paul maintained a modest pace. There were a couple of straightaways he tried to kick it up to third, but every time Paul drove faster the potholes, mud slicks, and overhanging branches reminded him to slow it back down to a crawl.

Paul could tell the trail had been maintained to a degree, but that didn’t mean it was free of any dangers. In some places the path was so narrow that one false slip would have sent the jeep rolling off a cliff and into the depths of the lush ravine several hundred feet below. In those cases, Roberto proved quite useful, warning the driver of the impending perils before getting out to guide Paul across the tight passes.

They continued the slow descent down the jade-colored hills toward civilization. It was starting to get dark, with the waning glimmers of light peeking through the twisting vine trees. With each passing minute, hazards on the trail were getting harder to see. Paul navigated around a wide ditch cutting across the trail, the jeep rocking down the path and narrowly missing a tree on the left. The passenger-side tire slid, kicking pebbles and dirt into the crevasse he was steering to avoid.

"I'd hate to get caught out here at night," Paul said. "How much further?"

Roberto said, "No more than twenty minutes or so. The ride into town would be a short one if not for the condition of the trail."

Claire held the roll bar with one hand and her gun in the other. She kept a close eye on the passenger in the backseat, while occasionally sizing up the driver. She couldn't help but notice Paul's increasingly nervous behavior: fingers drumming on the steering wheel, short and shallow breaths, and a twitching eye indicative of high anxiety. They had been through a lot, and Claire was concerned the stress was starting to get to him.

"Are you all right?" she asked.

"This is big, Claire. Who knows who's involved. The people at Asteria. Tanner. Hell, the CIA is probably looking for . . . my God." The realization that his family was at risk stopped him mid-sentence. "Michelle, Aaron . . . they're gonna get dragged into this, if they haven't already. What the fuck are we going to do? And who can we trust?"

"Well, keep in mind I'm a member of the press. At least that's something," Claire said. "The first thing we have to do when we get into town is tell somebody–"

"You're joking, right?" Paul was incredulous. "How long were you in there for? They've already killed my brother. At least that's what Tanner said. Who else do you think is on his list?"

"Jesus, Paul. I'm so sorry–"

"The first thing *I'm* going to do is find my wife and kid and get them as far away from Tanner's goons as humanly possible. You can do whatever you want. If you want to tell somebody, be my guest. Go tell it on the mountain, for all I fucking care. Good luck getting someone to believe all of this. But making sure my family's safe is my only priority."

"I get that you're upset," Claire said, "But we can't just let them get away with this, can we? You expect me to forget about what I went through back there? You don't think they're going to go after my family, too?" Her mouth twisted in disgust. "No way, Paul. No fucking way. We have to blow the cover off this operation, no matter where it leads."

"This isn't just about Big Pharma," Paul said. "Doyle worked for the CIA. So did Tanner. Running a covert testing facility in another country. These aren't the type of people you talk about, or play whistleblower with. These people will kill us, Claire. Plain and simple."

Paul stopped talking as the forest canopy finally opened up to clear, pastoral terrain. The clock seemed to move back half an hour as they splashed through the last puddle and onto the fork where the trail merged with a wider dirt road, the dark canopy of the jungle giving way to an orange-pink twilight.

For a few minutes the conversation ceased as they drove through the fertile valley cradled in the cloud-capped mountains of Costa Rica. They looked to see the volcano Doyle had mentioned to Paul back at the facility, smoldering in the distance. Paul took in the picturesque view. Despite the recent events, the Costa Rican countryside was quite beautiful in the evening. He took a deep breath to calm himself before breaking the silence.

"Look, Claire. Doyle is dead, and the guards were killing each other when Tanner bailed. For all he knows, we're all dead."

"Even if that's true, Paul, it's not going to stick. He'll go back there, or send someone else to. And when they don't find our bodies, they'll come looking for us. They'll exhaust every resource they have and they won't quit until we're silenced. You may be able to take off and hide for a little while, but the moment you stick your head up from the sand, that's it. This is powerful technology they're meddling with, Paul, and they're not going to give up on developing it willfully. The best we can do is strike now while the iron is hot; while they're still picking themselves up from this mess."

A voice rose up from the backseat. "I agree." Paul glanced in the rearview mirror. "She knows what she's talking about," Roberto said. "We've been synthesizing a new version of the drug, and it's light years ahead of the Ocula you know."

"What do you mean, a new version?" Paul asked.

"The first drug inadvertently gave patients the ability to broadcast levels of electromagnetic radiation capable of stimulating neural activity in certain life forms nearby."

"We know that already," Claire said.

"Yes. Well, what you don't know is how the signals are distributed." Roberto leaned forward and took a water bottle out of the cup holder. Claire tightened her grip on the pistol. Roberto put up his free hand. "Please. Let me demonstrate."

He set the bottle on the console. "Now, imagine this is a radio tower sitting high on a hill. The radio tower broadcasts the same type of electromagnetic radiation as our brainwaves do, just at a higher oscillation, or frequency. From the center of that tower, those waves effectively cover a specified radius around the tower." He circled his finger around the bottle, moving outward in a Fibonacci spiral until he reached Paul and Claire. "The further you move away from the center of the tower, the more your broadcast is going to fade into static."

"So the dreams have the potential to affect everyone within a given distance from the origin," Paul said.

"Yes," Roberto said. "But here's where it *really* gets scary. Ocula uses antisense technology to isolate specific gene sequences responsible for disruptive sleep patterns; sequences that are almost two million base pairs long. Some of those pairings–also known as introns–were once thought to be nothing more than useless filler. But the latest version of Ocula disproved that theory. By identifying sixty-four pairings within the original gene sequences, our researchers discovered what sets the clinical-trial outliers apart from everyone else. Once the sixty-four pairings were targeted, we were able to fine-tune the effects of the drug. Dreams that were once broadcast haphazardly can now be precision-targeted with uncanny accuracy."

Precision targeting, thought Claire. *Dawkins*. The last time she had seen her friend he was standing in a sweltering field, detached and taking gunfire just moments before Doyle had sucked her back into reality. She had hoped her last session with the spook was only a dream, but at this point she knew better.

Roberto said, "If Ocula 1.0 is like taking a shotgun to a shootout, then Version 2.0 is a laser-guided missile, capable of targeting specific organisms that are within range of the source. It also gives outliers more control over the neural activity of their targets, influencing the minds around them however they see fit."

Paul grumbled. "Like I said. We're all pretty much fucked."

"There *is* a light at the end of the tunnel," Roberto said. "The outliers. Both versions of the drug are completely worthless without the right gene sequence to act upon. For almost everyone else on the planet, these drugs lead to nothing more than a good night's sleep. Only a handful of people have the ability to make their dreams a reality."

Claire looked at Paul. “You know what that means, don’t you?”

Paul knew, and he didn’t like it. His brooding eyes focused on the shabby asphalt road ahead. He weighed his options and came up short. It didn’t matter how he felt about the situation; he was on board with the next step of the plan. He had to be. It was the only step they could take.

“Yeah. I know what it means,” he said. “We have to find the others.”

Chapter 22: Doubts

The cashier watched in bewilderment as Donny Ford dumped a pile of caffeinated drinks and B12 energy shots on the counter. One of the shots rolled across the counter and off the back edge, falling on the young cashier's foot and prompting a snort. Donny paid little attention, preoccupied with the phone that was wedged between his shoulder and ear.

"Sir," she said, smacking her gum. "You do realize we've got buggies and baskets for your convenience."

Donny stared blankly. "Just bag it." The voice on the phone piped up. "No, not you," Donny said. It was Marci.

"I'm in your room," Marci said. "Where are you?"

"I had to step out for a minute. Get some supplies."

"Okay. Where?"

"Right across the street."

"I could have run to the store for you, Don."

Donny grabbed his bag and receipt and rushed back to his car. "Sorry, Marci. I had to get away for a little while. Did you get the number I asked for?"

"Of course," she said, pulling a folded piece of paper from her pocket.

"Will you text it to me?"

Marci hesitated. "Don, I'm really starting to worry about you. Maybe you do need to go to the hospital. Just to get checked out. Even Dr. Yates agrees. The headache had us worried sick for days, and now you're acting the same way you did after–"

"Don't say it," Donny said. "I know what I'm doing." He cracked open an energy drink and chugged the entire can. "Just send me the number. Everything's going to be fine."

"Who are you planning to call? I looked up the number online and it's not listed."

"The people responsible for all of this. The drug people."

Marci had no idea what Donny was talking about, but she did recall their first pillow talk two months prior. They had maintained a platonic working relationship for over a year, but the combination of life on the road, a rigorous work schedule, and too many drinks at the hotel bar one night had commenced the current state of affairs. Marci had zestfully mentioned Donny's energetic demeanor both on stage as well as behind the scenes, to which Donny had replied, "You'd be surprised what a good night's rest will get you."

Marci walked through Donny's empty hotel room, peering over nightstands and looking for clues. She tossed open his luggage and thumbed through his clothes, expecting to find tiny vials of cocaine, twist-tied baggies filled with weed, maybe even a prescription or two. She turned up nothing but a bottle of ibuprofen and some questionable fashion choices.

"Donny, please," she said. "You have to tell me who these drug people are. You're not in trouble, are you?"

"No, Marci. It's not like that." He downed another energy shot. No way he was letting himself fall asleep again until he had this thing figured out. "Listen. I never told anyone this, but I've been taking some medication to help me sleep for a while now. The late nights, the constant traveling . . . it was weighing heavy, and I needed some relief."

"A lot of people take medicine to help them sleep," Marci said. "There's nothing wrong with that."

"Yeah, I know. But this stuff is new. It's the latest big push from the drug companies, and it's only available straight from the source. I had to participate in the clinical trials just to get my hands on the stuff. I also signed an agreement to check in periodically and report any strange side effects the moment they occur."

"You never told me about any of this," Marci said, unsettled. "You didn't call these people, did you?"

"No, not yet, but here's the thing. I thought the first headache was a fluke. Now I know this stuff is causing serious problems."

"Just stop taking it," Marci said. She rifled through Donny's toiletry bag. *No way sleeping pills are causing this*, she thought.

"It's not that simple. There's more to it than that. I . . . I just have to call. Now will you please send me the number?"

"Fine," Marci said. "But I'm not happy about any of this, Don. We really need to talk. Are you on your way back now?"

Donny started the car. "No. I'm going for a drive. Go ahead and book the room for the rest of the week. I'll call you when I find something out."

Donny hung up the phone and waited for Marci's text. He pulled out of the gas station parking lot, veering onto Old Highway 5 and heading north on the scenic route. He killed one more energy drink for good measure. Soon Marci's message came through, and he immediately dialed the number. Two long rings later a woman answered.

"Ryan Tanner's office. Sally speaking."

***

"The volcano," Claire said, pointing to the cloud-swept mountain through the windshield. "It's beautiful." It was dusk now, and purple and pink outlined the landmark in the distance. She turned to face Roberto, who was sitting in the backseat. "Do you know the name?"

"Yes, of course. That's Poás Volcano," he said. "It's not as active as many others, but it still surprises us every five years or so. It caused a terrible earthquake about ten years ago that killed a few dozen people. They were mainly local farmers, but some people died even as far away as San José. There's also the acid rain from the volcano, something that was a real concern for the people running the facility."

"How so?" Paul asked.

"You saw the horrible condition the building was in, right? One glance and you would think the facility had been there for decades. But it's actually the gases rising from Poás Volcano to the south causing acid rain in the area. It wreaked havoc on the surrounding ecosystem, as well as the facility. Acid rain is nasty. Park this jeep under that volcano and leave it during the rainy season and you won't find a speck of paint on it when you get back."

"Nasty stuff indeed, Roberto," Paul said. He looked in the rearview. "How much further?" Paul was silently kicking himself for bringing the tech along, even if he had saved their asses a time or two. They had crossed the same stream a half-dozen times on the way to civilization; common sense should have told him that the cascading waters would lead them down from the hills. No need for a tour guide.

Roberto said, “We should be about three miles to Bajos del Toro. Not much to the place, but they will have a phone. From there you can take passage over the mountains to Grecia, which is only ten or so miles from Juan Santamaria Airport in San José. The roads make driving slow, but it’s not too far. We could be there in two, maybe three hours.”

“Before we get there,” Claire said, “why don’t you tell us about the other outliers?”

Roberto shrugged. “Not much to tell really. You two were the first outsiders they brought into the facility. They simply called you the new subjects. You have to understand, the research lab was only informed on a need-to-know basis. We were able to work on the drug without knowing how they were going to use it.”

“The babe in the woods routine,” Claire said.

“I’m very serious,” Roberto said. “We knew about the clinical trials stateside, but that was it. We never needed test subjects in the lab. That’s not what lab work is about. We only needed their DNA to test the efficacy of the drug, to make sure the correct gene sequences were addressed. We were given a set of desired results, and instructed to meet those requirements. That was all. What they did with the medication afterword was above our paygrade.”

Claire asked, “But you must have heard more about the others. Names. Anything that can help us. You just said you were aware of the clinical trials; trials I just so happened to be a part of. Now you’re telling me you don’t know anything else?”

“No, ma’am. I am very sorry.”

“And no one else was taken to the facility before us?”

“Not a soul. You two were the only ones.”

Claire looked over at Paul. “Well, that gets us nowhere.”

"Not exactly," Paul said.

"What do you mean?"

"I might have a lead on some people back in the United States who were on the medication."

Claire nodded. "Your brother. Alex? Didn't you say–"

"I know what I said. The truth is, I'm not sure what to believe. For all we know, what Tanner told me could have been just another lie to induce some type of response. To get me good and upset and prepped for his little experiments. Anyway, we can't dwell on that right now. But if he's alive, it would be a start."

"You said 'some people'. Who else?"

"This guy. Donny Ford. A motivational speaker. Have you heard of him?"

Claire said, "The B-list murder suspect? Yeah, I've heard of him. He's been this year's high-profile Hollywood murder topic, although he's not exactly Hollywood." She asked, "How do you know him?"

"Tanner sent me to record one of the guy's seminars in Atlanta. At least, that's what I thought I was doing. Turns out it was to confirm suspicions that Ford was projecting the same electromagnetic radiation as the other outliers. Anyway, the seminar was a total disaster. The audience broke out in a riot and Ford went running off the stage, presumably to go shit his pants. The guy's a creep, but I'm certain he's on the medication. We should probably start with him. What do you think?"

Medication. The word triggered a memory for Claire. *Paul said he never took Ocula*. The escape from the compound had been hectic, and Claire hadn't thought about the claim until now. She might have believed him before the incident with the guards, but now it was all too clear. Paul had taken the medication. He was an outlier. A dreamer. Just like her.

That was unless Roberto was lying about the room vacancies at the Costa Rican Hotel from Hell. Claire thought it made a lot of sense, given the circumstances. Roberto wasn't going to implicate himself in anything illegal, plain and simple. And if he really was familiar with the detailed files of the twelve Ocula outliers, then he already knew she was a journalist. Everything he had told them was enough to build credibility, but not enough to indict him as a co-conspirator. He was an innocent bystander. A babe in the woods.

Claire held tight to her gun. The backseat passenger knew more than he was letting on, and she wasn't going to let him get the drop on her. She glanced over at Paul. He was still waiting for input on the lead.

She told him, "Yeah. I think you're right. We'll start with Ford once we get stateside." Paul nodded, and his focus returned to the road.

Claire checked the backseat. Roberto was quiet now, gazing out the window and watching the trees and fence posts pass by. He seemed oblivious to the conversation, but she still didn't trust the man, and for good reason. She decided to wait until she and Paul were alone to bring up the incident at the facility.

In a few minutes, they would be in the little mountain town of Bajos del Toro. From there they would head south, crossing the cloud-capped mountains of the southeastern Alajuela province before reaching the airport north of San José.

It was already dark and the moon was waxing full, rising slowly from the east and painting the asphalt ahead a silvery blue. The trail was lit for their nocturnal escape route back to civilization. Once they were on a plane, Claire could talk to Paul alone. Just the two of them.

Hopefully then she would get some answers.

Chapter 23:
Call Me

Ryan Tanner stood behind a desk littered with files. Forms had been removed and sorted through, many of them now lying on the floor. Filing cabinet drawers were left hanging open behind him, with papers sticking out and gently waving every time the man blew by. Tanner was a whirlwind, frantically searching case files for anything that could lead to other outliers. He cursed the mess on his desk, realizing he was guilty of the same offense he had reprimanded Paul Freeman for just days earlier.

This goddamn system. Here it was, twenty-one years into the 21st century, and Asteria Pharmaceuticals was still keeping clinical information in files. *Goddamn paper files.* If the Office of Clinical Research had a one-terabyte hard drive–a piece of hardware that would set them back fifty bucks–they could fit about eighty-five million pages of text on it. But filing efficiency wasn't Asteria's primary concern. Tanner could see that now.

The policy at Asteria Pharmaceuticals was to keep hard copies of information pertaining to clinical trials for security reasons. The rationale was simple. Without sharing files across a network, the company wouldn't have to worry about sensitive information being breached during cyber attacks. It was a clever take on security, with one inherent drawback. The system worked so well that even mid-level staff couldn't access the information without employing a small army of secretaries to do so.

"Sally! Will you get in here?" Tanner yelled. There was no response. He combed the inside of another file. It belonged to a clinical trial participant for Ocula. He thumbed through the papers, searching for specific fields filled out on page seven:

MEMO OF ODD DATA AND ERRATA
TRIAL PARTICIPANT: SAUNDERS, STEVEN F.
PROTOCOL ID: OCULA FDA III
PROTOCOL TITLE: SIDE EFFECTS
PRINCIPLE INVESTIGATOR: W. WILLIAMS
ISSUES: N/A

No issues. No documented side effects.

"Fuck!" He tossed the file across the room. The papers dispersed, then glided to the floor. He already knew finding other outliers was a shot in the dark. It didn't matter. He was still pissed.

To his right and lying in front of the computer monitor was the red envelope containing the files of the original twelve Ocula outliers. Unfortunately for Tanner, most of them had fallen off the radar. Eight clinical trial participants vanished shortly after Tanner's surveillance teams began following them. That left Claire, Ford, the younger Freeman, and poor Mrs. Edwards. As far as Tanner was concerned, Claire and Alex Freeman were out of the picture, along with poor Mrs. Edwards, who had made the choice to slit her own wrists after deciding a life on Ocula was just as bad as a life without sleep.

That left only one promising lead for Tanner to pursue: Donny Ford. The problem was that the showman had recently joined the ranks of the missing after a dismal performance at the Wyatt Conference Center just a few days earlier.

Tanner leaned back in his chair and rubbed his eyes. The last twenty-four hours had turned his world upside down. When it came to the joint operation between the agency and Asteria, the buck stopped with him. Once the higher-ups got word of the fubar that had taken place in Costa Rica, it would be his head on a platter. Every clandestine operation needed a fall guy. Tanner was theirs.

Not that Tanner could blame them. He never should have dropped his guard with Paul Freeman; he conceded that much. If Tanner had kept Paul awake long enough to make it to the stonewall chamber, Doyle could have countered what was already in his system with the manageable Ocula 2.0. From there the tests would have proceeded as planned. Instead, Tanner had provoked Paul to the point of an altercation, resulting in the prisoner being knocked unconscious, which directly led to the massacre of every guard in the facility.

Tanner knew the botched operation in Costa Rica put him in deep with associates past and present, but there was nothing he could do about that now. His only hope moving forward was to clean up the mess as quickly as possible, which meant tying up a few loose ends. He shouted once more at the door.

"Sally! What the *fuck* are you doing out there? Get in here!" He heard her ask someone to hold. She opened the door.

"Sorry, sir, but I've got someone on the line who says he needs to talk to you."

"Tell them to take a number, Sally. I'm fucking swamped in here."

"This gentleman, sir. He called the unlisted line. He says it's important. He's holding at the moment."

Tanner was stunned. "Next time, Sally, start with that." He pressed the blinking hold button and put the call on speaker. "Asteria Pharmaceuticals. This is Ryan Tanner. Whom do I have the pleasure of speaking with today?" He waved Sally out of the room.

The man on the other end of the line was a bundle of nerves; not the Donny Ford the public was used to. "My name's Ford. Donald Bradley Ford. I was given this number after a clinical trial I participated in. I was told to call if I ever had any negative side effects to report. So that's what I'm doing. Calling."

"Well, Mr. Ford, you did the right thing. This number was reserved for people just like you. We had thousands participate in the Ocula clinical trials. Thousands." Tanner stalled while he scrambled through the mess on his desk, searching for Donny's file. "Typically the evaluations only go as far as the final stage required before securing FDA approval for a particular drug. But here at Asteria Pharmaceuticals, we like to go the extra mile."

"Yes. Well, I wouldn't have called if something weren't wrong. Something's happened, and I need help. I need answers. Can you help me?"

"Of course we can help you, Mr. Ford. But first we'll need to know a little more about your reason for calling. Tell me what happened, exactly."

"I've had some . . . side effects. From the medication. Things I can't explain."

"Try to explain, Mr. Ford. Please, do try."

Donny started in. "Well, when I started the medication during the clinical trials, everything seemed to be going just as expected. I was getting eight hours of sleep every single night. It was incredible. And the sleep. The sleep was like nothing I'd ever experienced before. Like waking up from an operation. At least, that's how I would describe it. Ocula was anesthesia in a bottle. Whenever I felt restless, I was only a pill away from saying lights out for the evening."

"Sounds like the perfect drug to me," Tanner said, "but I'm biased, of course. When did the side effects begin?" Tanner was staring at Ford's file. He already knew the answer.

"Last year, during the clinical trials. That's when the first migraine occurred. I'd never had headaches before in my life, so I reported it to the program manager. He didn't seem too concerned at the time."

"A lot of people get headaches from medication, Mr. Ford. It's a common side effect, right up there with nausea, fatigue, upset stomach. It's something that's expected in every clinical trial. Results don't always live up to patient standards. Someone is always going to have a discomforting experience." Tanner's voice was leading. "So, is there anything else you'd like to tell me, Mr. Ford?"

Donny paused, then said, "Yes. There's something else. Something that followed these headaches. I had these . . . these dreams. The first was about a good friend of mine. Only, in that dream, we weren't getting along too well. We were fighting, one thing led to another, and then I killed him. It was horrifying, but at least it was just a dream, right?"

Tanner listened intently.

"Well the next day, he passed away. Now maybe it was a coincidence, maybe it wasn't, but . . . let's put it this way: he's dead now, and I feel responsible. And I wouldn't think much of it happening just once, but it happened again this morning. Maria

Moreno, the Action News Atlanta anchor. She's been in an accident."

"And you were dreaming about her this morning?" Tanner asked.

"She was on my mind the moment I woke up. I turned on the news, and there was the headline."

Tanner was relieved. He had found his next mark, and in a relatively short time, nonetheless. No more combing through bullshit stacks of worthless documents searching for another variable in the equation. Donny Ford would do just fine.

All Tanner had to do now was convince Donny to meet at his office. There he could subdue the salesman with the same device he had used on Paul. Then he would call the Consultants and stage another EMT call, just like before. A quick trip to the roof's helipad and they would be on their way back to Costa Rica to clean this whole mess up. But first, Tanner had to get him there.

Tanner leaned in to the speakerphone. "This is all very interesting, Mr. Ford. The welfare and safety of our clinical trial participants is always of the utmost importance to us here at Asteria. We'd like for you to come in to the facility in Atlanta. Here we can discuss your condition in more detail, and document everything you've just told me so we can update your file. Then we can work toward coming up with a viable solution. What's your schedule look like at the moment? Can you make it in today?" He leaned back and made a steeple with his hands, anticipating a favorable response.

Donny replied, "I'm sorry, Mr. Tanner. A meeting today just isn't possible. Can we get together to discuss my case sometime next week?"

Tanner silently mouthed a few curses. Then he said, "Yes, sure. We can meet next week."

Tanner thought on his toes. He needed to wrap the Ford situation up today. He tapped on the desk, yearning for a smoke. It was time for a Hail Mary. "Listen, though, Donny. If this medication is affecting you this badly, you need complete rest. Possibly medical attention. Let me send my personal physician to check in on you, make sure all of your vitals are looking good. Consider it a free physical, courtesy of Asteria. Just give me your information and where you're staying and I'll send–"

Click.

Donny Ford was gone.

"FUCK!" Tanner picked up his speakerphone and threw it across the room, the cords dangling like kite tails before crashing into the wall beside the office door. The one phone call he received from an outlier, and he blew it. He could already think of half a dozen mistakes he had made over the course of the call. His tradecraft was rusty, and the blunder had cost him his only lead. He stormed across the office to examine the dearly departed desk phone. Busted. Just like his chances of bringing Donny in quietly.

Only one option remained. Tanner would have to call the Consultants. He had used the ex-CIA special operations group on a few occasions, most recently during the Paul Freeman extraction just three days earlier. The higher-ups had warned him about using the group's services habitually; the team of mercenaries was supposed to be considered a last resort. But Tanner knew no one else could find Ford as quickly as they could. He also knew that time was working against him.

Tanner pulled out his cellphone and dialed a number. If the Consultants were still operating in the Atlanta area, they could have Ford in custody by sundown. He just hoped the motivational speaker hadn't told anyone about his condition yet.

If Tanner's plan was going to work, he needed Ford alive.

Chapter 24:
Come Fly with Me

The only seats Paul and Claire could secure for the flight back to the U.S. were on a twin-engine Piper Navajo leaving for Corpus Christi at 7 a.m. sharp. The plane must have been over thirty years old, complete with mismatched panels on the rear fuselage, poly-fiber field repairs on one of the wings, and dry-rotting tires accentuating the landing gear. Claire met with the pilot on the runway prior to takeoff, and could tell right away he was a little drunk. Paul even noticed a few pieces of duct tape running along the wings of the plane and flapping in the breeze, but he didn't care. He was desperate to get home. Given the recent events, the complementary accommodations were sure to feel like first class.

The trip from Bajos del Toro to north San José had been a fast one, taking less than two hours to get across the mountains and into the city. Paul didn't bother to obey the speed limit, working the gears of the five-speed around the steep mountain curves like a professional wheelman. He hauled even more ass once they could see the bright city lights glowing on the horizon.

They were a few miles south of the mountain pass when Roberto escaped. Paul had been watching the road and Claire was dozing in the wee hours of the morning when they heard the back flap of the soft top open up to the sound of the rushing air outside. When Paul checked the rear view, he caught a glimpse of Roberto sneaking out the back of the Jeep, jumping into the night and rolling down the grassy hill on the side of the road. Paul instinctively slammed on the brakes, sending Claire crashing into the dash as he threw open the door to run after Roberto, but it was too late. He ran a few steps and then stopped to watch the young scientist disappear into the trees.

Roberto was the only person who could verify Paul and Claire were still alive; everyone else–with the exception of Doyle–had taken off long before the duo made their escape. While they hoped Roberto didn't run to the nearest payphone to give Tanner a status report, they had to assume that was exactly what had happened.

On a positive note, at least they were traveling lighter. Claire had already called in a few favors while on assignment in San José a few years back, and she was reluctant to ask for help again. Fortunately, she had underestimated her benefactor's inherent generosity. Once they reached Juan Santamaria Airport, she made the call and laid out her needs. Private passage to the states. Enough cash to last a few days. Clean clothes. And no questions asked. The aristocrat enthusiastically obliged.

Claire's investigative journalism into child abductions three years earlier had led to the rescue of the man's nine-year-old daughter, kidnapped by ransom seekers and dropped off in a park the moment the media put the heat on the offenders. It was a debt no father could ever repay. But for now, a flight back to the U.S. on one of his private planes would have to do.

Paul drew the curtain to watch from the rounded-square window as the plane took off, rising quickly above the medley of lush tropical landscape and urban development below. Once they were airborne, his attention turned to the cabin.

"Look, they've still got ash trays in these things," he said, flipping the lid on his armrest open and shut. "Are you sure this plane doesn't belong to Tanner?"

Claire sat across from him. "Ummm, no. Alejandro Aguilar is an honorable man. Deals in a little contraband from time to time, but nothing too deplorable."

"How do you know him?" Paul asked.

"I had the pleasure of helping his family out a few years back with a high-profile kidnapping case. I was working as a foreign correspondent in San José at the time. He was convinced–in his words–that the *Yankee coverage* led to his daughter's safe return. He thinks he owes me for the rest of my life. Of course, I would argue otherwise. But this is the second time he's helped me out of a pinch down here, so I've gotta be running low on favors at this point."

"He must not think he owes you that much," Paul said, pulling a piece of rotting tape from the armrest. "Didn't you say the guy was wealthy?"

"He is. There's just no way he's letting anyone borrow his Gulfstream."

"Well, he could have let us borrow a cellphone." Paul looked back out the window and thought of Michelle and Aaron. He hoped Tanner hadn't gotten to them yet, but he couldn't help thinking the worst.

Claire said, "A cellphone wouldn't work around here anyway, Paul. Besides, I thought you called home when we got to the airport?"

"Yeah, I did. No one answered the house phone. I also had Michelle program her new cell number into my phone."

Claire shot him a crooked smile. "You didn't memorize it, did you . . ."

Paul was quiet.

"First world problems," Clair said.

"I know, I know. Modern-day conveniences. We never realize how dependent we are on our phones and watches and tablets until something like this happens. I can't remember a single number I've plugged into my phone over the years. Funny thing is, I can still remember all my friends' phone numbers from elementary school."

"Back when we had to perform the painstaking task of memorizing ten whole numbers and then pressing the corresponding buttons on a telephone keypad," Claire reminisced. "Trust me, I can relate. My old friend Dawkins used to call modern-day conveniences the new-age crutches. Probably the most accurate definition I've heard yet. We rely on digital maps to get us places, never realizing that anything from a dead battery to a solar flare could render digital devices useless in a fraction of a second. We count on mobile tech to store important contact information, passwords, and account numbers; use it to buy groceries, order room service, and purchase transportation . . ." She motioned to the window. "And look how lost we are without them. We literally have a better chance of getting stateside with a drunken pilot at the helm than we ever would by ourselves without our new-age crutches."

"Can't disagree with that," Paul said. They were at cruising altitude now and flying much slower than a 757. "So how long do you think it's going to take to get back to Atlanta?"

"That's the thing about traveling off the radar. It'll take at least another day to get back, maybe longer. We can't fly direct. Odds are we'll have to refuel in Mexico just to get to a friendly airport outside of Corpus Christi."

"Friendly?" Paul asked.

Claire chose her words carefully. "Let's just say Señor Aguilar can be a little liberal with his imports. Don't worry about it. Compared to many of his South American counterparts, the guy's squeaky clean."

Paul still wasn't convinced, so Claire explained. "The San José bureau had suspected Aguilar was involved in the drug trade long before covering the story of his daughter's kidnapping. To outsiders, the man seemed like a typical cartel baddy–daughter gets targeted for the father's wealth and dubious behavior. The kidnappers assumed he was a man likely to pay up without making any waves.

"Turns out Aguilar's illegal activities weren't as incriminatory as the kidnappers had hoped. Of the many businesses Aguilar was vested in, the one acting as a front for smuggling drugs into the United States involved non-narcotics. Antibiotics and antivirals, to be exact. Drugs like amoxicillin, doxycycline, and amantadine were on the cheap in Central America. They were also impossible to get off-the-books in the U.S. The exports helped illegal immigrants secure basic medicinal needs without risking deportation just to get a cold treated, and the locals loved him for it."

Paul smiled. "Defending the poor majority from the tyrannical few. Like a Costa Rican Zorro."

"Well, it's not like he's losing money from his side business," Claire said. "I think he's a good man, but he also knows how to play the game. The antibiotic runs make for good local publicity, which helps build his political clout. Fewer things are more important in Central America. Struggling Columbians loved Pablo Escobar, and public admiration is what kept him on top of the world down here for so long. I'm sure Alejandro has read up on the strategy."

A gust of turbulence rattled the plane, but the pilot was unfazed. He turned around to address his two passengers. "Little bumpy, no?" They nodded their heads and pretended not to worry.

Claire whispered to Paul, "I think he's been sipping on Grandpa's cough medicine all morning." She motioned like she was turning a bottle up.

"I wouldn't worry too much," Paul said. "You know it's legal to drink and drive in Costa Rica? Honestly, I'd be worried if the pilot *wasn't* drinking."

Claire forced a laugh, but the memories of her tortuous ordeal were beginning to rise to the surface. She remembered her friend Dawkins, whose weathered face was central to the last dream sequence induced by Mr. Doyle. She could still feel the sensation of bullets whizzing by her face; hear the explosive sound of fully automatics sending armor-piercing rounds across the field; and smell the soil she clung to as she hit the deck and ducked for cover. She shuddered to think she might have had something to do with any of it. She knew she had no control over the situation at the time, or her own mind for that matter. But she couldn't shake the feeling of responsibility for the death of so many.

She diverted her attention to Paul, leaning in to speak in confidence. "Paul," she said, "There's something I've been meaning to ask you. It's about the drug. You said you never took Ocula before, that you weren't on the sleep medication. Was that true?"

Paul's response was matter-of-fact. "Yeah, it's true. I told you I haven't taken it."

"I know you said–"

"Even if I wanted to, it's not even available to the general public. They're still awaiting FDA approval."

"Yes, of course. I get it. But what I don't get . . . what doesn't make sense, is the fact that all of those guards murdered each other back at the facility, and you were the *only* one who could've dreamed something like that up."

"You were there, too, Claire."

"You're right, but I was locked away in my cell, remember? Those cells were built to contain electromagnetic radiation, kind of like the inside of a microwave. Nothing gets out for the protection of the others working in the compound. There's no way it could have been me. Plus–and this is a big plus–I wasn't asleep! The moment the door swung open and I left my cell, all of the guards were already dead. There's just no way it was me."

Paul looked up and away, visualizing the people he ran across in the facility on his way to the holding cell. "Okay, so the guards didn't decide to make an exit by drinking a bad batch of AR-15 Cool Aid. We can agree on that, right?"

"Yup."

"We also know that Tanner isn't one of the outliers. He has that shitty little device, but I don't think he can use it to harness any kind of influential power or anything like that, do you?"

"No. The device seems to detect and target individuals who are producing trace levels of electromagnetic radiation within close proximity, but it can't help him reproduce the signals emitted from the outliers. If he wanted to influence anyone, he would need an Ocula outlier to do his dirty work. Probably someone like Doyle, too."

"And we were the only two emitting anything at the facility."

Paul was baffled. No wonder it was easy for Claire to assume he was on the medication. He knew he had never taken anything like that before; he didn't even have access to the drug. So how could any of this be possible?

"Just us two, Paul," Claire said. "No one else could have caused the event, and I was locked away at the time. But if you're convinced you've never taken it, then I really don't know what else to say."

Claire laid her head back in the chair. She had clearly given up for the time being. Might as well catch a little shuteye, she reasoned. They would be landing to refuel in a few hours, and she hadn't slept properly for weeks. She yawned before making a final suggestion.

"You know, Paul. You could have taken the medication and you just don't know it."

You just don't know it. Claire would have witnessed Paul's light-bulb moment if she hadn't already closed her eyes. Paul remembered how well he slept the night before all of this mess began. It was the night before Tanner sent him to the Donny Ford seminar; before he was knocked out and whisked away to Costa Rica; before his life was turned upside down.

It was the night that marked the best sleep of his life. And the following day, Michelle had been eager to know all about it.

Chapter 25:
Tibetan Greeting

The tires of Donny Ford's rental car squealed as he raced up the winding asphalt driveway leading to the Vajrayãna Monastery. The two-story palace on a hill was inspired by traditional Tibetan architecture, the only building of its kind in the rural outskirts southwest of Atlanta. The stone exterior walls were whitewashed and coarse. Merlot-red window treatments complemented matching latticework on the fascia surrounding the flat roof. Canary-yellow canvas awnings hung over every window. The building sat atop the highest point in the middle of a ten-acre estate, surrounded on all sides by groves of white oak trees springing up from the gently rolling hills below.

The monastery was the home of Dawa Shakya Graham, a reputable Buddhist and Atlanta investigator Donny had met in Tibet over a decade ago. Dawa's unconventional life was twofold. Part of his time was devoted to helping a select group of students pursue the spiritual path to Nirvana, while his day job involved pursuing murderers and their accomplices as a detective with Atlanta Homicide. The dual undertakings weren't without challenges. Dawa had been in incredible shape before making Detective First-Grade three years earlier; now a dark receding hairline and a pudgy waist reflected the effects of witnessing the worst of humanity on a regular basis.

Working homicide was tiresome, but Dawa was far from jaded. When he wasn't on duty, the thirty-eight-year-old detective taught Tibetan Buddhist principles passed down from his mother's side to a handful of students who frequented the monastery. Teaching for free and working for APD weren't profitable endeavors, but both gave him a fulfilling sense of purpose. It also didn't hurt that Dawa was able to augment his government salary with a handsome inheritance left to him by his American father.

Dawa had taught Donny everything he knew about Tummo meditation when the two were traveling the Himalayas together some ten years earlier. Their initial plans were to bring the Shakya family teachings to the U.S., but they soon discovered the chasm separating their core beliefs was too vast to reconcile. While Dawa wanted to take an esoteric approach, reserving the sacred teachings for a small and select group of practitioners, Donny wanted to share Tummo with the entire western hemisphere, establishing the first-ever East-Coast outpost for Tibetan Buddhism and spreading the familial teachings to every sentient being in the New World.

When Dawa balked at the notion of commercializing Tummo, Donny took what he had learned sub-rosa and went his own way. Donny's motivation had little to do with bringing others to enlightenment, and more to do with the pursuit of the almighty buck. He teamed up with his old high school buddy Bill Stevens, and the rest was history.

Naturally, Dawa went a different route. He had used part of his inheritance to turn the Graham family property into a Tibetan Buddhist monastery, accepting qualified individuals who would honor, protect, and respect the teachings of the ancient religion. In the time Donny had spent peddling his own perversion of Tibetan culture and beliefs, Dawa had turned his dream of spreading the knowledge and truth of his family's religion into a reality.

Donny knew Graham was the better man. He also knew showing up at the guru's home unannounced was in poor taste, but it was highly unlikely his old friend would turn away a sentient being in distress, no matter how tainted their history was.

He brought the car to a screeching halt in front of the monastery. He jumped out and ran to the front door, pounding his fist against the solid oak entry and praying for Dawa to answer. His voice was panic-stricken.

"Dawa! Are you home? I need your help! It's an emergency!" He rapped on the door five times, then paused to listen for signs of life. Nothing. He knocked and waited again, this time adding a third act to the routine by jiggling the door handle. Finally, he heard feet shuffling on the other side.

"Who is it?" a voice asked.

Donny considered giving a fake name just to get his foot in the door, but there was no point. His hair had a little more gray in it since they last spoke, but Dawa would easily recognize his old friend. Donny had been an on-again, off-again national headline for the last year; surely the detective was keeping close tabs.

"It's your old friend. Donald. Donald Ford." There was no reply. Only silence.

"Dawa. I'm sorry to come here like this. And for everything that's happened. I wouldn't . . . I hate putting you in this position, but there's no one left to turn to." He wrung his frigid hands, choosing his words carefully. "I know I betrayed you, Dawa. And I've made many, *many* mistakes. But I'm in trouble, and you're the only person who can help me. Please, I'm begging you. Will you help me, Dawa?"

Donny stood at the door and waited, warming his hands with his breath. The winter cold ached his bare fingers. He was about to give up and return to the warmth of his car when the door cracked open. A pair of eyes peeked out from the dark interior on the other side. The eyes looked the desperate and shivering man up and down.

The door flew open and out came a solid ball of knuckles, the right hook flying straight into Donny's face and busting his nose.

"What the fuck?!" Donny yelled as he stumbled back, cupping his hands over his busted nose. Blood ran between his fingers and down the front of his shirt. He closed the leak with his thumb and forefinger and held his head back, looking to the sky while keeping a safe distance from Dawa.

"That's some compassion you've got there, Dawa. *Fuck*!"

"My compassion only goes so far, Donald. It's something I'm working on." He took a step forward and Donny took a step back. He halted, gesturing toward Donny's face. "It's never going to stop bleeding if you keep holding your head back like that. The blood needs to coagulate. Tilt your head forward."

Donny cautiously obeyed, bringing his watering eyes level with his attacker's, the gusts of air chilling his tears and sending cold streamers down his face. He glared at the temporarily relapsed Buddhist.

"Are you sure you still need my guidance, Donald?"

Donny reluctantly nodded. "Yes. Of course, Dawa. I need your guidance."

"Then take off your shoes," the host commanded, "and come inside."

***

Buddhist shrines lined the maroon walls to the left and right of the vaulted meditation room inside the home of Dawa Shakya Graham. Wooden columns held the high ceilings over the two-story chamber. Faux-gold cornice filled every corner and capped every angle. Colorful Asian artwork told centuries-old tales of Buddhist traditions. At the back and center of the room, three prominent Buddha statues sat atop pedestals looking over the main meditation floor where Donny and Dawa were sitting, eyes closed and legs crossed.

The impromptu meditation session was Dawa's idea; a non-negotiable requirement before the sage would listen to anything Donny had to say. The practice was more for Dawa than his guest. Donny had wandered so far from the selfless teachings of Tibetan Buddhism that sitting on a pillow and calming his mind was a near impossibility. Still, Donny didn't want to insult his host, so he sat quietly with his eyes closed and tried his best to go through the motions.

The light from the glass chandelier hanging above the two meditators filled the room with a warm ambiance. The winter cold had kicked the furnace into overdrive, blasting heat through the vents and causing the interior woodwork to crackle and pop. It wasn't long before Donny began sweating profusely. He felt a single bead of sweat drip slowly down his forehead to the bridge of his swollen nose, giving rise to an unbearable tickle he was forbidden to scratch. His eyes shut hard as he tried to block out his external environment, but he found it impossible to ignore his surroundings. His mind was frenzied and his nose was throbbing.

Donny peeked out of one eye toward his old friend. The man sitting across from him was calm and content. No sweating, no angst. A true symbol of inner peace.

Donny couldn't take it anymore. He had to break the silence. "Dawa, you haven't once asked me–"

"Shhh," Dawa replied.

Donny nodded and obeyed. He closed his eyes and tried to return to his meditation, but he couldn't concentrate. He sat in silence for another five minutes, each passing second lasting an eternity. He cleared his throat before he chimed in again. "Dawa, I'm sorry to break from tradition, but I need to talk to you about why I'm–"

"Break from tradition?" Dawa said, opening his eyes. "Nothing in the past has ever stopped you from breaking tradition, Donald." He rubbed his chin and leaned forward to examine his old friend.

"It doesn't look like time has been good to you, Donald." Dawa could see the weariness in Ford's eyes, adorned with dark circles and carrying heavy luggage. "Tell me, Donald. Do you think your actions have anything to do with your current condition? Maybe the karma you studied so long ago has returned to pay you a visit? Did you come here believing my devotion to the teachings of the Dalai Lama would force me to ignore your betrayal? Because if that is the case, Donald, then you are quite mistaken."

"I didn't mean to make you angry, Dawa."

"Your presence here could lead to little else. Did you believe you could walk into my home, my temple, after all that has happened, and leave your poisons at the door?"

Donny hung his head in silence.

Dawa continued, "Three poisons I warned you about when we first met. Just three. And you could not resist a single one. Now I have allowed anger to seep into my well and poison my water. Tell me, Donald, do you even remember the other two?"

"Of course. There is anger, and then greed and ignorance, Dawa."

"So you do remember," Dawa said. "And here you sit, reveling in all three. How am I to maintain peace and tranquility while suffocating under the poisonous cloud you've brought to my door? At least the criminals I deal with on a daily basis don't pretend to be my friends before betraying my family's goodwill."

Donny lifted his head. His eyes were misty. Dawa analyzed his guest, trying to decide whether it was Donny's shame or his potentially broken nose that had turned on the waterworks.

"Dawa, I cannot begin to tell you how sorry I am for misusing your teachings. I never meant to hurt anyone, the least of which you. I made so many mistakes. I have only myself to blame. You trusted me to keep and honor the teachings of Tibetan Buddhism, and I did not. You taught me a powerful path to enlightenment through Tummo, and I exploited it for nothing more than monetary gain.

"I mean look what you've done here," Donny said, admiring the room. "Teaching others the principles and practices we dreamt of so long ago, welcoming them into your home. This is the other side of the coin. The side I regretfully chose against. I knew it was wrong the moment I met with Bill Stevens. But one thing led to another, and I just got caught up in everything. I couldn't see a way out. Now all of the greed and ignorance I've embraced my entire adult life has led you to anger." He hung his head and put his face in his hands. "I am truly sorry, old friend."

Dawa tried to be empathetic; after all, his religion required compassion and wisdom to achieve enlightenment. But like most practitioners of any faith, what his religion called for and how he actually felt were occasionally on opposing sides. He tried to rid his body of harmful feelings like anger and disappointment through a brief meditation session, but the session was interrupted and the wounds were still fresh on his mind.

Dawa knew that evil did exist in the world; he witnessed it every time he was called to the scene of a crime. Donny was no evil man. Misguided, yes, but far from evil. Dawa took a deep breath and calmed himself. He focused on the sensation of anger clouding his mind, then worked to rid his body of it. Finally, he spoke.

"Donald. Listen to me. My anger belongs to me. For that, you needn't be sorry. You know as well as I do that even the most devout Buddhists are overcome with anger from time to time. It is a force to be reckoned with, but it is nothing we can't control. Mine has passed for a time, and for that I am thankful. But that doesn't mean I can forget what has happened. The way you took our most sacred traditions and peddled them to audiences around the world; the way we warned you how dangerous these teachings could be in the wrong hands; your refusal to listen, as well as your abandonment of the life you so emphatically embraced in the Himalayas." Dawa shook his head. "For the sake of our traditions and principles, I cannot allow myself to forget.

"So," Dawa said, "tread lightly when telling me what has brought you here. Should I detect deception of any kind, I will have no choice but to ask you to leave."

Donny uncrossed his legs and moved to his knees, sitting on one of the many red pillows lying in the meditation room. "Dawa," he said. "Something has happened to me recently. Something I've traced back to two things: a prescription I've been taking, and the meditation techniques you passed down to me ten years ago."

"You're not taking pain pills, are you?"

"No. No pain pills."

"Good. It seems like every homicide I'm called to these days involves substance abuse somewhere along the line."

Donny's voice had a hint of impatience to it. "These pills are a little different, Dawa. A friend told me about a company seeking volunteers in a clinical trial for a promising new sleep medication. Life on the road was taking its toll, and I never slept. After hearing about the anticipated outcomes for the medication, participating in the trials seemed like a good idea at the time."

"Why did you choose not to rely on the Dhammapada? Why seek answers in the things of this world? In pills?"

"You're right," Donny said. "I should have leaned on the scriptures, and on the teachings passed down from your ancestors. I know I wouldn't be in the situation I'm in had I done things differently. But at that point, I had strayed far from my adopted home. I was tempted by greed, and I thought turning to the Precepts would mean turning away from the life I was living. Away from all the money. I was just too far gone, Dawa. Too far."

"I see," Dawa said. "You strayed far from the path, and you lost sight of the crossroads. So goes the endless cycle of death and rebirth. *Samsara*." Dawa looked up toward the seated Buddha statues. "Sometimes I am afraid I will be caught in this endless cycle, too. With my job, the things I see every day, whether or not I'm really helping others . . . It's all a part of this life, but that doesn't mean we are ever too far gone, Donald. As long as we are in this world, we can always find our way back." Dawa meditated on the Buddhist concept, his eyes drifting into the distance. Then he broke his silence. "So tell me about this prescription. For sleep, you say?"

"Yes. A sleeping pill; one that was supposed to produce the best sleep anyone's ever had." Donny leaned in. "And let me tell you something, Dawa: the way this stuff worked? Make the hairs on the back of your neck stand at full attention. It was the perfect drug. Flawless. Well, for a while, at least. The pill seemed to be working fine . . . and then Bill Stevens was murdered."

"Your business partner?"

"Yes, or rather, my soon-to-be-former business partner. We were in the process of breaking the business up when he was murdered in a Las Vegas hotel room, just a few doors down from where I was staying."

Dawa's voice inferred suspicion. "Angry business partner murdered during the process of business dissolution . . ."

"I know it looks bad, but there's no way I could have murdered him. I was in my room, fast asleep. My door didn't open all night."

"Except when you went to his room to argue over the business."

"Well, yeah. I mean, after that." Donny was flustered. "Look, I didn't do it, Dawa. It's still an open investigation, but there's nothing rock solid pointing to me. It's all circumstantial. But still. I feel responsible. I feel like there's blood on my hands."

Dawa was puzzled. "I don't quite follow you, Donald."

Donny reached in his pocket and pulled out a pill. "It's for sleep disorders. It's called Ocula. Asteria Pharmaceuticals makes it."

"Asteria. Don't they have a building downtown?"

"Yep. That's company headquarters." Donny handed the pill to the inspector. "I was taking that stuff for months leading up to the first event. I had been arguing with Stevens about the future of the business the night it happened. Things got pretty heated, I told him where to shove it, and then I left. That night in my hotel room, I had a dream about killing him."

"Goodness, Donald."

Donny put up his hand. "I know, I know. I'm ashamed to admit it, even if it was only a dream. But damn it, Dawa, I was mad. When I woke up the next morning, Stevens was dead. Now I realize this should have been nothing more than a horrible coincidence, but just this morning I had a dream about a reporter from Action News Atlanta swiping my bottle of ibuprofen and swallowing every last pill. That same reporter is now in the hospital and listed in critical condition."

Donny's anxiety was apparent, a result of terrifying events mixed with an excess of over-the-counter pick-me-ups. He paused for a moment to catch his breath and wiped the sweat from his forehead.

Dawa held the pill up to the light. He carefully looked it over, then gave it back to Donny.

"Do you remember the first principle I taught you? The principle of mindfulness?" Dawa asked.

"Of course. Focusing on the present, on sensations and feelings and–"

"And everything you're experiencing within your own mind and your own body," Dawa said. "Meditation is about improving one's inner self; embracing the free flow of thought; nurturing self-awareness on the most personal level. Tummo goes a step further to help practitioners take control of certain body processes, but it cannot be used to control another person. Nothing in Tummo meditation or Tibetan Buddhism claims to hold power or persuasions over others."

Donny stood up and paced the room, unable to contain himself any longer. "Come on, Dawa! You know as well as I do that connections do exist! The principles of interconnectedness, karma, dependent origination . . . we're all in this thing together, right? And I fear because of this drug and because of my knowledge of Tummo, those connections have somehow led to murder. My body may not have been in the same room as Stevens the night he was murdered, but I can't say the same about my mind."

The investigator was patient. He attempted to calm his old friend from a seated position. "It's true that every living thing shares a connection, Donald. But that does not mean we can influence others at will. Not through meditation, and certainly not through pills."

Dawa referenced the pill that was in Donny's hand. "That poison you speak of. That is the reason for your pain. Your ignorance. Your suffering. All of your training, your determination to learn the old ways, and you've already forgotten the Fifth Precept. The basis of heedlessness lies with intoxicants. Alcohol. Drugs. Little sleeping pills. I must tell you, my friend, I believe Tummo may have actually helped you in your time of need. But . . ." He shook his finger at the pill. "Relying on that? That is taking the wrong path, my friend."

Donny stopped pacing. "I know, Dawa. You're right. I know it all sounds crazy. Of course you're going to lean toward the most likely cause of these hallucinations, dreams, whatever you want to call it. You're a good investigator, Dawa. And you always were the pragmatic one."

Donny spoke, but he didn't mean a word he was saying. He was convinced both the Stevens and Moreno events were caused by combining a gene-regulating sleeping pill with his previously acquired skills. What else could explain the out-of-body-like experiences of his dreams? He could still feel the frigid air blasting from the AC unit by the window in Stevens' hotel room, and smell the pot smoke drifting in from the stairwell down the hall, flaring his nostrils and giving him a contact high.

The dream with Maria was just as sharp. The sound of pills rattling down a plastic bottle as the reporter ate her ibuprofen sans chaser echoed in his ears. The only other time Donny experienced anything as evocative as the nightmares was when he was practicing mindfulness–the ancient Buddhist tradition of purifying awareness without clinging to worldly things. Once the mind loosed the shackles of judgment, internal conflict and self-doubt, the mind was free to explore inner truth without the anxieties and stresses of this world holding it back.

Donny had freed his mind once before after spending two years with Dawa and his family in the Himalayas. At that point, the spiritual plane felt as real as the suede-covered pillow he had been sitting on in Dawa's meditation room. But there was one crucial difference between the devastating dreams of late and the transcendence he discovered in the Himalayas: when he crossed over to the holy realm through meditation, he was completely alone. Party of one. No reluctant guests around to poison with pills or stab to death with the bartender's ice pick.

In Donny's mind, Ocula and meditation must have worked together to amplify connections with other people through his dreams on a similar plane. But to Dawa, that was all crazy talk. Donny couldn't accept the detective's simplistic rationale.

"Still, don't you at least think it's possible? That in some inexplicable way I am the one causing these things to happen?" he asked.

"The pill is of this world," Dawa said. "So are pain and angst and murder and death. All of these things are a hindrance to the enlightenment you once sought, but that does not mean enlightenment comes to those who ignore reality. Far from it. When you ask me if breaking barriers between your dreams and this world is a possibility, a part of me wants to say yes, because I believe anything is possible. But we are still bound by the scientific laws of this world, such as the laws of physics. These laws can't be ignored. So are you causing these things to happen? I simply don't think so."

"You just said anything is possible."

Dawa sighed. "I did. But as a Buddhist, I can't condone such thinking. Exploring unknowns is a waste of time that could be better spent meditating on the things we *do* know."

"Then what should I do now, Dawa? Just pretend this never happened just because I can't be sure *how* it happened? My life will never be normal again. I can't turn to these people at the pharmaceutical company, and they're not going to forget about me, either. Something happened here, and I have to get to the bottom of it."

"You came here seeking advice, and now I will give it to you. But before I do, I have to ask. Are you still taking the medication?"

"Not for a few days now. I took Ocula Sunday night, and then had a migraine attack during Monday's seminar."

"Hmmm, I see." Dawa thought long and hard about the possible reasons behind Donny's current condition. Either the man was lying about taking the pill and was still exposing himself to a potentially mind-altering drug, or he was telling the truth and had replaced the medication with something else, perhaps an opioid of some sort. The third possibility, based on Donny's implausible assumptions, was one Dawa refused to entertain.

"Well," Dawa said. "At least you are off the medication. That is the first step. The second step would be to look into this company to see if they have any active complaints filed against them with the FDA. Maybe this drug has interacted with something else you are currently taking, causing these problems."

Donny chewed his lip through Dawa's borderline derision.

"I can also make a few phone calls, beat the bushes to see if I can find out anything about some of the people working for the company. Tell me though, Donald. What is it about the drug company that has you so rattled? I assume you've spoken with someone recently?"

"Yeah, a guy named Tanner. Ryan Tanner. He answered the emergency 800 number Asteria gave us after the clinical trials ceased. We were supposed to call if we had any negative side effects from the drug. I called on my way here and got a spooky vibe from the guy. He was way too eager to get me into his office today." Donny was fidgeting. "Something's going on. I just know it."

Dawa stood and placed his hand on Donny's shoulder. "Don't worry so much, Donald, and do try to calm yourself down. I'll look into this Tanner fellow and see if anything pops up on the radar. In the meantime, you just need to relax. Why don't you consider staying here for a while? I have a guest room open that you're more than welcome to use. I think the rest would do you good."

"Just like that, Dawa?" Donny skeptically asked. "You're not going to wait for me to go to sleep before punching me in the face again, are you?"

Dawa laughed. "No, Donald. I would never wait for you to go to sleep before punching you in the face again. I would very much want you to see it coming."

The two walked to the door leading out of the meditation room when Dawa turned to his guest. "One more thing, Donald. Have you told anyone else about these events?"

Donny froze.

Marci.

She was still at the hotel and waiting for Donny to return. There was a chance Tanner would be looking for him after he terminated their phone call earlier, and if that were the case then Marci was in serious danger. Donny quickly reverted back to panic mode.

"I've got to get out of here, Dawa. I have to leave now."

"Donald, I don't understand. You just got here, and I don't believe you are in any condition to–"

"I'm sorry, Dawa. I'll explain later." He rummaged through his wallet to find a business card. "Here. Take this. My number's on the back. Please call me if you find out anything on Tanner."

"Where are you going?"

"There's someone I have to check on back in Atlanta. Someone who may be in a lot of trouble."

Without another word spoken, Donny bolted out of the meditation room and through the front door, letting in a heavy gust of cold winter air. Within seconds Dawa heard the engine starting and the tires chirping on Donny's rental car as his old friend made haste back down the same driveway he was so eager to get up just an hour earlier.

Dawa frowned, uncertainty in his eyes. He looked down at the business card in his hand.

CHANGE YOUR MIND.
CHANGE YOUR LIFE.

If only it were that simple.

Chapter 26: Drug Run

"We're landing where?" Paul was standing at the entrance to the cockpit and talking to the captain as the Piper Navajo prepared for its descent onto Texan soil.

"On the runway, señor." The pilot pointed out the window to a narrow clearing in a dense field of scrub brush, palms and persimmon trees. "Over there."

"Jesus, man, where? All I see is that grassy strip." Paul turned back to Claire. "Is this guy serious?"

Claire fastened her seatbelt. "I told you it was under the radar," she said. "I'd buckle up if I were you."

The plane banked on the approach to line up with the landing strip, causing Paul to stumble on the short walk from the cockpit back to his seat. He sat in front of Claire and fastened his seatbelt, giving the old waist strap a couple of tugs for good measure.

"Don't worry. It looks scarier than it really is," Claire said.

"Who said I was scared?"

Claire grinned and played it cool, but her nonchalant attitude couldn't hide her firm grip on the armrests. It wasn't the first time she had landed in a questionable location, but hard landings were something she never got used to. She watched as details of the landscape below quickly came into focus. She clenched her jaw and waited for impact.

The plane touched down on the grassy runway with a jolt and a thud, unnerving the passengers and rattling the seats. The second bump was less jarring, followed by a succession of shudders down a pothole-ridden runway that obviously wasn't designed to accommodate heavy traffic. Soon the plane slowed to a halt, the twin propellers winding down as the noise and intensity of their landing dissipated into the calm of the remote farmland.

Paul's head was spinning, his grip still tight on the armrests. Claire was a little shaken from the kamikaze landing, but she did a good job of hiding it. The pilot cut the engines, took off his headset and addressed the passengers. "That wasn't so bad, no?" There was no response.

Outside the plane, the three travelers stretched their legs and observed their surroundings. The grassy runway cut from the thinly wooded terrain wasn't the only sign of development in the area. A small hangar, barely enough to squeeze a twin-engine plane into, was hidden in a stand of trees with the opening facing the landing strip. The roof of the hangar was covered in a mixture of camouflage netting and kudzu vines, concealing it from aerial view. Claire looked down the end of the runway and noticed a dirt road leading into the trees. She made a visor with one hand and motioned to the pilot with the other.

"Is that the road out?"

"Sí." The pilot was unloading the plane's external storage compartment. He turned to address her as he wiped his brow. "The road leads into Highway 44. From there you can head south into town. It's not too far. Maybe a two or three-hour walk from here."

"And Corpus Christi?"

He pursed his lips. “Hmm. Maybe another hour driving. Don’t worry. I’m sure you can find a ride into the city once you hit the highway.”

“What about you?” Paul asked.

The pilot smiled.

“You didn’t think this plane ride was just for you two, did you?” He pulled several medium-sized boxes from the storage compartment and stacked them by the plane. “I’ll be waiting here for the bolleros to pick up the delivery. They won’t be here until after dark, but you should leave well before then. If they see me with two gringos, they’re going to think something is up.”

Paul noticed one of the boxes was labeled *ANTIBIÓTICOS.* He looked back at Claire and silently mouthed, “What the fuck?”

She shrugged a shoulder. “Hey, when I’m offered a free plane ride, I tend not to ask too many questions. Besides, we’ve got another drug to worry about at the moment, don’t we?”

Paul agreed. They had wasted enough time just getting to Texas on a plane fit for the scrapyard, and now he was getting sidetracked. The two stowaways bid farewell to the drunken pilot and hit the trail.

The dusty road leading out crossed through authentic south Texas backcountry. The same scrub brush and palms they saw coming in could be seen for miles in every direction, with no signs of civilization in sight. There wasn’t much to hear, either, save the occasional gust of wind howling or distant birds calling. At one point Claire thought she had picked out the songs of a dozen different birds ahead, only to spot a mockingbird plagiarizing tunes from the comfort of a mountain laurel branch hanging over the next bend in the road.

"These days even the birds can't be trusted," Claire said. Paul nodded without responding, his mind wandering back to the Aguilar Operation.

In a way, he admired the man. Who cared if Alejandro Aguilar was sneaking antibiotics into the United States? Paul supposed one could argue that Aguilar's drugs were putting patients in danger primarily because they weren't FDA-regulated, but he also knew FDA regulation didn't always protect consumers from life-threatening drugs.

Paul had only recently become familiar with a list of FDA-approved drugs that had harmed thousands of patients in the past. Cerivastatin was meant to lower cholesterol, but instead killed over one hundred thousand patients by shutting down their kidneys. Troglitazone was designed to treat diabetes, but inadvertently led to hepatitis. Valdecoxib would have been a promising anti-inflammatory, if only it were also anti-heart attack and anti-stroke (it wasn't). And those were just a handful of drugs featured in a four-page whitepaper Paul had found in the marketing department's break room.

He couldn't imagine Aguilar's time-tested amoxicillin or pseudoephedrine putting users at risk; otherwise there wouldn't be a market for his products. But the most devastating preparation ever conceived by mankind was well on its way to FDA approval–another example of a dangerous drug falling through the industry-complacent cracks.

Ocula was also a drug Paul was convinced he had been given without his consent. The night before his abduction marked the most restful night of his life, and there was only one person he could think of who had a vested interest in his sleep patterns—his wife Michelle. But as long as Paul had known her, she had never given him a reason not to trust her.

In his eyes, their relationship was sound. There was no jealously, no history of lies or deceit, no suspicious texts or phone calls or after-hours rendezvous that were characteristic of marriages on the rocks. They weren't drifting apart; they were just getting started. Paul had been under the impression his marriage was stronger than ever.

Maybe that was why this latest revelation had cut so deep. As far as he knew, Michelle had never tricked him like that before. After years of being brutally honest with one another, now she decided to start sneaking pills into his nightcap? How long had the deception gone on? Just the one night, or for weeks prior to that? How long had those pills been building up in his system?

Paul hoped he was wrong, but he couldn't think of another explanation. He kicked a rock and watched it skip down the hard-packed road. He had a hundred questions he wanted to ask Michelle, and no way of getting in touch with her. Claire noticed her partner-in-captivity walking in silence just a few steps ahead.

"Everything okay up there?"

"Yeah. I was just thinking about something you said on the plane. About taking Ocula and not knowing it."

"Yeah? Did it spark something?"

"Well, kind of. I was thinking about my wife."

"Aha," Claire said. "Michelle, right?"

"That's right. Been together since we were seventeen, but I've known her since junior high. My dad moved my brother and me to a small town after mom passed. We've been in Georgia ever since." Paul slowed his pace to let Claire catch up.

"I've known Michelle almost ten years now," he said. "She's never lied to me about anything. Well, as far as I know. I mean there's really no way of knowing a lot of the time, is there.

Anyway, now I'm starting to ask myself, 'What kind of person drugs their spouse like that?' If she wanted to help, why wouldn't she just sit down with me and have a discussion about my health or sleeping habits or whatever it was that was bothering her. You know, like adults are supposed to do?"

"There's a central flaw in your theory," Claire said. "Ocula is almost impossible to get your hands on. I had to jump through countless hoops just to participate in the clinical trials. Even if Michelle wanted to slip you a sleeping pill, where would she get it?"

"Tanner told me Alex participated," Paul said. "Maybe Michelle called him to bum a pill or two."

"They talk much?"

"Not that I know of. But if she lied about drugging me–"

"Technically she didn't lie," Claire reasoned. "And even if she did, maybe she was afraid of your reaction."

"True, but it still doesn't justify the deception."

"If she's even the one responsible."

Paul was dithering. "I don't know. I just don't see how anyone else could have drugged me like that. And Michelle was ultra-curious about how I had slept the night before I was abducted."

"Uh huh," Claire said. "Well if it was her, then it sounds like she was just trying to help. But what do I know about wives and husbands and all that mess. I mean I have heard things. Troubling things," she said playfully. "But honestly, I have no desire to ever find out. I have a hard enough time keeping myself in check. I can't imagine having to report to another person."

"It's not like that, believe me. This is the first time she's tricked me."

"That you know of," Claire said.

Paul tried to hide his festering agitation, but the investigative journalist was reading him like an open book. "Let's just drop it," he said.

Claire didn't press the issue. The two had already been through enough to break down the most impregnable personas, and she had no desire to spend the rest of the trip back to Atlanta with a pissed-off married guy. If they were going to shed light on the corruption lurking in the shadowy depths of Asteria Pharmaceuticals, then they were going to have to work together.

Claire knew how important it was to find the other outliers before they were culled from the herd like sick cattle; the problem was figuring out who they were. Tanner had mentioned The Twelve on several occasions, but only let slip the identities of a few. Claire counted them out in her head. There were the Freeman brothers, Alex and Paul, and blind Mrs. Edwards made three. Claire was number four, and Donny Ford was five.

Five out of twelve. Those were the only names she had ever heard, either from Tanner or Paul or the rambling Mr. Doyle. And only one of those names was a solid lead. Not a great start.

There was something else bothering Claire, too. After the heated conversation in the Jeep on the way to San José, Paul seemed reluctant to get on board with finding the others. Claire understood his concern for his wife and child, but she also knew scooping up the family and running and hiding under a rock somewhere wasn't going to solve anything in the long run.

Sooner or later, Tanner's people would find Paul, and when they did, they would kill him and anyone else around–wife and kid included. Claire knew all too well what Tanner and company were capable of, and there was no doubt in her mind that cleaning up the mess in the field was priority number one.

She also knew they had to reach Ford before Tanner did, and that she would need Paul's help to do so.

The sound of feet crunching gravel resonated through the air as the two continued their march toward the faint sound of traffic in the distance. Claire figured the main road was a mile or so away. Once they reached the highway, Paul would have the option to take off on his own. She had to make sure they were on the same page before getting back to civilization.

"Didn't you say this Donny Ford guy was in Atlanta?" Claire asked.

"That's where he was the day I was abducted. Tanner sent me to his seminar to record him with the device. Who knows where he's at now."

"We've got to find him, Paul. No matter where he is."

Paul stopped in the road and turned to Claire. "Look, I already told you we'd go searching for the others, but first things first. I'm getting back to my family. I have to make sure they're okay. I could really care less about anything else."

"Care less?" Claire was stunned. "What about your brother, Paul? Don't you want to bring the people who murdered him to justice? What about me? Do you have any idea what they did to me in there? What they were going to do to you? And you couldn't care less. Wow. You really are a shortsighted son of a bitch, aren't you?"

"I don't have to stand here and listen to this sh–"

"No, you do, Paul. And here's why. You're a dead man walking. We both have targets on our backs now." She pushed her finger into his chest. "It's just that you're the only one in this little party of ours that hasn't come to terms with that yet. And until you do, you're never going to stand a chance."

Claire turned to walk away, leaving Paul standing in the road. He cursed under his breath. There was no clear choice. He could forsake his family for the time being and find Donny Ford first, or he could abandon Claire and get his family to a safe place, maybe his father's old farmhouse. It was highly unlikely Tanner knew about the rural outpost. If he chose the latter, Ford would likely be dead by the time Paul came out of hiding. Both choices sucked, but they were out of time. Paul had to choose.

He picked up his step and caught back up to Claire. "You said I have to come to terms with being a dead man. What exactly did you mean by that?"

Her eyes were on the horizon, searching for the highway. "You're not thinking practically, Paul. You're thinking with your heart. It's a noble response, but thinking that way in a life or death situation will get you killed."

Paul smirked. "You know about life or death situations, huh?"

"Cut the condescension, Paul. I've reported from countries you've never even heard of, about conflicts you–how would you put it–could care less about?"

Paul held his hands up and his face down as if to call a truce. "I'm not trying to be condescending, Claire. I'm just not sure where you're going with this."

"Think about it, Paul. The first thing Tanner's going to do is go after Ford and the other outliers and wrap up this entire situation the only way he knows how. He's at least a day ahead of us, and there's already a good chance he's gotten to some of them. Since Ford's the only other one we know about, he's our only play."

Claire spoke louder, competing with the sound of passing cars on the highway coming from over the hill ahead. "If you decide you want to split up now, fine. I can't stop you. But what I can tell you is this. You're signing your family's death sentence by thinking you can hide them away. Odds are your wife has already filed a missing person's report, and these people aren't going to allow a grieving widow to stir up trouble downtown at the last place you were seen before your abduction. They'll silence everyone they can to protect their interests. The only way we're going to stop them is to stop worrying about the things we can't control and use our fucking heads."

The dirt road had led them right to the highway, just as the pilot had said. Traffic was moving fast and steady. Bursts of air shot out from each passing car that flew by. Hitching a ride was their only option, but the chances a driver would ever pull over on the fast-paced stretch of highway were slim to none. They started walking south. Claire pleaded her case while Paul tried to wave down any car going under eighty.

"Who knows what Ford can tell us about the program," Claire said. "Don't you want to know what's happening to us? To the other dreamers?"

"What makes you think he has a clue about what's going on, Claire? The man's a 21st century trickster. Even if he didn't have the same experiences we did, he'd probably make some shit up just to be a part of a conspiracy he thought he could make some money off of later. He's an asshole, Claire. Right up there with the likes of Jonas Perch."

"The televangelist?"

"The one and only. He had a knack for appealing to people at rock bottom and then promising to lift them up out of the trenches–for a reprehensible fee, of course. The guy stole millions from poor retirees, low-wage workers, and offered nothing but platitudes in return. This guy Ford? Cut from the same cloth as Perch. Seriously, Claire. Why in the hell would I ever put my family's safety over a piece of shit like that?"

Claire was listening, but her attention was turned to the slowing pickup truck she had flagged down. The truck driver hit his hazards and pulled up on the shoulder alongside Paul and Claire.

"Y'all need a lift?" he asked through a half-cracked window.

"Yes," Claire said. "We heard this road leads into Corpus Christi?"

"Sure does. Headed that way now." The truck driver looked at Claire and liked what he saw. He opened the door to let her in. She was willing to take the risk.

"Thank you so much. We've been walking for a while now."

The driver looked at Paul and curled his lip. "Don't mention it, darlin'. But I believe your boy here's gonna have to ride in the back. Single cab an' all."

Paul looked at the driver, then at Claire. She shrugged. "Well, beggars can't be choosers. Have fun, Claire." He hopped in the truck bed and sat in the corner next to the cab, facing the tailgate. Claire climbed into the truck and rode shotgun, sticking closely to the passenger door.

The driver asked, "Ya'll hikers or what? I didn't see any backpacks on you."

Claire spoke on the fly. "Our car broke down a few miles up."

"I didn't see no car–"

"That's what happened," she snapped.

"Okay, okay. Just makin' a little small talk's all. No need to be a firecracker."

The driver played offended, but Claire could tell he was far from it. She looked back to see Paul sitting in the corner, the wind blowing his hair in all directions as he watched the cars zoom by on the other side of the highway. She felt bad for the man, and she desperately hoped his family would be safe. She wasn't a callous person at heart, but she could play the part when times called for it.

Paul was her best shot at finding Ford, and Ford was one step closer to exposing the wrongdoings at Asteria. Claire didn't have to be a journalist to know the more people Tanner got to first, the less believable their story would be. It was also possible Tanner thought Claire and Paul were dead, an advantage that would disappear the moment Paul showed up at his house to evacuate his wife and kid.

There was nothing Claire could do to stop Paul from splitting once they hit the city. He was adamant about securing his family first and foremost, and she could understand that, even if it did mean an exponential drop in their chances of survival.

She gazed out the window, counting the passing telephone poles like sheep and closing her eyes before she reached fifty. She was so tired again, even after getting some sleep on the flight into Texas. She knew falling asleep in a stranger's truck wasn't the smartest move, but she couldn't help herself. At least Paul was with her; that was all the assurance she needed. She dozed off quickly, with just enough time to entertain a single thought in her head before drifting off to sleep.

If only I slept this good before.

Chapter 27:
Trouble

The traffic light clicked over from yellow to red, but Donny didn't care. He knew he could make it. He stomped the gas and blew through the intersection, forcing cars to hit the brakes and honk their horns and wave their middle fingers at the reckless driver. By the time the halted cars started moving again, Donny was long gone.

Donny was testing the limits of his rental car, and so far, the black sedan was holding up. He barreled down I-75, his white-knuckle grip tight on the wheel as he weaved in and out of a mélange of tractor-trailers, minivans and sedans in a race to get back to his midtown hotel room. Hopefully, Marci would be waiting for him there.

Donny figured the odds of Tanner looking for him were slim, but he didn't want to take any chances. While it was true that nothing during their phone conversation hearkened to malice or ill will, there was a disturbing and undeniable fact Donny had taken away from the brief exchange that gave him the creeps. Tanner knew about the dreams.

It was the only explanation for Tanner's desire to see Donny right away. The yarn Ford had spun over the phone earlier that day should have been classified as science fiction, fantasy, or outright lunacy by any pharmaceutical rep's standards, but Tanner hadn't been fazed one bit. No snickers heard, no long sighs detected, no barnyard epithets muttered. Every vocal cue

Donny could pick up on pointed to a man who unequivocally believed every word Ford was telling him was true. And that worried Donny more than anything else.

Donny pulled under the hotel vestibule and hopped out of his car, whirling through the revolving glass doors, running for the elevators and catching a lift just as the elevator doors were beginning to shut. He frantically pressed the button to the seventh floor. Marci said she would be in room 710, right next door to Donny's room. If he could convince Marci to go with him to Dawa's for a few days, that should give the three of them enough time to figure out their next move.

The seventh-floor light flashed and the elevator dinged. It was Donny's cue to calm down and tread carefully. He peeked out from the elevator car, first looking left, then right. The halls were empty. No one in sight. He stepped out and commenced the slow walk toward the end of the corridor.

The green doors to rooms 700 and 702 were right in front of the elevator, with room numbers ascending upward to the right. His purposeful steps were undetectable on the soft carpet leading down the hallway. He had to move both quickly and quietly if he was going to get to Marci's room before meeting another guest sharing the same floor–a meeting he would very much like to avoid.

Donny looked to his left: 704 and 706. He stopped and looked back. The floor was still quiet and empty. Just a little further. He could see the doors to 708 and 710. Both doors were shut, with no sign of a forced entry. That had to be a good thing. Donny fished around in his pocket for the room key Marci had left him and opened the door.

At first glance the room appeared to be in order. It was bright inside, with the curtains drawn back to let the daylight in.

The starch-white sheets were ruffled and pulled back on one side. The television was on but the volume was muted. There was no sign of Marci.

"Hello? Marci? You here?" The room was mostly silent except for the white noise of the bustling city coming from the streets below. Donny noticed Marci's cellphone lying on the nightstand. It wasn't like her to leave her phone behind.

"Marci?" he called again as he walked toward the bathroom. The door was shut. He looked down at his feet, and that was when he saw water running from under the door, darkening the carpet on his side.

Jesus.

He burst through the bathroom door. His eyes followed the floodwaters to their source. There was Marci, lying in an overflowing bath with her head drooped over to one side, her left arm dangling outside of the tub. She was motionless. Her face was already blue and her eyes were wide open, fixed on the torrent of water streaming across the ceramic-tile floor.

"Oh *God,* no!" Donny cried as he fell to his knees alongside the tub. He rapidly tapped her cheeks and tried to wake her. He swept the wet hair away that was covering part of her face. He pressed his thumb deep into her wrist and waited in vain for a pulse. There was nothing. Minutes passed before it finally set in that she was gone. He pulled her in close and embraced her while trying to hold back tears over the death of his lover, but the emotions crept up fast. The water was still running and cascading over the side of the tub as Donny broke down, holding Marci one last time.

***

"You wanted to see me, sir?" Tanner asked as he opened the door to George Sturgis's office.

The CEO of Asteria Pharmaceuticals was sitting behind a solid-oak desk at the far end of his massive office on the top floor of Asteria's downtown headquarters. Windows lined the entire south side, with curtains drawn back to let the winter sun warm the large vaulted space. Angled beams of light from the tall exterior glass cast long rectangles on the office floor. A built-in mahogany bookcase occupied the back wall behind Sturgis's desk, filled from top to bottom with medical and pharmaceutical research journals spanning the last fifty years. Sturgis was sitting in the shadow of the short wall blocking the sun to his right. He looked up from a stack of documents on his desk and spoke in a gravelly voice.

"Yes. Come in, Mr. Tanner. We've got a lot to talk about."

George Sturgis had always been an intimidating man. He was taller than most, with broad shoulders to match a solid frame built on years of athleticism starting at an early age back in the 1960s. He wasn't afraid to lean on someone to get what he wanted, but most of the time the slightest insinuation of brute force was enough to make his targets cave long before it ever came to that.

Sturgis was also a high achiever. He had been accepted to the University of Florida at the age of seventeen on a wrestling scholarship after winning the state tournament two years in a row. He completed his MBA before his twenty-first birthday, and by the summer of 1975 George Sturgis had earned his PhD in organic chemistry, effectively setting himself up for a lucrative career as a research chief and the eventual CEO of the largest pharmaceutical company in the southeast.

Now in his late sixties, the man with the silvery receding hairline and piercing gray eyes was more domineering than ever. Only a few people at Asteria could look him directly in the eyes when talking to him. Ryan Tanner was one of those people.

"What's this about?" Tanner asked. He stood in front of Sturgis's desk. His boss noticed his twiddling fingers.

"Looks like you're dying for a smoke, Tanner," he said. "How much is a pack now, $20? More?" He shook his head. "Sometimes, Tanner, I think we pay you too much."

"Really? I was just about to ask you for a raise."

Sturgis cracked his knuckles and raised his voice. "Honestly, Tanner, you've got to be out of your goddamn mind coming in here and talking to me like that after the shitstorm you've caused around here."

"I don't follow."

"Your little side project in Costa Rica. The project you said would stay under wraps. The one you assured me you could handle." He leaned forward, his fists clenched atop his desk. Sternly, "How's that going for you, Ryan?"

Tanner swallowed hard and pulled at his collar. His plan was to keep everything under the radar until he could tie up all of the loose ends, but apparently someone had already tipped off the boss.

Sturgis answered for him. "I got a call from one of your techs at the facility. I hope you didn't think when I put you in charge of this project I was just going to let you run with it without someone down there to keep an eye on you. My informant told me some incredible things. Unbelievable things. So when exactly did you plan on telling me what happened at the facility? Did you think you could simply sweep all of those deaths under the rug?"

For a moment, Tanner had thought he could. But now the truth was out. He had to explain.

"There was a disruption. One of the project participants caused a disturbance outside of the safe zone and we had to take action. He was knocked unconscious when, in retrospect, we should have gone ahead and terminated the threat. These things tend to happen with experimental research from time to time, but I can assure you, steps are being taken to prevent an episode like this one from happening again."

"Tell me something," Sturgis said. "Do you think I rose to the top of one of the world's most advanced pharmaceutical research firms by letting mistakes like this go unanswered? Don't think for one second you can brush this off as some tragic accident, write a report and continue on with your research. Do you know who else I got a call from today?"

Tanner didn't.

"Diego Ibanez with the Costa Rican state department. He tells me your workers talked, Ryan. Told local reporters about a clandestine research facility in the jungle with ties to a drug company in the U.S. Said the Costa Rican government knew all about it and was being paid to keep things quiet. Now our insiders have washed their hands of all allegiances and the government is taking action. I received word through our back channels this morning that they're planning on sending security forces to the facility as soon as tomorrow." Sturgis stood up from his desk, towering over Tanner. "Now I don't give a goddamn what kind of strings you've got to pull or favors you have to call in to get the job done, but you've got less than twenty-four hours to make sure nothing at that facility can be traced back to Asteria. Do we have an understanding?"

Tanner understood. "You can rest assured that everything will be taken care of." He stood up and walked to the door. Sturgis stopped him halfway. "One more thing, Ryan. I know you've got connections. That's one of the reasons I hired you. But don't forget. I've got connections, too. Do *not* disappoint me on this."

Tanner nodded, then left. He walked to the stairwell on the west side and lit up a smoke. He had played it rather cool in Sturgis's office; something he carried over from Langley. The seriousness of the situation, however, was not lost on him. Even worse, he could only think of one last play he could make on such short notice. He still had a contact of his own working in the Ministry of Public Security. If he could convince him to lay off the facility investigation long enough to get a team down to Costa Rica, he could have the place wiped clean before local authorities arrived.

If that didn't work, Tanner feared there was little else he could do before security forces ransacked the place. Asteria would be implicated in a scandal of epic proportions. It would not only be the end of his career, but once the lurid details emerged, he would likely end up spending the rest of his life behind bars.

Tanner took a long drag off his smoke, then snuffed it out and kicked it to the corner where a half-dozen other cigarette butts had been left over from previous meetings with the top brass. It was time to go to work, and the sooner he could get a hold of his friend Prado in Costa Rica, the better.

But if Prado couldn't come through, Tanner was lost.

Chapter 28:
Cat's out of the Bag

Marci's phone sat on the hotel nightstand, ringing and vibrating to the point of almost falling off. Donny got up and left the bathroom to see who was calling, but he didn't make it to the phone in time. He picked it up and read the screen. ONE MISSED CALL: MOM.

Jesus. He rubbed his eyes with his thumb and forefinger. He wondered why this had happened. Marci was lying in the tub with a half-empty bottle of pain pills spilled over on the bathroom counter, with the other half unquestionably resting in Marci's stomach. Next to the pills was an empty bottle of Jack Daniels. To the untrained eye, it didn't look good.

Donny wasn't buying the set up one bit. It was too cliché, too staged. A layperson might have seen an open-and-shut case, but to a man who made a living based largely on presentation, he knew this one didn't fit the bill.

An orgy of evidence, he thought. Just the pill bottle would have been enough, but throwing in the liquor bottle and placing her in the tub was about as original as leaving a note that read, "Goodbye, cruel world." Plus, Marci couldn't stand Jack Daniels. She had gotten sick off of it at a party in college and she hadn't touched the stuff since.

Donny began looking around for other clues, but the killers had done their homework. Even determining something as basic as how the killers got into the room was a mystery. Marci wouldn't have opened the door for just anybody, and there was no sign of a forced entry. Donny examined the windows; they were sealed insulated glass panels that couldn't be opened. The shades were also pulled back; apparently, the perpetrators weren't too worried about being seen (Of course, they *were* on the seventh floor). The scenario had Donny stumped, but one thing was for certain. Whoever did this was ultimately looking for him and was sure to be close by.

He returned to the bathroom and kneeled down to kiss Marci onc last time. He ran his hand up the side of her neck, and that's when he noticed it: a small bump, almost like a tiny pinprick right above her carotid artery. *An injection site.*

She had been drugged all right, just not in the sense the killers would have had the local investigators believc. Donny had suspected a faux crime scene, but now he was certain. These guys were professionals who would stop at nothing to silence anyone close to the Ocula program, doe-eyed assistants included.

Donny hastily went to the door. He knew he had to get out of the building undetected. He looked down one end of the hallway, then down toward the elevators. The coast was clear.

He was halfway down the corridor when he heard the elevator chime and the doors open. Footsteps followed. Donny was transfixed by the sound as a man wearing a black overcoat came around the corner. Their eyes met, and for a moment they were both frozen in a standoff.

It was one of Tanner's goons.

The man pulled his coat to the side, brandishing his weapon. "Sir, I'm going to need you to come with me."

Donny ran.

Without hesitation, the man pulled his Glock and fired three rounds toward the runner. All but one missed, grazing

Ford's left shoulder the moment he hit the door to the emergency stairwell.

Donny didn't notice. The pitchman was running on pure adrenaline, flying down seven flights of stairs all the way to the main floor. He hurried through the revolving door and made it to his rental car before noticing two more goons coming from the parking lot in front of him, guns drawn and running his way.

He slammed his car in reverse and floored it, tires screaming and laying down a thick coat of rubber as two shots pierced his windshield. Donny kept his head down, peeking back just enough to see where he was going. He waited for an opening and violently cut the wheel, righting the car and shifting into drive before flooring it again. A quick glance in the rearview revealed the goons running back to their car.

Donny had a modest head start on Tanner's Consultants, but rush-hour traffic quickly threw a wrench in his escape. He could already see lines of cars at the top of the hill, sitting in gridlock just a quarter mile away. He checked his mirrors again. The goons were gaining. He was coming up fast on the standstill traffic and he had to make a choice. He saw an opening on the sidewalk to the right of the stopped cars. He could jump the curb and plow through the four-way intersection. No one would be crazy enough to follow him through a five o'clock medley of cross-street traffic.

There was no time left. He cut the wheel right and hopped the curb, sending a hubcap spinning off the front wheel and rolling into one of the parked cars. Once he hit the sidewalk he could see the blur of speeding cars ahead, packed tightly together like train cars rushing down the tracks. His eyes widened as he realized there was no way he could make it. He glanced at the speedometer: 80 MPH. He stood on the brakes with both feet, but it was too late. The sedan slid and fishtailed right into the middle of the busy intersection.

That was when Donny looked out the driver-side window. He heard the horn blowing and the brakes screaming as the front grill of a minivan was violently introduced to his driver-side door. The impact threw Donny into the passenger seat as the van pushed the black sedan onto its side and down the busy highway, sparks blasting from underneath as aluminum and steel swiftly scraped down a football field's worth of concrete. There was so much noise, followed by so much pain. And then there was silence.

That was the last thing Donny remembered.

***

"Prado! Como estás, amigo?" The relief in Tanner's voice was tangible. He had been trying desperately to get his old Central American contact on the phone for hours, and now he was finally getting a call back. Apparently, it had been a busy day for the Costa Rican official. Prado was sitting at his desk and chewing on a cigar when he rang the former company man.

"Tanner, my friend. It's been a long time. How are you doing these days?"

"I can't complain. Just trying to make a living. How are you, old timer?"

"Still younger than you, cabrón."

"Is that so?" Tanner quipped. "Well, age is just a number, amigo, and I'm doing a lot better now than you were a decade ago. What was it, August 2010? I know you remember the hell week I'm talking about."

Prado nodded. “Ah, yes. The joint task force assigned to monitor the Guerrez cartel’s cocaine operation. Five days in the jungle with triple-digit heat. Era fuego, amigo. What I remember is that you almost had a heatstroke. And the bugs. Dios mío!”

Tanner laughed. “Hey, now. Talk all the shit you want about my trouble acclimating to the equator, but you were the one who almost gave away our position when you insisted on bringing your cellphone to the jungle in case the flavor of the month called. What was her name? Do you even remember?”

“Maria.”

“Yeah. Maria. Couldn’t have guessed that. That was a nice ringtone, by the way.”

Prado laughed and played the good sport before getting to the point. “So what do I owe the pleasure of your phone call today, Señor Tanner?”

“I need to call in a favor, Prado. There’s a facility in Costa Rica, halfway between Pueblo Nuevo and Poás National Park. It’s got ties to a company located here in the states. Has anything come across your radar in the last couple of days?”

“Oh, yes.” Prado lit up his cigar. “Everyone down here is talking about the frightened workers who are claiming there is a secret laboratory in the jungle. It’s all over the local news here in San José. What do you know about it?”

Tanner held his hand over the receiver and exhaled one long fuck before returning to the call. “The facility in question, Prado. My company has ties to it that can’t be disclosed. We had a contact in the state department, but apparently they’re claiming they can’t keep a lid on it.” Tanner rolled his fingers on the desk. “Is there anything we can do about this?”

Wearily, Prado asked, “What do you need, Ryan?”

"Delay the security forces for a couple of days. Give me time to get some people down there to clean things up. Then we'll be gone and out of your hair for good."

Prado was shaking his head before Tanner could finish. "Ryan. My friend. What you are asking me to do is impossible at this point. I could have delayed an investigation had one or two people walked out of the jungle with wild stories, but we've got a dozen men in San José swearing they were abducted by gringos, and now they have the media's full attention. Unfortunately, there's no covering anything up here, Ryan, because the cat is already in the bag."

"Out of the bag," Tanner said.

"Yes. Well. I don't believe I can help you with this, Ryan. I am very, very sorry, my friend."

Tanner was pleading now. "Prado. Listen to me. This can't get out. It's not just about my job, Prado. My life depends on it."

"What is in this laboratory that has gotten you so worried, jefe? Because if our police get up there and find it's drogas, it's going to be just another Friday."

"It's not drugs, Prado, but it's bad. I wouldn't ask if I didn't need help. You're my last resort. Please. Delay the search. Just a day or two."

Prado sighed. "I'm sorry, Ryan. I simply cannot help. Now I must go. As you can imagine, the police force is having a very busy day here in preparation for tomorrow."

"Prado, wait!"

The receiver clicked and Prado was gone. Tanner went into an immediate rage. He reared back and hurled another phone at the wall again. It was the second one he had destroyed in under a week. For whatever reason, smashing something against an innocent wall seemed to have a calming effect in situations like this.

He sat behind his desk, massaging his forehead with his thumb and index finger. There was little else he could do now. Prado and the security forces would reach the clandestine facility by midday tomorrow, maybe sooner. The security to the lab below would stall them for some time, maybe even days, but it wouldn't change the fact that the entire upper level was riddled with the bodies of a couple dozen armed guards–at least what was left of them, at that point. After all, they were in the middle of the jungle.

Allowing Doyle to carry out his experiments in the stonewall chamber on the top floor had probably been Tanner's biggest mistake. The security to the main labs below might have bought him enough time to get a cease and desist from authorities by calling in a favor from his buddies at Langley, but Costa Rican police would already have everything they needed to implicate Asteria Pharmaceuticals in an international human rights scandal right there on the top floor, long before any paperwork could halt an investigation.

Tanner was doomed, and he knew it. His hands were shaking as he pulled his smokes from his shirt pocket to light one up. Smoking always helped him think. He leaned back and contemplated his next move. The situation was dire and called for drastic measures. He seemed to be completely out of options.

Except for one.

Chapter 29:
The Big Easy

Paul looked up through the windshield and into the night sky. The full moon diminished the light from the stars behind it, and was accompanied by a few bluish-gray clouds that were huddled in close like old friends. It was just after midnight, and Paul and Claire were driving on I-10, an hour east of the Texas-Louisiana state line. The road was a lonely one, marked by the solitary stretch of highway they were riding on eastbound. Occasionally they would spot headlights in the westbound lane traveling in the opposite direction, but the passing of fellow nightriders was few and far between.

Claire was scrolling through the navigation on the dash of the rental car they had picked up in Corpus Christi, looking for the fastest route back to Atlanta. They were making good time; early estimates had them arriving in Baton Rouge by 2 a.m., and already they were close to city limits just after midnight. Claire took note of the discrepancy. The last thing they needed was to run into a cop shooting radar.

"You know, Paul, we're almost to Baton Rouge and it's barely midnight." She referenced the revised navigation. "This has us in Atlanta by seven. Maybe we should slow down a little?"

"No time," he said. "Tanner's already back in Atlanta. Hopefully he's still scrambling to figure out what he's going to do next. We've got to get back before he starts going after people, after my family. After Ford."

"That's going to be hard to do if we get caught speeding. You've been pushing ninety the entire time. Maybe I should drive the rest of the way."

Paul started to answer, but was interrupted by a traffic notification coming from the navigation screen:

TRAFFIC ALERT: MAJOR ACCIDENT ON I-12 EASTBOUND AT MILE MARKER 6 EAST OF BATON ROUGE LA. ALL LANES BLOCKED.
SEEK ALTERNATE ROUTE.

Paul glanced between the road and the dash, evaluating the news. "I-12. That's the interstate we were supposed to get on in Baton Rouge, right?"

Claire scrolled through the options. "Yep, I-12 was basically the New Orleans bypass. Now it looks like we're going to have to stay on 10."

"Which takes us right through New Orleans. Great. That's going to set us back a minute."

"That's right," Claire remembered. "Carnival season. I think Mardi Gras is next Tuesday, but the party down here goes on for weeks leading up to it." She searched for a better route before conceding. "I think we're just going to have to head south and go through the city. Navigation says it'll only tack on an extra thirty minutes without traffic."

"Key words being *without traffic*," Paul said. The digital line marking I-12 was flashing bright red on the screen, with I-10 heading into New Orleans one long and bright green line.

Claire pointed to the screen. "I don't think we have much of a choice."

***

The bright city lights created a golden haze in the fast-approaching distance. It was nearing 2 a.m., but while the rest of the western world was fast asleep, New Orleans was pulling an all-nighter. Paul made the choice to exit off the interstate on Basin Street in search of a twenty-four-hour gas station near the city center. There had been few opportunities to pick up a cellphone on the late-night drive from Texas to Louisiana, and he wasn't going to miss another chance to call his wife by sticking to the perimeter.

They followed the prompts of the navigation system, turning south on St. Louis Street and into the heart of the French Quarter–a risky endeavor given the height of the season. The car idled slowly down the narrow street as partygoers packed the sidewalks, holding drinks and throwing beads and making bad decisions that were destined for the Internet. A group of rowdy twenty-somethings gathered below a balcony, all eyes on the show above. A young woman was gripping the bottom of her shirt, pulling it just below her breasts and teasing the crowd before fully committing. Street voyeurs chanted in unison: "Dooo it! Dooo it!"

The girl laughed and blushed and looked to her friends for approval. They gave the nod, and up went the shirt. The crowd roared. Cellphones were held high with cameras set to record. Her quasi-bashful performance would be gracing social media pages and party blogs by sunrise.

"Oh, to be young and dumb," Claire said.

"I can't quite imagine you venturing to Mardi Gras during your college years."

"Well, don't try," Claire said sternly.

Paul smirked, keeping his eyes peeled and looking through the crowds for the gas station that was supposed to be ahead on the left. Unfortunately, not a single building in sight appeared to be newer than the 19th century edifices New Orleans was known for. Victorian-style two- and three-story buildings were painted in a rainbow of colors ranging from bright canary yellow to weathered fire-engine red, with a variety of creams and greys and whites in between. Cast-iron balconies fronted most of the higher buildings; many with hanging fern baskets draped from the elaborately designed rails. The live oaks privileged enough to secure what little space was left on the sidewalk sporadically burst from their grates and hung over the street, obscuring Paul's view of the road ahead.

"This fucking navigation," Paul bemoaned. The crowded streets of stumbling drunks and promiscuous patrons were nerve-racking. All he wanted was to get to a phone; something he never would have thought would be so difficult in the 21st century.

He had tried calling the house phone from the airport in San José, and again at the rental-car agency in Corpus Christi, but all he had gotten was the answering machine. He desperately needed a cellphone so he could leave his wife a number with instructions to call. He had been missing for days, and he knew she was probably ringing the long-distance landlines off the hook by now. He was about to launch into another tirade of classic pedestrian-induced swearwords when the narrow passage opened up to North Rampart Street. An all-night gas station was brightly lit and calling from the corner.

"Thank God," Paul said.

He pulled to the front and ran inside. Claire watched him talking to the clerk from the car before checking her mirrors, first the center rearview, then the passenger side. A car that was sitting a block away behind them caught her attention. It was a Crown Vic, parked with the headlights off. Two silhouettes were sitting motionless inside. Then she saw one head turn to talk to the other.

Claire had always been a little suspicious of her surroundings; her natural skepticism was part of what made her an excellent investigative journalist. But the recent events had exacerbated such proclivities to a level bordering paranoia, and she knew it. She forced herself to forget about the car behind her and focus on something else, starting with the air conditioner. With all the car's technology, the heat was in disrepair, and no amount of knob-turning or vent-slapping was going to fix it.

Paul came out of the store tearing open the packaging of his new flip phone. He motioned for Claire to roll her window down. "Yeah?" she said.

"Hey, I'm gonna be out here on the phone for a minute. You probably don't wanna hear all this."

"Works for me."

Paul walked to the nearest light post, kicking a foot back and leaning on it as he dialed home for the third time in two days. He said a little prayer inside, hoping the third time was the charm. After two excruciatingly long rings, someone picked up on the other side.

"Hello?" It was Michelle.

"Michelle, thank God. It's me."

"Jesus! Paul? Oh my God, where are you? I've been trying to call your phone for days! What's going on? What happened?" Michelle was understandably frantic, but given the urgency of the situation, Paul had to cut through the formalities.

"Listen to me, Michelle. I'll explain everything, I promise, but this is very important. Has anyone contacted you in the last two days? Anyone from my work?"

Michelle had to think before answering. "Yes. A man. Your boss, I think."

"Did he tell you his name? Ryan Tanner?"

"That sounds right," Michelle said.

"When did he call, and what did he want?"

"Just this morning. Well, yesterday morning, rather. Around eight or nine. He said you hadn't shown up for work in three days and he was concerned. He wanted to know if I had spoken with you."

"What did you tell him?"

"The truth! That I hadn't talked to you since you left for work on Monday. That I knew as much as he did. I called everyone I could think of. Your friends, your coworkers, your brother. Half didn't know where you were, the other half didn't answer. By Tuesday night I had to call the police to file a missing person's report, but that seemed more like a formality than anything else. The two officers that came by the house were convinced you were going through a crisis or something, that you would show back up sooner or later."

"Is that everything? You didn't tell him about any missed calls, did you?"

"No, of course not. I mean, I didn't really think to, either. A couple of numbers showed up on the caller ID, but they never left a message. Was that you? Why didn't you leave a message?"

Paul paused to put a finger in his free ear. A boisterous Mardi Gras crowd had made their way down the street, howling and catcalling as they stumbled past the station. He turned to face the other direction. "Michelle, I've been on the move since

Monday. I didn't get a chance to call you before Thursday morning, and I didn't have a number you could call back on until now."

"Where's all the noise coming from? Where are you right now?"

"New Orleans."

"Where?"

"It's not what you think, Michelle. I was kidnapped at work Monday and I've been trying desperately for the last several days to get back to Atlanta as soon as possible. Michelle, this is very important. Do you have a pen and something to write on?" He looked up toward Claire sitting in the car. She pointed at her watch. He nodded okay, then went back to his call.

"Yeah, I've got a pen right here."

"Write down this address. 550 Flat Shoals Lane."

Michelle repeated, "550 Flat–Shoals–Lane. What's this for?"

"Remember my dad's old farmhouse I told you about out on Highway 20? I need you to take Aaron and get there fast. I think the men who kidnapped me think I'm dead, but we can't risk it. You need to leave and go someplace safe. Don't tell anyone, just go. I'm leaving New Orleans now, and I'll meet you there in about nine hours. Okay?"

"You're kind of scaring me, Paul. What's this all about?"

"It's got something to do with Asteria and the drugs they're making there. Listen, I don't have time to explain, but I promise I'll fill you in on everything when I get there. Just take Aaron, fill up some bags with food and water and go. I'll be there by lunchtime, okay? You've got to trust me on this, Michelle."

"Okay, Paul. I trust you. I'm just a little scared."

"Don't be, sweetie. Like I said, this is just a precaution. The farmhouse will be safe. Be careful driving out there, Michelle. Give Aaron a kiss for me, would you?"

"Of course. I love you, Paul."

"I love you, too. Wait!" He had almost forgotten to ask. "What the *hell* is your cellphone number?"

***

Paul climbed back in the car and put it in drive. Claire asked, "How's the family? Everything okay on your end?"

"Yeah. They're fine. Apparently Tanner or someone pretending to be Tanner called her yesterday and asked if she'd spoken to me. I told her to head to my dad's old place in the country. Her and Aaron should be safe there."

It was almost three in the morning, but the streets were still packed as they slowly drove out of the French Quarter and back toward the interstate. Claire watched and listened as the city lights dimmed and the sounds of Carnival faded into the distance. Once they hit the interstate again, they were back in the dark.

Claire said, "Tanner's putting out his feelers to see if we've talked to anyone since the event."

"Yeah, either that or someone is pretending to be Tanner. After what you saw, wouldn't you think he'd be convinced that everyone in the facility is dead?"

"We can't risk making such a huge assumption," Claire said. "Although it does seem like he called your wife to put his mind at ease. What did she tell him?"

"The truth. That I was missing and she didn't know where I was."

"Think he bought it?"

Paul shrugged. "Who knows. Maybe."

"Well, hopefully that got us off his radar for a little while, but we're not off the hook yet. Either way, Tanner will be focused on the others, too, including Donny Ford."

"Damn, I almost forgot about him for a minute."

Claire turned to face Paul. "You're still on board with the plan, right? Wasn't that what the call was all about, making sure your wife was safe?"

"Of course," Paul assured her. "We'll find Ford, and hopefully he will lead us to the others. The more people we have to go public with, the better."

"Right." Claire waited for Paul's eyes to return to the road before scrutinizing the driver. Sure, he had promised they would stick together and see the task through, but something told her there was a side to Paul that couldn't be trusted.

She turned her attention to the road. The rental car's headlights formed a steep pyramid of light on the fast moving asphalt ahead. The terrain around them was pitch black. The highway was free of cars, the trees were shrouded in darkness. Even the moon had set over the horizon, the clouds working hard now to deny what little starlight was left to the world below.

She checked her rearview, searching for any glimmer to replace the darkness outside. Finally, she saw a light in the distance, directly behind them. What began as a small and unified twinkle turned into two distinguishable beams of light growing larger by the second. Headlights. She spotted them at least a mile out; now they were a few hundred yards away.

"See that?" she asked.

Paul watched his mirror. "Yeah. Guy came up fast, didn't he?"

It was true the car had closed a significant distance in a short amount of time since Claire first spotted it, but now the vehicle was hanging back and pacing them, maintaining a cool eighty-five miles per hour from a couple of hundred yards behind.

"We're obviously being followed," Claire said.

"We don't know that yet."

"Who the fuck do you know that drives like that?"

"You're joking, right?" Paul dismissed. "Probably some dumb teenagers speeding who got scared when they ran up on another car. This rental does have a kind of *five-o* feel to it, doesn't it?"

"Maybe. I don't know."

Paul considered her rising paranoia. When they first met, Claire had been calm and collected, even after being tortured for weeks on end. Now Paul wondered if she was on the verge of a nervous breakdown. How long had she been in captivity? What had they done to her? And what about the way she had executed her tormentor Doyle with zero hesitation or remorse thereafter? No one could murder someone like that and feel nothing, right? She couldn't keep up the tough girl act forever, Paul concluded. Sooner or later, everyone broke.

Paul turned on the radio and searched for something to calm her nerves. "You like classical?"

"Oh yeah. Chopin's my jam. See if you can find his funeral march. That's fitting for the occasion."

Paul picked up on the sarcasm and pulled away from the dial. "Okay, no music then."

They continued driving into the night, keeping a watchful eye on the car tailing them from a distance. Claire stared into the side mirror. She could only make out a couple of dark shadows occupying the front seats. Were those Crown Vic headlights? From this distance, she couldn't tell.

She leaned her head against the glass, never taking her eyes off the mysterious sedan. Maybe Paul was right. Maybe it was just a carload of drunken teenagers trying to keep it between the lines, or a couple of late-night commuters heading home from a business trip. It could be anybody, and she knew she should probably just let it go.

Her thoughts distracted her long enough to let the car slip into the distance. She leaned her head up and watched as the headlights on the sedan faded back into one, and soon the car was gone, lost to the darkness on a seemingly abandoned Louisiana highway.

She rested her head back on the glass and stared into nothing. *Maybe I am just being paranoid.*

Chapter 30: Emergency Medicine

When Donny Ford woke up he was in the hospital, boxed in by curtains with white fluorescent lights shining down in his face. He squinted and looked around. A heart rate monitor was to his left, spiking gradually as he returned to consciousness. The monitor beeped loudly as the lines jumped and scrolled across the screen with each passing rhythm.

He took note of his heart rate. Seventy-four beats per minute. He saw the numbers below that next to NIBP. Must be his blood pressure, because it was showing 147/90. A little high, thought Donny, but he had just been in an accident that, in his mind, he never should have survived.

That was when the pain kicked in. Donny tried to reach down with his left hand to locate the source of the dull, aching pain in his left leg, but his arm couldn't get there. He looked to find a sling was restraining it. He could wiggle his fingers, but he couldn't do much else.

Then there was the leg. It felt like a baseball player had used his shinbone for batting practice. He lifted his head to try and get a better look at the splint wrapping the injured limb, but the cervical collar wrapping his neck choked him like a tightly wound scarf. The more he investigated the pain, the worse it got.

He relaxed his head back on his pillow. His neck was excruciating. *Whiplash*, he thought. He was lucky to be alive. Under normal circumstances, the injuries recorded on his patient assessment chart would have been enough to worry about, but something else was causing his heart rate to climb even higher.

Tanner's goons. They had tried their best to murder him back at the hotel with no regard for the people around them or any authorities that might have been lingering close by. Their actions were bold and determined, and they were willing to operate above the law to achieve a common goal. It was clear they would let nothing get in their way–especially not some inner-city emergency room with zero security and a six-hour wait.

The ER was packed. Nurses and doctors scrambled from one bed to the next, working to treat a variety of patients with conditions ranging from critical to go-home-and-take-an-aspirin. Donny could see a nurse through the slit in the curtain next to his bed. She was working a large, whirling machine next to the patient. The whirling grew louder before ending suddenly with one big click, like a large camera shutter capturing an old-time photograph.

Down the hall and through the white noise of ringing phones and CB radios Donny heard a woman singing what sounded like an old gospel hymn. He couldn't quite make out the words over the nurse politely asking the woman to stop moving so she could administer an IV, but the tune sounded a lot like *Leaning on the Everlasting Arms*. He recognized it from childhood, something his mother used to sing when she was folding laundry in the living room of their tiny two-bedroom house. But while his mother's rendition evoked fond memories of childhood innocence, the tune resonating from the distressed woman down the hall gave Donny a haunting sense of mortality.

Donny's stiffened neck kept him from seeing much, but from what he could hear, the place sounded like it was in the midst of utter chaos. Tanner's men would have no trouble slipping in and finishing what they started back at the hotel. He was still shaken from the wreck, but he was already scrambling to figure a way out of the hospital and into hiding.

Donny was peering down at his toes when the curtain yanked back. A nurse set his chart on the table beside him and walked to his bedside.

"Sir? Do you know where you are?"

He struggled to find his voice, clearing his throat. "Ahem. Um. Yes. In the hospital."

She leaned over him with a penlight and examined his pupils. "Good. Can you tell me your name?"

"Donald. Donald Ford."

The nurse stuck her pen in her shirt pocket. "Mr. Ford, you've been in a serious automobile accident. Do you have any family members we can contact?"

It took a moment for the words to register. "Um. No. No family to contact." He noticed he couldn't move his left arm in the sling holding it steady. He asked, "How bad is it?"

She referred to the chart. "You've sustained a handful of injuries, Mr. Ford. CT found a hairline fracture in your tibia, just a few inches above your ankle. Your left arm is broken at the radius four inches up from your wrist and is being immobilized until we can get it reset by one of the doctors. You've got two broken ribs–not much we can do about those–and you're suffering from severe whiplash; pretty common in a case like this. It may sound like a lot to take in, but given the circumstances, I'd say you are a very lucky man, Mr. Ford."

"Lucky," he repeated. He tried to wiggle his fingers. They were stiff and sore, but seemed to be in working order. "Do you have any idea when I can get out of here?"

"A couple of days. Maybe three. You were in a severe accident, Mr. Ford. The doctor will probably want to monitor you for at least another forty-eight hours."

Donny groaned with disapproval. The nurse noted Ford's vitals on the chart. "Okay, Mr. Ford. I'm going to leave you to it. If you need anything you can push the call button and we'll be right here, okay?"

Donny struggled to lean up in the bed. "There is one thing," he said. "The people–" He winced, a sharp pain catching him in the ribs. He pushed through. "The people chasing me."

"People are chasing you, Mr. Ford?"

"Yes. They're dangerous people." He looked around the blue-curtain room. "I can't stay here. It's not safe. You need to move me somewhere else."

"Uh huh." The nurse's tone quickly turned incredulous.

"I'm serious! I can't be in the middle of this place. I need my own room. Security. Protection." His voice rattled. "You have no idea who's after me!"

"Okay, Mr. Ford. We'll see what we can do. You just lie back and try to get some rest."

She walked out and drew the curtain. Ford could see two shadows on the other side, one much taller than the other. He picked up on bits and pieces of the conversation.

"He says people are chasing him."

"Is that right?" a man replied.

Donny heard something about confusion. Then he heard the man say, "Let's go with Haldol and Ativan. IM."

"Dose?"

"Fifty on the Haldol and . . . what do you think, one milligram of Ativan?"

There was more whispering, and then the two shadows parted ways. The nurse returned a few moments later. She pulled two shots from the pocket of her scrubs.

"Okay, Mr. Ford. We're going to give you a couple of shots to help you–"

"I don't want any shots," he contested. "I want a secure room. You have to move me!"

"Sir, I'm going to have to ask you to calm down."

"I'M NOT GOING TO CALM DOWN UNTIL YOU GET ME THE FUCK OUT OF HERE!" Donny clawed at the tape on his arm, peeling it away and removing his IV.

"Doctor! I need a little help in here!" the nurse yelled.

Immediately, medical staff descended on the curtained room. Donny was rising off the bed when the team forced him back down. The doctor laid on Donny's chest while a technician held his legs to the bed. Donny's body squirmed and twisted, all of his energy exerted into a fledgling attempt to get off the bed.

The doctor yelled, "Jesus, Megan. Get that IM in his leg *now!*"

The nurse timed the two intramuscular shots in between kicks, pushing the drugs into Donny's thigh as he jerked and screamed and demanded to be let go. The three medical professionals continued to hold Donny down. Slowly, his wrenching slowed and his tense muscles relaxed. His hands turned from fists to jelly as he felt his body slip out of his control. His eyes were heavy, and his anxiety fleeting. The voices filling the room morphed from coherent tones into garbled noises. Everything was a blur, and then the blur turned to black. His head fell to the side and he passed out.

Chapter 31: Priorities

The rain was coming down hard when Claire pulled up to a set of brownstone townhomes in south Atlanta. She had taken over driving duties shortly after merging onto I-65 north in Mobile, convincing Paul he needed to try and get some rest before getting back home. The heat in the rental car had been busted since Corpus Christi, making the overnight haul back to Atlanta a cold one. Paul had his suit jacket turned around backwards and was using it for covers. The car rolling to a slow halt in front of Claire's temporary safe house was enough to wake the weary passenger. He rubbed his eyes and looked outside.

"This is your friend's place?" Paul asked.

"Co-worker's. Number 202. We journalists have to look out for one another in times of paranoia and peril," she said. "Should be safe. It's not home, but at least we'll have a chance to clean up. Probably be a good idea to ditch the rental, too, just to be safe." She pointed to the car parked in front of them. "Company car. Keys should be inside."

Paul yawned as he fumbled in his pockets for his cellphone. Sleeping in a car was rarely fulfilling, and this time was no different. He dialed his wife to check in; it was the first time calling since New Orleans. There was no response.

Claire looked over. "She didn't answer?"

"Nope," he said. "I called her cell and the house phone. No answer on either."

"What about the farmhouse you sent her to? Do you know how the service is up there?"

Paul could have kicked himself. "Fuck. I didn't even think of that. I haven't been there in years, but it's in the middle of nowhere. Probably isn't a cell tower in sight."

"At least she's safe from Tanner," Claire said. "Don't beat yourself up over it. Getting off the grid is a good thing. Smart. She'll be harder to find, if he's even looking for her in the first place. But honestly, Paul, I think Tanner's got bigger fish to fry."

A moment of silence followed, filled only with the pitter-patter of a slackening rainstorm outside. Paul watched a wet-weather stream run down both sides of the street, forming rapids over the gutters along the way.

He nervously tapped the armrest and changed the subject. "Gotta love winter in Georgia," he said. "Never cold enough to snow, but damn if it doesn't get close."

"You're right. I hate winter here. Just months and months of cold rain."

"And when it *does* snow, everyone loses their damn minds. One mention of a snowflake and the entire state shuts down; milk and bread flies off the shelves; alarms sound and sirens blare; traffic grinds to a halt, with meteorologists declaring the end is near."

"You forgot about the assholes who don't go home."

"Yeah, the guys in the two-wheel drives who think cars work just as well on ice as sleds do."

Claire cupped her hands and warmed them with her breath. She said, "Surely you don't want to sit here and talk about the weather, Paul." He was staring at the rain cascading down the windshield. She could tell the decision to find Donny first was weighing heavily on him. "Listen, I promise you, we'll get to your wife and son. But right now, there's someone out there just like us who is going to die if we don't find him before Tanner does. We have to be smart about this." She put her hand on his shoulder. "Trust me. You're doing the right thing."

Paul dismissed the consolation and reached for the door. "Well, I guess we don't need to be sitting here worried about getting our precious little heads wet then, do we?" He hopped out of the car and hustled up the front steps to 202 before Claire had a chance to respond. She followed, and soon they were standing in the foyer and shaking off the cold.

Paul asked, "Do you know where I can find a towel?"

Claire pointed. "Sure, second door on your left."

She threw the keys on a small table by the door and then walked down the hall in search of the office. She had been inside her coworker's home once before following an office Christmas party where too many drinks led to an awkward morning after. She had been in such a hurry to leave that she hadn't taken the time to properly case the place, a curious act she usually performed while unsuspecting hosts were still asleep.

She found a small cluttered office at the back of the home. The computer sat on a timeworn oak desk facing the east wall. She blew the dust off the top of the monitor. The old computer's best days were obviously behind it. Tall bookcases took up the remaining space, with stacks of old newspapers blocking the bottom shelves from view. A large bay window let in the daylight from the south end, dividing the office from the kitchen and overlooking the rose garden in the backyard.

Claire booted up the computer and waited. Paul was still towel drying his hair when he walked in the room. He handed a spare towel to Claire.

"Thanks," she said.

He pulled up a kitchen chair. "So what are we looking for?"

"On this dinosaur? It's not looking good so far. But if we can get online, I'll start with a basic people search. I've got the password to a business account we can leverage. If we can find some contact numbers, then we can make some calls and hopefully get in touch with Donny before anyone else does."

The computer continued to lag. The noisy fans and grinding hard drive spoke to its age. Paul picked up a pen off the desk. "You need this?" he asked.

"Be my guest."

"Great. While you're working on that, I'm gonna check out the news."

Paul slid the pen in his pocket and walked to the living area, adjacent to the kitchen and just out of Claire's view. He found the remote and flipped through the local channels. Three clicks in and he saw it. A news helicopter was covering the scene of a car accident at a busy local intersection. The traffic cam panned out, showing a massive traffic jam that went on for miles. At the bottom of the screen the news ticker read:

TV PERSONALITY AND SELF-HELP AUTHOR DONNY FORD BELIEVED TO BE IN SERIOUS CONDITION FOLLOWING WRECK ON HIGHWAY 41. COMMUTERS ARE BEING ASKED TO SEEK ALTERNATE ROUTE . . .

Paul jotted something down on a scrap piece of paper and stuffed it in his pocket. Then he leaned around the corner. "Hey, Claire," he said. "I think I found Ford."

Claire jumped up from her chair and joined him in front of the television. Her eyes scrolled with the ticker at the bottom of the screen. “They got to him. FUCK! We were too late.”

“We don’t know that for sure yet,” Paul said. “Serious condition can mean a lot of things.”

“I know exactly what it means. It means if he’s alive, he won’t be for long. Tanner’s men aren’t going to total a car and call it a day. They’ll see this thing through, which means we’ve got to get to the hospital. Did they say where they took him?”

“They didn’t. If the wreck was on Highway 41, that still only narrows it down to three area hospitals I know of, maybe four if you count Grady downtown. I really wouldn’t be the person to ask.” Paul clicked through the neighboring local news channels. There was nothing more on the accident; just cheesy soap operas and tabloid talk shows.

Claire pressed her fingers to her lips and thought. With her credentials and a couple of calls to some local first responders, she could easily track down the hospital Ford had been taken to. She just needed to find a phone.

“I’ve got an idea. Borrow your cell?” she asked.

Paul gave her a look of dismay. “Sorry,” he said. “Battery’s dead. Guess flip phones aren’t what they used to be.”

Claire looked around the room. “Surely there’s a phone here somewhere.”

“I didn’t see one in here,” Paul said. “Why don’t you check upstairs? I’ll check online to see if I can get some directions to these area hospitals.”

“Sounds like a plan.” Claire marched up the stairs to the second level while Paul walked down the hall and back toward the office. He stopped halfway, listening for Claire’s footsteps above. It sounded like she was rustling through some drawers in one of the bedrooms.

Paul made his move. He grabbed the car keys off the foyer table and quietly snuck out the front door. He ran to the driver's side of the car, stopping briefly to look up toward the townhouse, double-checking to make sure Claire wasn't on to him.

She wasn't. Not until she heard the car door slam and the engine start. She ran down the stairs and out to the front steps, but Paul and her rental car were already long gone. She looked back to the small table where she had left the keys. A crumpled note had replaced them. She opened it and read:

Sorry. Must help family. Call when you find Ford.
555-9035

Chapter 32:
The Old Farmhouse

Paul didn't feel good about stealing Claire's rental car, but the journalist was obviously delusional. How could anyone expect him to put a stranger, a motivational speaker, over his wife and kid? And what exactly would rescuing Ford accomplish? How would it make them safer, and what would it do to stop Tanner?

Not a damn thing, at least from Paul's perspective. He sped up the interstate, heading north toward the old farmhouse, far away from the madness in Atlanta. He dialed Michelle's number with one hand while driving with the other. The phone went straight to voicemail. There were only two reasons why she wasn't answering. She was either out of service, or something had happened.

Paul tried to be optimistic. He reasoned a north Georgia farmhouse lacking cellphone service and far away from the big city was probably the safest place to be. Still, he couldn't get there fast enough. The pedal was glued to the floor. The mere thought of losing Michelle was enough to make his chest hurt. She was the love of his life, second only to his infant son. They were his top priority now. He could focus on nothing else until they were safe.

That didn't mean he wanted to abandon Claire, either. The savvy journalist had already found a phone, confirmed with a single text message stating, "What the fuck, Paul?" All he ever wanted to do was make sure his family was out of harm's way.

When he could guarantee their safety, then he would go back to Atlanta to help Claire expose Asteria for the felonious pharmaceutical company it really was.

Paul recognized the danger they faced from Asteria. The company in question had both the capital and the connections to make anyone stirring the pot disappear without a trace. Part of that power came from the industry's strong ties to several federal agencies. Most people already knew that Big Pharma had kept the lights on at the FDA for decades; it was part of the reason why obtaining FDA approval for a new drug was typically as easy as issuing a stop-payment on a check, so long as the pharmaceutical company didn't completely botch the clinical trials.

But what few Americans realized was the influence Big Pharma had on other agencies like the DEA. When clinical research began building a strong case for medicinal marijuana in the early 21st century, the Department of Health and Human Services petitioned the Drug Enforcement Agency to consider moving marijuana from Schedule I (a classification shared by LSD, heroin, mescaline and ecstasy) to Schedule III. The move would have placed marijuana in the same category as low-dose hydrocodone and codeine, lifting antiquated barriers to research and prescriptions for debilitating conditions like cancer, multiple sclerosis, Parkinson's, and epilepsy. Once Big Pharma began expressing opposition to the petition, however, the DEA rejected it. No reasonable explanation was given.

Paul knew the reason behind the DEA's reluctance to label marijuana less addictive than oxycodone, morphine and fentanyl (all Schedule II drugs): because Big Pharma wasn't in the weed business. And when he asked himself why the DEA could give two shits about the interests of Big Pharma, it all came back to the original two factors that made Asteria

Pharmaceuticals a force to be reckoned with. Capital and connections.

No one person could take on an opponent like Asteria alone, Paul gathered, but Claire had the power of the press on her side. Claire would be able to leverage her position as a nationally syndicated journalist; few occupations were more fitting to blow the lid off an international human rights scandal involving one of the largest drug companies in the world. To accomplish that, Claire would need to gather as many credible sources as possible to back up the wild assertions. She couldn't go off half-cocked like some late-night commentator or tabloid journalist. She needed all of the facts, with witnesses to corroborate her claims.

But even if the entire roster of clinical-trial outliers were available to give full depositions about the unbelievable side effects caused by Ocula, who would believe them? Paul ran the scenario through his head. He had experienced the drug firsthand, and even he was having trouble buying it. He imagined a tabloid headline:

Sleeping Pill Leads to Deadly Mind Control

The whole thing sounded pretty thin. The best evidence they had at this point was circumstantial, and with such a game-changing hypothesis to begin with, the science would never be given a chance. Paul compared it to debating the long-term effects of global warming with a dissenter who couldn't get past an online meme of a snowy spring day in the South. It didn't matter what the long-term data showed; people would only believe what was right in front of them. And in the time it would take Paul and Company to convince the American public they weren't bat-shit crazy, everyone linked to the Ocula outliers would already be dead.

Trying to take down a drug company based on the farfetched side effects of their latest sleeping pill seemed pointless. But there was one haymaker that would deliver a monumental knockout punch to Asteria: the Costa Rican facility. At least two-dozen bodies were left to rot in the subtropical jungle, accompanied by plenty of evidence to implicate Asteria in a genocidal scandal that would shake the pillars of the entire industry. Tanner had escaped less than forty-eight hours ago, and if he was calling Michelle yesterday morning to inquire about Paul's whereabouts, then there was a good chance the company man wasn't back in the jungle giving dead bodies their unceremonious acid baths.

As Paul slowed to exit off the interstate, it was clear that Claire's best bet was to contact her friend Mr. Aguilar in Costa Rica and break the story from there. If locals caught wind of what had happened in the jungle involving a Yankee corporation, every cable news outlet in the world would be swarming San José by the weekend.

Paul turned onto Highway 20, a rural two-lane leading west toward his father's old farmhouse. The road stretched through remnants of the countryside north of Atlanta. Long spans of pasture and farmland were separated by development and clear-cut, with entrances to new subdivisions hugging the side of the highway every mile or two. The further Paul got from the interstate, the fewer neighborhoods and stores he passed, until finally he was out of the developed world and into the wilderness.

The highway parted thousands of acres of land protected by the state for a ten-mile run before opening back up in the next town over. There were less than a dozen clearings in the forest. One was a small patch where the wildlife management district office sat right off the highway; others were rural homes that predated the 1951 State Land Protection Act. Homes owned within the protected wilderness that had gone into disrepair were condemned and then consumed by the surrounding forest, while those that were still in good condition remained the property of the original deed owner (or the deed owner's heirs). The farmhouse Paul had spent so many summers in was passed to Paul and Alex following their father Frank's untimely death; a relic of a past Frank had spent with the wife he could never let go of, even in death.

As Paul pulled off the highway and onto the long gravel road leading to the rustic home place, old memories began rising to the surface. The first thing he remembered was the smell. The cold mixed with a thick stand of evergreens had a unique scent that reminded him of Christmas. His father was constantly traveling when Paul was just a boy, and the family had only spent a couple of Christmases on the property, but the piney aroma stayed with him.

It was cold and overcast, but he rolled down his window anyway to take it all in. He could hear a woodpecker in the distance, and the occasional crow cawing overhead. Potholes were scattered down the length of the gravel drive. Tree limbs hung over the road and clawed across the rental car like a cat sliding down a popped car hood. Paul could see the tracks of another vehicle in the road ahead.

Michelle, he thought. *Good, she made it here*. No one had any business coming down this road, and the tracks were fresh. Overflowing puddles and waterlogged branches indicated the storm that had rolled through Atlanta earlier made a lengthy pit stop north of the city. Michelle couldn't have beaten him by more than a couple of hours.

As he neared the top of a hill, he could see light from the clearing. It was the pasture surrounding the old home place. The gravel road split the ten-acre expanse into two equal sections. One side with rolling hills leading back into the forest at the base of Bear Mountain, with the other side covered in tall fescue and relatively flat compared to the surrounding terrain.

A creek flowed down the mountain and into the pasture on the hilly side. Paul could hear it bubbling from the car. The waters flowed from the hills and came within a few yards of the screened-in porch on the right side of the old house. He could remember sitting on the porch when he was little, watching flashes of lightning bugs mirrored on the glistening stream right after dusk, accompanied by the bluish light of the rising moon.

Paul knew why his father had had such a hard time getting rid of the place after his mother died. He was just a teenager when it had happened, leaving Frank Freeman to raise two boys on his own. He hadn't understood at the time why Frank would force them to leave the comfort of the burbs behind to spend weekends working around the property, doing little more than keeping the place up to code so the state wouldn't condemn the family heirloom, but now Paul got it. It had been a way for Frank to make a connection with his deceased wife. It was supposed to be the place where they would grow old together, but as it sometimes did, life had other plans.

The dirty white paint covering the two-story home was chipped and cracked. Paul could see a patch of shingles on the roof covering the open front porch. A shingle lay in the yard just below the repair. Paul thought perhaps Alex had picked up where his father left off. The front porch spanned the entire front of the house and wrapped around to the screen porch on the right. To the left was a parking area where Michelle's black four-door Jeep sat. Paul noticed the front door to the house was wide open, but the screen door was shut. Michelle must have been airing the place out.

He parked behind Michelle and walked to the door. The old porch floorboards creaked with each step, an old-timey alarm system warning the people inside that someone was at the door.

"Michelle?" he called from the porch before walking in. No one answered. Opening the screen door was even louder, the ear-wrenching screech resonating the length of the outstretched spring at the top. Surely she heard him by now.

The house was dim; the power had been cut off long ago. The lanterns his father had left behind sat idle on the hearth and end tables. The overcast light shining through the wavy glass windows cast ripples on the floors. Paul called once more as he walked into the den. No one answered, but he thought he heard a footstep toward the back where the kitchen faced the creek. He stepped through an open doorway and was greeted by an old acquaintance standing by the sink.

"Ah, Mr. Freeman!"

It was Tanner. He was holding a gun on the side closest to Michelle, who was tied to a dining chair beside the small table in the kitchen. Her mouth was duct-taped shut. Her eyes were misty and her makeup was running. In the corner was Aaron, whimpering in a playpen and sucking fretfully on his pacifier. They both appeared unharmed.

Paul's chest hitched at the sight of his worst nightmare come to life. "What the fuck is this, Tanner?"

"Oh, I think you know what this is, Paul. You must have known I would come looking for you. And now you're going to do something for me, or I'm going to kill your precious little family. Do you understand?"

Paul could sense a change in his former boss. Urgency filled his voice. His eyes were wild and twitching. He was sweating profusely in a house without heat in thirty-degree weather. This was not the calm and collected Tanner he remembered from the facility. This was a man behaving erratically, in panic mode and unpredictable. The ex-CIA man had lost his mind, and he was holding Paul's family at gunpoint.

Chapter 33: Escape

Donny was still delirious when he heard footsteps returning to his bedside in the ER. The towering man standing next to him was a dark blur, but he could tell the suspicious character didn't work for the hospital. He tried to open his mouth and call for help, but all that came out was an incoherent moan, joining in the chorus of anguish being sung by the rest of the emergency room choir. He shut his eyes hard and refocused. The man wore a black overcoat and a crew cut. He was holding a syringe in one hand and drawing from a vial in the other. He filled the syringe full, five milliliters of the mysterious solution, then reached for Donny's IV line.

Donny was helpless. He tried to muster all of his strength to emit a final plea for help, but the assassin was on to him. He dropped the IV line and pulled a handkerchief from his pocket, stuffing it in Donny's mouth and muffling his screams. He then returned to the task at hand, locating the port to Donny's IV line.

Donny watched the needle go in. This was it. He was going to die and there was nothing he could do about it except lie there and take it. What a miserable twist. *Man survives car wreck only to die in the hospital from unrelated injuries.*

The Consultant was just about to push the poison into the IV line when another figure came up behind him. "Drop the needle," she said.

It was Claire. The man turned to look but halted when Claire pushed the barrel of her 9mm deep into his back. “Don’t turn around and back away from the patient.”

He complied, and the two slowly stepped back in unison toward the foot of the bed. Swiftly, Claire slammed the butt of the gun into the back of his head, knocking him out cold. His body fell next to the bed. Claire knelt down beside him and searched for a wallet. She found nothing to identify the man with.

“Who are you?” Donny asked.

“A journalist. Claire Connor. I was on Ocula, too.” She stood up and ripped the medical tape off Donny’s arm.

“Fuck!” He jerked. He would have reached for the taped arm if the other arm hadn’t been broken.

“Sorry,” Claire said. “I’ll let you pull out the IV.” She peeked through the curtain and checked the perimeter. “Hurry, though. We’ve got to get you out of here. I’m sure more of those guys are nearby.” She noticed Donny’s hospital attire and immediately regretted not bringing a change of clothes. No way she could sneak him out of the building with his ass showing.

“Got anything to wear?”

He didn’t. The paramedics who pulled him from the crushed automobile had to cut his jeans off to treat his injured leg. His Hawaiian shirt, he had been told, was also a loss. Barring the hospital standard issues, Donny had nothing to his name except his wallet, a cellphone, and his birthday suit.

Claire improvised, rolling the unconscious hitman out of his long dark overcoat. Donny sat up in bed and she helped him put it on, tying the belt tight around his waist. “Tanner’s guys must go shopping together.”

"Tanner?" Donny knew the name. "That's the guy who wanted to see me yesterday. He had to be the one who—" He stopped himself. No point in rehashing the hotel incident now.

Claire didn't pry. She pointed out the splint wrapped around Donny's lower leg. "Can you walk?"

Donny said, "I don't care if I have to crawl. I'm getting out of here."

Claire moved to Donny's good side and helped him out of bed. Donny gritted his teeth, anticipating the pain. He threw his arm over her shoulder and put his weight on his good leg. The drugs the nurse had given him earlier were quickly wearing off. Every jarring movement sent pains shooting from his leg up through his broken ribs.

He tried to keep his grunting to a minimum as the two hobbled down the hall, Donny using Claire as a makeshift crutch while the tiny journalist fought to keep him upright. They were twenty feet from the double doors leading back into the lobby when Claire pulled Donny through a windowless steel door on the right.

"Where are we going?" Donny asked.

"Employee exit. I noticed two guys hovering around the main entrance, so I parked down the street. This way should be safe."

They hit the door leading to the employee parking lot. A nurse yelled at them to stop, but they didn't look back. Claire's only thoughts were to get Donny to the car and then get the fuck out of Dodge.

The door led to the ground level of the employee parking deck. They walked past the gate and a security guard who paid them no mind; chasing after hospital patrons for using the wrong doors was above his paygrade. Donny tried to keep his composure as they walked down the sidewalk, but every step felt like a lightning bolt was searing through his fractured leg.

"How much further?" he huffed.

"We're almost there. It's the white sedan just up the block." Claire checked the perimeter as best she could with Donny's arm draped over her shoulder. The sidewalks were busy. Dozens of faces were in the crowd, making it nearly impossible to tell if the two were being followed. A few people noticed Donny's bare feet and pained grimace, but were unwilling to intervene. It was the middle of the Friday afternoon lunch rush, and everyone had somewhere else to be.

Claire had parked her coworker's company car two blocks from the hospital. Although she took reasonable precautions, she wasn't convinced Tanner's men would be after her before making contact with Ford first. She knew Tanner didn't have a solid lead on neither her nor Freeman, and was likely focusing all of his attention on disappearing the man now clinging to her side and struggling to stay upright.

Donny weighed heavily on Claire's left as she searched her right pocket for the car keys. She opened the back door and eased him into the backseat of the sedan, laying him flat before starting the car. She checked her mirrors one last time before finding a gap in the traffic to blend into. Soon they were on Hill Street and heading toward Claire's safe house on the south side. Donny gasped with every bump in the road.

"How are you holding up back there, Ford?" Claire asked through the mirror. He gave her the okay with a nod, but it was clear he was in agonizing pain. He guarded his left side and his breathing was shallow. The arm in the sling was useless, and the leg below wasn't much better. Horses had been put down for less. She had to get him off his feet and somewhere safe.

"Listen," she said. "I've got a house we can go to. It's on the south side, about fifteen minutes from here. That should give us somewhere to hide for the time being. I know a doctor who makes house calls. We can call him when we get–"

"Can't go," Donny mustered. His adrenaline was still flowing from the hospital escape. Now that he was resting again, the pain had eased enough to let him focus on the current state of affairs. His speech was as short as his breath. "Calling someone, anyone. It's too dangerous. There's a man, Dawa Graham. We'll be safe there."

"Donny, I'm not sure you're in any state to be making decisions here."

He leaned up on his elbows. "Claire, listen to me. Graham is with Atlanta PD. He's already helping me look into Asteria."

"I'm just not sure about bringing anyone else into–"

"Look. You have to trust me." Donny paused to consider the statement while catching his breath. "Hell. I say that, but I'm not sure I would trust anyone if I were you, either. I understand your reservations, but you can look Graham up before we get there. He's been a detective with APD for years. He's a good man. He can help you with the case, and he'll help me with the pain. Please, just take me there. I'm begging you, Claire. It's as safe a place as any." With a long sigh, he laid back down, exhausted from the lengthy request.

Claire thought about what Donny said. *As safe a place as any*. He was right. There was no reason to think her coworker's home was any safer than the detective's. She had two options: retreat to the brownstone on the south side, or take Donny's advice and seek the help of his detective friend.

Both choices ultimately came down to trust, a notion Claire had become apathetic to. Paul's duplicitous actions hadn't helped on that front. Still, she had little choice. The man in the backseat–the very man whom she had preached to Paul about the importance of rescuing–was asking her to trust him. There was little else she could do but listen.

***

Donny told Claire how to get to the Monastery from the backseat in short and exasperated steps. "Left here." "Straight." "Keep going." "Little further." "Watch the gate."

His blunt directions were a far cry from the pleasant suggestions of most navigation systems, but they got the job done nonetheless. In less than half an hour they were parked under Dawa's grand portico entrance. Claire had phoned the detective on the way to prepare him for their arrival. He met the couple at the door and helped Donny inside.

"Goodness, Donny. What's happened to you? I've been watching the television; they said you were in a horrible accident."

Donny confirmed the news as Dawa laid him down on a daybed in one of the guest rooms. "Yes, Dawa. It happened shortly after I left here." Donny could see Claire casing the place just out of earshot. He pulled Dawa in closer and whispered, "Marci. She was at the hotel I was staying at. I was afraid they would come looking for me, and they did. They killed her, Dawa."

"The people you asked me to look into?"

"Yes. And I'm not sure how high this thing goes, Dawa, but I know that son-of-a-bitch Tanner made this happen. He was the guy begging me to come in yesterday. A couple of hours later, Marci is dead and I'm getting shot at."

Dawa rubbed his chin. "I heard a call come in over the radio about shots fired at the Marriott yesterday."

"I'm telling you, Dawa: This thing is big. Those guys looking for me at the hotel were the ones who forced me into a four-way intersection." Donny struggled to speak, but he had to ask. "Exactly who are we dealing with here?"

"Maybe you should ask your friend," Dawa said as Claire walked in the room.

"What are we talking about?" she asked.

"Donny was telling me about the people who tried to kill him yesterday. We believe they are affiliated with Ryan Tanner, Public Relations Director at Asteria Pharmaceuticals. Beyond that, everything is a mystery. I made some inquiries earlier, but either no one knows who this person is, or no one is willing to talk about him."

"I would go with the latter," Claire said. "Ryan Tanner's a spook. He worked closely with Dick Doyle at the CIA for over twenty years. Doyle was a lead researcher on the CIA's Yosemite Seven program; a program focused on the development of mind-control methods for the purpose of influencing national elections around the world."

Dawa and Donny exchanged glances. "How do you know all of this?" Dawa asked.

"Because I was held captive by Tanner and Doyle at a top-secret facility in Costa Rica, funded by Asteria Pharmaceuticals."

"And they just offered up this information to you, a captive?"

"Yeah," Claire said resentfully, crossing her arms. "I guess some people just don't know when to keep their mouth shut. Know what I mean?"

Donny mediated. "Okay, now. There's plenty to worry about without turning on one another." He clutched his side as he spoke. "Claire, you mentioned before that you were on Ocula. Do you think that has anything to do with the mind control program?"

"I would almost guarantee it."

Dawa said, "Sounds like the MK-ULTRA project from the sixties. I didn't know the CIA was still interested in things like that."

"They used to be," Claire said. "I can say with certainty that the Yosemite Seven program was the utter failure that led to Tanner and Doyle's resignations. Remember the rumors of foreign persuasion surrounding the Venezuelan elections in 2018? Those guys were responsible, although the outcome was opposite what the CIA had anticipated."

"I'm not sure why," Dawa said. "MK-ULTRA was no better, or so I've read. The U.S. Senate held hearings on the mind-control program in the late seventies, exposing the illegal experiments behind it. Drugging U.S. citizens without their knowledge, behavior modification, influencing the masses. So you are standing here telling me such programs still exist?"

"Like I said, the ball was in Tanner's court in 2018, and he apparently dropped it. Fast forward three years later and he's found a way to carry on his previous research by retaining dismissed colleagues from the Yosemite days using his new position at Asteria Pharmaceuticals."

Dawa studied Claire as she spoke. Years of investigative experience had led to an unsullied gut feeling deep within the detective; a feeling that usually conformed to the logic in his mind. This time, however, was different. While Dawa's head told him her story was too incredible to be true, his gut was urging him in the other direction. Her conviction, her mannerisms, and most importantly her eyes, were all pointing toward the truth. At least, she thought she was telling the truth. There was also the very real possibility that she had escaped from the Milledgeville Asylum and would soon be asking him for a roll of aluminum foil to fashion a hat with.

Dawa asked, "So what is your relation to Donald here?"

"Tanner held me captive at his facility for two weeks before I escaped. I just got back to the states yesterday, and I've been trying to find others involved with the program, starting with Donny." Claire could tell she was being interrogated. "Look, I know this is unbelievable, but if you're already familiar with the CIA's history of secret programs, then you must admit it's a possibility." She pulled up a news story on her phone and handed it to him. He read the headline:

AFTER TWO WEEKS, DISAPPEARANCE OF JOURNALIST REMAINS A MYSTERY

"This is about you," he said.

"Sure is. And I wasn't hiding in some spider hole in the Middle East, either. I was in the tropics being tortured and experimented on by Doyle and Tanner and a whole host of others." She reached for Dawa's arm. "A lot of people are dead in Costa Rica because of these people. You can help us bring them to justice."

Donny interrupted her impassioned speech with a loud groan. His hair was soaked and his fever was high. Dawa's concern for his wayward friend was evident. He knelt beside him. "Poor Donny. He is in such bad shape. Such a shame what he has let this world do to his spirit."

"I know a doctor who makes house calls," Claire said. "We need to get him here as soon as possible. It's obvious your friend is in a lot of pain. He may have an infection, too. And who knows how bad his leg is after being forced to rush out of the hospital on it? What do you think? Sound like a plan?"

Dawa nodded in agreement, never taking his eyes off his old friend. The world had turned him into a stern man, but his compassion was always overflowing in the presence of someone in need. He took a towel from the bedside table and wiped the sweat from Donny's forehead. The patient's grip on the sheets was tight. He was wrenching in pain and moving in and out of consciousness. There was no pain medication in Dawa's home, not even so much as an aspirin. He only knew of one way to help his friend.

"Donald. You need to listen to me. You do not have to experience this pain. You do not have to feel this way anymore."

Donny's wrenching eased. Dawa had his attention.

"Remember the technique we practiced? The transcendence away from the pain and suffering of this world?" Donny remembered. Dawa said, "You need to go there now. Your body cannot continue with this pain. This is the only way I can help you. Are you ready to go there, Donald?"

He was ready. Dawa placed a hand on Donny's chest and instructed him to focus on his breathing. He began by performing a series of breathing exercises. Breathe in for three seconds, out for four. Each sequence was designed to relax the body just a little more than the one before.

Soon Donny's erratic breathing steadied. His grip on the sheets loosened. His body lay still on the daybed and his sweating ceased. He slipped into a deep meditative state, almost like a patient undergoing hypnosis. His eyes could be seen moving rapidly under the closed lids. Dawa withdrew his hand.

For the moment, his old friend was somewhere else, far away from any pain.

Chapter 34:
Time's A Wastin'

Paul took a step toward Tanner when the gun came up. He could almost see down the barrel.

"Don't think about it," Tanner said. Paul halted, then took two steps back. His hands were up.

"Tell me what you want," Paul said. "What's the play here, Tanner?"

Tanner pulled a cigarette from his shirt pocket with his free hand and lit up. He tossed the lighter on the kitchen table. "You're going to do something for me. Something no one else on this planet can do. You remember the facility, don't you Paul? I *know* what you did there; what you're capable of." He was smiling through his nerves.

Paul spoke calmly. "There's no proof I did anything, Tanner. I know you believe in this stuff, but there could still be a reasonable–"

"Cut the crap, Freeman. You know goddamn well what you did. How else could you explain the guards shooting one another the moment you were knocked unconscious, Ocula still coursing through your veins? You dreamed it would happen, that the guards would kill each other, didn't you? DIDN'T YOU?"

Paul caved. "Yes, Tanner. I dreamed they would kill each other, and that's exactly what they did."

"*I KNEW IT*! The moment I realized what was happening at the facility, I just knew it was all *oozing* out of that tiny little brain of yours. I just prayed there wasn't anything about me in there. Imagine what that would have felt like, to know someone else's thoughts were pushing you do to something irrational. Something deadly."

"Yeah. Imagine that." Paul looked to Michelle, his hands still in the air. "Tanner, please. Let my family go. They've got nothing to do with this."

"Fraid I can't do that, Mr. Freeman. You know the rules. I get what I want, then we'll talk about your family."

Paul racked his brain, searching for a way out of the situation. A set of kitchen knives sat in a wooden block by the cast-iron sink behind Tanner. Old Mason jars full of canned vegetables filled the shelf on the wall to his right. He could see a baseball bat through the window separating the kitchen from the screened-in porch. His eyes searched for options.

Tanner said, "I know what you're thinking, Paul. But there really is no way out of this. Not unless you do what I ask of you."

"Once again, Tanner: What the fuck is it you want me to do?"

"The facility . . . do you remember where it was at, geographically speaking? Do you remember the landmark to the south? You must have passed it during your escape. It was the only way back to San José."

Paul had to take himself back to the jungle. He remembered the facility itself, surrounded by dense forest. There was a small town just a few miles south of the facility; what was it . . . Bajos del Toro?

"Are you talking about the town?" he asked.

"Jesus. No, Paul. The volcano. The fucking volcano you passed going into San José. Poás National Park. The facility was just three miles north, practically at the foot of an active volcano."

Irritated, Paul opened his hands and asked, "Where are you going with this, Tanner?"

He took a drag off his smoke. "I want you to blow it up for me."

Paul laughed. For a moment, he thought Tanner was joking. Tanner's face proved otherwise.

"You're serious," Paul said. "Tanner. *You're* the one who sold me on the science behind this whole endeavor, remember? We take a pill and our minds project our thoughts and dreams into other organisms nearby. *Living things*. Last time I checked, making a fucking volcano erupt to swallow up a secret facility didn't meet the requirements."

Tanner shook his head in fervent disagreement. "You're not hearing me correctly, Paul. Everything I told you before came directly from Doyle. He was the scientist–not me. I don't care what you *think* you're capable of; I *know* what you're capable of. Do you want to know how I know, Paul?" He flipped the safety off on his Beretta and pointed it at Michelle's head. "Because if you don't do what I ask, I'm going to kill everyone that matters to you."

"*STOP!*" Paul yelled. He started to lunge again, but Tanner pressed the barrel hard into Michelle's temple.

"Don't make me kill your wife, Paul. Now back the fuck up. *NOW!*"

Aaron began crying. Paul was breathless and Michelle was shaking. An uneven leg of the chair she was tied to was tapping like Morse code on the old oak floors. Tanner smiled at

Paul, still holding the gun to Michelle's head. He reached in his pocket and pulled out a bottle of pills. He shook them at Paul.

"Figure it's been a while. Let's make sure you've got everything you need to get the job done. Come on now. Time's a wastin'."

"How do you know I won't focus on killing you, Tanner?"

"You underestimate me, Paul. This is the good stuff. Ocula 2.0. All I have to do is wait for you to fall asleep, and then I'll walk you through the whole scenario frame by frame. Paint the scene, so to speak. You wouldn't believe what this stuff can do with a little inspiration. Just ask your friend Claire."

"This is crazy! How do you ever expect this to work?"

Tanner smirked. "Just call me a believer." He tossed the bottle his way, and Paul caught it. "No more stalling, Paul. Now take the pills."

Tanner was grinding his teeth. He had gone mad, and everyone else in the room knew it but him. Michelle could feel the cold steel barrel quivering on her temple. Paul counted a pack's worth of cigarette butts snuffed out on the floor by the sink; Tanner had been chain-smoking since he got there. Even little Aaron peered up from the safety of his crib, giving the intruder a fearful glare with leftover tears now crusted on his cheeks.

There was no other play. All Paul could do was take the drug, fall into a deep sleep, and pray he could somehow will himself to overcome whatever directives Tanner was going to throw his way. He untwisted the cap and immediately thought of Claire. For two weeks she was given Ocula 2.0, and for two weeks she had no control over her thoughts and actions when in the throes of an REM sleep cycle. She must have tried to resist, but the affliction in her eyes she worked so hard to conceal indicated to Paul that she never could.

The outlook was grim, but Paul had little choice. He wasn't worried in the least about Tanner's impractical request: there was no way neural activity–no matter how magnified or concentrated–could make a volcano explode. It was utter nonsense that defied all logic and reason, dribbling from a psychopath who had exhausted every viable option in his dwindling arsenal. Even if it were a possibility, they were too far away for it to have an effect. All of the organisms affected in prior experiments were within a relatively close range, making it plausible that neural activity could act as a kind of organic radio transmitter, persuading other organisms to fall in line. But causing a volcano to erupt while taking a drug-induced nap a continent away? It just wasn't going to happen.

What did concern Paul was the fact that he would be voluntarily knocking himself out for an indiscriminate amount of time. Who knew what would happen while he was under? And what if Tanner was monitoring the situation in Costa Rica through a contact? In all likelihood he would execute Paul's entire family the moment he realized the bogus plan didn't work.

But Tanner was itching to pull the trigger, and Paul could sense it. The madman's patience was wearing thin, and Paul was all out of options. "Okay, Tanner. You win." He took a pill out of the bottle and swallowed it dry.

"Take a step forward, open your mouth and lift up your tongue," Tanner demanded. Paul complied while Tanner leaned in, taking a long, hard look. "Well, I'll know soon enough whether or not you took it." Tanner pulled out the mysterious scanning device and set it on the kitchen table. "Remember this?"

Paul remembered. "I should have gotten rid of it the day you sent me to the Donny Ford seminar."

"That's actually a very good point, Mr. Freeman. Had you never brought back a busted device in the first place, I never would have identified you as one of the dreamers. Interesting to think about, isn't it? What are the odds! To think you, out of a million people–" Tanner stopped to clear his throat, fighting the urge to cough. "Out of a million . . . ahem . . ."

Tanner couldn't finish his sentence. He tried taking a deep breath, but ended up in the midst of a coughing fit instead. Paul watched as Tanner hunched over, choking and gurgling as he struggled to breathe. Something serious had overwhelmed the spook. He was like a fish out of water, his chest puffing in vain as he fought to find air.

Tanner dropped the gun on the floor and stumbled back against the sink, kneading his throat as if he were trying to free an object that was blocking his airway. It was no use. The passage was sealed off tight. He panicked. He lunged at Michelle and clutched her face with both hands. His strained voice was barely audible as he gasped, "*Help! Help . . . me!*"

Paul pulled Tanner away from Michelle, then picked up the gun. His first instinct was to shoot, but when he looked down and saw the man on the brink of suffocating, he held back. Tanner was on his knees, grasping his throat and begging for his life. Paul watched Tanner's complexion change from light blue to dark purple. Blood vessels in his eyes had burst; a result of the tight grip he had on his own neck. Finally, Tanner's grip loosened. His hands fell to his side, and his body fell over on the kitchen floor. Just like that, Ryan Tanner was dead.

Whatever relief Paul felt from watching his adversary keel over was soon met with the realization that he had just taken Ocula 2.0 moments before. He ran to the kitchen sink and stuck his finger down his throat. He dry heaved several times, but nothing came up. It was no use; the drug was already starting to take effect.

Paul knew it would be quick. He untied Michelle from her chair, then told her he would be a minute. He stumbled out onto the screen porch. Light shone through peepholes in the clouds, adding sparkles to the creek cascading down the mountain and across the field. For a moment, Paul felt a brief sensation of déjà vu. His wife's voice grew faint as she called on him from the doorway. He couldn't respond.

They're safe now, he thought. He found himself a place on the old porch swing and drifted off to sleep.

Chapter 35: Troublemakers

"Donny? Are you awake?" Claire stood over Ford. A man in a button-up shirt was holding a leather bag and standing next to her. "This is Dr. Peterson. He's going to be evaluating you now."

Donny rubbed the sleep from his eyes. He had been unconscious for a few hours, drifting into a deep sleep after allowing Dawa to guide him in meditation. The effects were powerful. His pain, though still agitated by the slightest movement, had momentarily subsided. He was careful to lie still while addressing the room.

"Why, hello, Doc. Bet you haven't seen a mess quite like this in a while, have you?"

"Go easy on yourself," Claire said. "You've been through a lot. I'm sure the good doctor here can get you fixed right up."

Claire and Dawa left the room while the doctor assessed his patient. They discussed plans to bring the people responsible for a number of human rights violations to justice. Claire would break the story the moment she got the word from sources in Costa Rica that local authorities had raided the secret facility. Dawa would then have enough evidence to submit a written affidavit implicating Ryan Tanner in the conspiracy to murder Claire Connor and Paul Freeman, along with the actual murder of Paul's brother, Alex. With such a preponderance of evidence, no judge would have a problem signing the arrest warrant.

The doctor joined the two outside of Donny's room. Claire asked, "How's he feeling?"

"Better now that he's resting. Nothing seems to be life threatening, but I would insist you find a way to get him to my clinic. Without medical records to go on, I'll need to perform a series of MRIs and CAT scans to ensure we're only dealing with the fractures you mentioned before." He pulled two bottles from his bag. "I've also started him on amoxicillin to ward off any infection, just to be safe, as well as some medication for the pain. That should help him get some rest."

The doctor handed the bottles to Claire. Dawa didn't like it, but it wasn't his call. If Donny felt like he needed pain pills, they were his for the taking.

Claire shook the doctor's hand. "Thank you so much for coming by on such short notice. I owe you big time for this."

"You don't owe me a thing, Claire. Tell your father I said hello." She nodded, and the doctor left.

Dawa said, "It pays to grow up in a small town, doesn't it?"

"I don't know if I would call Atlanta small, but it certainly helps to know the right people."

They returned to Donny's room. A glass of water sat on the bedside table with a small white pill lying next to it. Donny was sitting upright and in brighter spirits; it was the first time Claire had ever seen him smile.

"Someone's looking better," she said.

"Someone's feeling better. I assume he told you guys he wants me in his clinic ASAP?"

"Yes," Claire said. "But I think it would be wise for us to stay put until Atlanta Police can secure an arrest warrant for Tanner."

Dawa agreed. "I've already spoken with the department. What we've got now isn't much, but the moment we hear back from Costa Rican authorities we should have everything we need to bring these people in for questioning. Then we can get you the medical care you need. We want to make sure those limbs of yours heal up right, Donald."

Donny lay back on the bed. "Works for me," he said. "I've been running for the last twenty-four hours. I really don't feel like going anywhere right now."

"I don't blame you," Claire said, pulling up a chair. "You know, Donny, we really haven't had a chance to talk. I was hoping you could tell me more about the program. About Asteria Pharmaceuticals and your connection to Ryan Tanner."

"Really isn't much to say," he replied. "I had never spoken to Tanner until yesterday morning. I participated in the Ocula clinical trials–"

"As did I," Claire said.

"Then you know about the contact information we were given in case something came up after the trials ended. Well, something definitely came up. I started having these incredibly vivid dreams. Dreams that were impossible to discern from reality. I knew it must've had something to do with the medication. That's why I called the number. A guy named Ryan Tanner answered and basically demanded that I come in to see him. It freaked me out, so I hung up the phone. That's when bad things started happening."

Claire found the story all too familiar. How she had participated in the FDA clinical trials for Ocula; had contacted Ryan Tanner voicing concerns after a series of impossible events involving the dreams she was having; had been drugged on a plane and whisked away to a secret facility. The last part, she imagined, would have been a similar fate to Donny's had the program not imploded in the jungle. Now it seemed Tanner was hellbent on sweeping everything under the rug.

Claire asked, "Do you know about any others involved with the program? Have you spoken to participants who experienced similar side effects?"

"Only one," Donny said. "A guy named Wayne Rider. The meeting was pure luck. As I'm sure you already know, Asteria lobbied the FDA to keep a tight lid on the clinical trials. Participants were generally kept away from one another. I didn't talk to Wayne until long after the trials had ended, following the death of my business partner Bill Stevens. I couldn't shake this feeling that the drug had played some part in it, so I took to the Internet to do a little investigating.

"Wayne had submitted a question about Ocula to a health forum to see if anyone involved in the trials had a similar experience. We emailed back and forth for several weeks. To this day, I'm convinced he had the same experience with the drug as I did. Then one day he sent me a text telling me he was disappearing, and suggested I do the same. Haven't heard from him since."

"You said he texted you," Dawa said. "Do you still have his number?"

"Sure, but I'd almost guarantee it was from a burner phone. Hell, I doubt Wayne Rider is even his real name."

Claire said, "Well, at least it's a start." She was about to continue her line of questioning when her cellphone rang. She excused herself to the next room to take the call. Dawa took her place in the chair by the bed.

"So, Donald. You found relief from your pain through the meditation, yes?"

"Yes, Dawa. In fact, I'm still feeling pretty good, although it could be because I haven't moved much since I got here."

"I noticed the pill by your water. No need?"

"No need, Dawa. The pain's gone. Unbelievable, really."

"It was a basic meditation exercise, Donald. We've practiced it a million times before."

"You're right. But there was something else."

Dawa was intrigued. "Really? Tell me what happened, Donald."

"Well, I know you're skeptical about this whole idea of the sleeping pills affecting my dreams and dreams affecting reality and so on and so on."

Dawa was stone-faced.

"Still," Donny said, "I know there must be something to it." He leaned up. "You see, Dawa–it happened again. Just before the doctor arrived. But this time, the dream wasn't brought on by a migraine attack like before. This time, the dream started the moment I fell asleep, right after meditation."

What Dawa heard was making him uncomfortable. He didn't like the idea of Donny implying that a sacred meditation technique had been used to conjure up false realities. Such practices weren't meant to fill the delusions of the lost; they were meant to bring sentient beings to balance and peace. He lowered his head and sighed.

"Donald, my friend. We've been through this before. How could your dreams possibly have an effect on the world we live in?"

"And I've told you, Dawa. It's happened twice before. Stevens? Moreno? Have you already forgotten about them?"

Dawa shook his head. He was tired and didn't want to argue. He felt he had no choice but to play along.

"Okay, Donald. Two of your dreams have come true. Now you've had a third. What did you dream about this time?"

Donny painted the spectacular scene while Claire paced outside the room, still talking on the phone.

"I was at the foot of a mountain," Donny said. "It was winter, but there wasn't a snowflake in sight. I felt cold, but it wasn't intolerable. Actually, it was kind of pleasant. The best winter days are always the ones without wind, and this one was no different. It was perfectly still. The sky was blue and the sun was shining down on my face. I was at complete peace."

Dawa said, "That's good, Donald. Very good."

"I was watching the mountain," he continued. "Taking it all in. Most of the trees were barren, but the evergreens were thriving. Various shades of deep greens and light browns covered the mountainside. Down the middle of the mountain, toward the gulley, I saw the bluest stream I've ever laid eyes on. Breaking whitewater marked the gentle rapids cascading down the length of the stream. The stream zigzagged from one side to the other, falling down the mountainside like the way a leaf falls down from a tree.

"Suddenly, the clear skies turned to dark clouds, overcast and grim. I heard a voice ahead, coming from a dark figure that wasn't there before. The figure was now standing between me and the mountain, blocking my view of the stream. It called to me. *We'd like for you to come in, Mr. Ford. We'd love to chat.'*

"It was Tanner. He was asking me to come closer, but I wasn't buying it. I tried ignoring the shadowy figure, but the longer I ignored him, the more agitated he became. Suddenly the figure grew taller, and was now standing at least ten feet high. I tried to run, but I was paralyzed. Couldn't move. He continued to call, extending his hand. *Come on in, Mr. Ford.'*

Donny stopped to take a long sip of water. Dawa didn't believe the supernatural twist, but his old friend's story had him hooked. "And? What happened next, Donald? Get on with it!"

Donny set the glass down. "Water," he said. "The water from the stream that was blocked by the shadowy figure now rose above it. The mountain stream swelled and grew like a massive tidal wave. The wall of water hung in suspense for what seemed like an eternity, and then in one fell swoop it engulfed the figure, Tanner, and swallowed him up whole. The waters quickly calmed and receded, but as they drew back into the mountain I could see Tanner gasping for air and struggling to stay afloat. Finally, he went under, a chain of bubbles marking the place where he drowned."

"That's some story," Dawa said. "But most of our dreams have rational explanations, Donald. For example, you spoke to Tanner on the phone. That's how you knew his voice. The figure just represents something, or someone, ominous and scary. You said as much about Tanner. I'm a little lost on the mountain; perhaps it represents peace, tranquility. The soft flowing waters almost certainly point to a sense of calm and relief, something you experienced recently through our meditative exercise."

Dawa stood up. "It's an interesting dream, Donald. But still, my friend, I believe these episodes are little more than just that."

Donny was getting ready to counter when Claire walked back into the room. She stuffed her phone in her pocket. "That was the other Ocula patient I was telling you about. Paul Freeman. The one who helped me escape from the facility in Costa Rica."

"What did he want?" Dawa asked.

"It's Tanner," she said. "He says Tanner is dead."

***

George Sturgis sat at his desk and cracked his knuckles, listening intently to the dark-haired man in a tailored suit sitting across from him. The man was reporting the current state of affairs involving missing employees and a secret facility in the jungle funded by Asteria Pharmaceuticals. Sturgis rarely worried, and when he did, he never showed it. The current situation, however, was one he couldn't afford to take lightly. One misstep, one detail left unattended to, one loose end, and it wouldn't just be the end of his career. Both his life and the life of his company were on the line.

"Run me through the Costa Rica situation again: how can you be so sure Tanner's little side project isn't going to come back to bite us in the ass?"

The man said, "I got off the phone with one of our guys outside of San José earlier today. It doesn't seem to be making the news here, but apparently there's been a volcanic eruption just a few miles south of the facility. They're calling it catastrophic. Local authorities have called off the investigation into the facility until further notice. It sounds like they've got their hands tied up in other matters, for the time being."

"Good. That will give us time to get a team down there to clean things up before the police have a chance to raid the place."

The man smiled. "No need. Satellite imagery shows the volcanic plume is extending northbound. Catastrophic volcanic designations are given to volcanoes with a destructive radius of three to fifteen kilometers, meaning there's thousand-degree lava oozing toward Tanner's place in the jungle as we speak. In all likelihood, the eruption has taken out the facility, along with everything in it."

Sturgis grinned. "My God, what are the odds of that?"

"Apparently, the volcano erupts on average once every five years. But yes–very fortuitous."

"I'll say!" Sturgis smacked his leg and leaned back. "Couldn't have planned it better myself! Your man in Costa Rica has been quite resourceful during this whole fiasco. I'll have to send him a bottle of scotch. And you say this was the technician who tipped us off about Freeman and Connor?"

"Yes, he's the one. Pretty useful for a UM grad."

"We'll have to get him up here once he gets back to the States. We need a good man heading up any post-approval studies the FDA shoots our way."

"You're sure Ocula is getting approved for sale soon?"

"Within the month," Sturgis said.

"Well, sounds like you'll have your hands full here. I'll pass the word along to Roberto next time we speak. I'm sure he could use a break from working in the far reaches of hell with the likes of Tanner and Doyle."

"Doyle." Sturgis thought on the name. "It's a shame what happened. And your man's sure he's dead?"

"Well, he never saw the body," the man replied. "But based on what Paul Freeman said, Doyle's a goner."

Sturgis pondered the recent events. Asteria had dodged a bullet; one that was a direct result of Tanner's obsession with Ocula and mind control. To Sturgis, the pseudoscience taking place in the jungle had always been preposterous, but Tanner's promise of treasury-backed riches had clouded his judgment. *Never again*, he thought.

Sturgis leaned forward and crossed his arms on the desk. His voice was skeptical. "There's something I have to ask. Do you really believe in all this garbage? About changing our realities with our dreams? That people have the ability to influence the minds of others, all by taking our little sleeping pill?"

The man was stung by the mockery. "Of course I believe it, Sturgis. Although I must say, it's disheartening to think you don't have more faith in our research."

"Yes, well. The government can afford to run on faith. Private companies cannot. Tanner was convinced he could sell a new version of Ocula for a premium to his old contacts at Langley, so I advised him to proceed. Promised triple-digit returns. Nothing beats a government contract, he said. Well, I let Tanner run his own show, and look where that's gotten us. We're weeks away from Ocula's public debut, and all we can talk about is keeping a lid on the scandal of the century. Guess that's what I get for working with spooks like you to begin with."

"If you didn't believe our reports, then why did you sign off on the deaths of the clinical trial outliers to begin with?"

Sturgis scoffed. "Isn't it obvious? Do you not realize what we've accomplished here? This isn't just the most effective sleeping medication ever developed–it's the most effective medication ever developed, period. Antisense therapy is a first for mankind, and Asteria is leading the way. Just think. In ten years, cancer will be a thing of the past. Conditions like ALS, Parkinson's, and heart disease will all join the ranks of polio and smallpox; a sorrowful chapter in the history of healthcare, but history nonetheless."

"You make it sound like it's about saving lives."

"It is about saving lives! And it starts with the lives of those working for this company. We put everything we had into the research and development of this drug. Did you really think I would let a dozen troublemakers jeopardize Asteria's future? And to think, those fools made bogus claims about our medication's side effects, when almost two thousand other clinical trial participants sang its praises. I would've been insane not to shut these people up once and for all."

"So it was never about their claims? You don't believe this drug gives them any sort of power or abilities beyond our current understanding?"

Sturgis's laugh was condescending. "You're joking, right? As my father would have said in his day, 'it's all horseshit.' Every bit of it." Sturgis waved his arm. "Look around you for a moment, would you? I'm running one of the most successful pharmaceutical companies in the world. That doesn't happen by betting on pseudoscience."

"Some would say the same about antisense. You know as well as anyone that dozens of international pharmaceutical companies have bankrupted themselves chasing after antisense therapy."

"Antisense is different. There was always solid science to back up its claims. The companies you're talking about never had a legitimate game plan for success. They set their eyes on the presumptive noble causes of the day. Chasing cancer. Heart disease. Alzheimer's." Sturgis huffed. "Might as well have been chasing unicorns. We could have dumped millions into antisense research for cancer, but then what? No solitary antisense regiment is going to cover every type of cancer, because every type of cancer stems from mutations in a specific line of genetic code. Sleep disorders, on the other hand, were linked to a genetic sequence we could manage–a single line of code. Putting our antisense efforts into creating a drug like Ocula was the logical first step. Plus, let's face it: there's nothing sexy about cancer drugs, and rarely is the end user satisfied with the results. But a pill that guarantees eight hours of sleep, all night, every night?" He tapped hard on the stock report on his desk. "The numbers don't lie. Investors are drooling over Ocula, and the pill hasn't even hit the market yet."

"So this was always about the money. Nothing else."

Sturgis was indignant. "Jesus, you government spooks can be some real self-righteous bastards, you know that? Listen. I answer to one governing body, and that's the shareholders. Of course it was about the money. Isn't it *always* about the money?"

The man replied, "Yes. For some people, Sturgis, it's always about the money." His demeanor had grown caustic. He buttoned his coat and stood to leave. "Will that be all for today?"

"We never discussed the situation at hand. We've still got these outliers running around out there. Nothing has changed from the original plan. We must eliminate these threats before word gets out there's a problem with Ocula. It's not just my job that's on the line, mind you. Your ass is hanging out there, too. They've all got to go. Connor, Ford, the Freemans."

"Freeman. There's just one now. The Consultants took care of Alex Freeman over a week ago, although they seemed to have misplaced the body."

Sturgis's eyes widened. "Misplaced? Are you fucking kidding me?"

The man calmly put up his hand to stop him. "Sturgis. This is what we're here for. I told you we would take care of it, and we will."

"Easy for you to say. Your company isn't going anywhere. If this thing goes south, mine will."

"You have nothing to worry about. I've already got a team tracking the others now. We'll have everything wrapped up by your next quarterly conference call, trust me."

"Trust . . ." Sturgis snarled and dismissed his associate. The man let the door slam on his way out. Sturgis sat in a quiet office and looked out the window. He watched the clouds form shapes and objects he hadn't seen in years. One looked just like a dog he had when he was a kid. His name was Merle. The droopy-eared bloodhound was running across the sky and chasing the rooster cloud that was sitting in the top right corner of his window. He twiddled his thumbs as he watched the scene play out like a movie. Then the clouds dissipated, the characters exiting the stage.

He returned to his earnings report. Asteria's stock was up another three percent. Given the circumstances, the week was ending on a positive note. George Sturgis hit the remote, closing the blinds and getting back to work.

Chapter 36:
Rising Sun

The drive back home for Paul and Michelle was poignant. The overcast clouds had dissolved from the day before, replaced by a slow-rising sun washing over the road and the trees and the hills on the horizon. It was a beautiful Saturday morning. Aaron was in the backseat of Michelle's Jeep, sucking on a pacifier and shaking his sock monkey by the tail. Michelle sat in the passenger seat, her hands folded in her lap. Her eyes spoke of an apprehension cleverly concealed by the warmth of her purposeful smile. They were on the same two-lane Paul had followed in the day before; only this time he was leaving with his family intact.

Paul wanted to forget everything that had happened–if only for a moment–but the events covering the last twelve hours were domineering. Tanner had forced him to take Ocula 2.0, sending him into a predictable eight-hour sleep cycle. It wasn't until midnight that he had woken up in his parents' old bed, tucked in by his wife after passing out on the old porch swing.

How she got him inside was still a mystery, but he was thankful she had taken the time. The night had been cold and dreary in the old rustic farmhouse, but the handful of logs Michelle had rustled up was just enough to keep them warm until morning. She watched the lanterns burn while patiently waiting for her husband to wake, never leaving his side as he slept off the drug.

When Paul finally came to, he was manic.

"I've got to call Claire. I've got to tell her what happened. There could be more on the way. And Alex. I have to call Alex. He might be alive!"

Paul tried to lunge out of bed, but Michelle was quick to calm him. She pulled the old quilt back over his chest and told him to relax. She looked into his eyes and tried to fight off the urge to cry, but it was no use. They embraced one another and wept until Michelle drifted off to sleep in the same bedroom Paul's parents had shared so many years ago.

Paul left Michelle and Aaron to rest in the bed while he stepped outside to call Claire. He broke the news about Tanner's death, and then Claire filled him in on the case. He was relieved to hear an Atlanta police detective was working with Claire and Ford to bring in Asteria employees who could be tied to the Costa Rica facility; all they were waiting on was confirmation of the company's ties to the secret jungle compound. Once Costa Rican investigators raided the facility, they would have everything they needed to link Asteria to the crimes. Paul wished the operation well, and asked Claire to keep him posted.

Then it was time to get to work. He went to the kitchen to get Tanner. The company man's lifeless corpse was already stiff and reeking of death. Paul thought eight hours was a little fast for the stench of decomposition to arise, and he hoped Tanner hadn't shit himself. He grabbed his old boss by the feet and dragged the body from the kitchen to the cinderblock porch steps leading into the field.

Moving the corpse outside was like pulling a two-hundred-pound wheelbarrow without the wheel. Near the creek and shaded by a century-old oak tree was a small graveyard. Crude headstones with etched-in pet names like Tracker and Bullet and Rascal were nestled under the leafless branches. It was a good a place as any. Paul took a shovel from the storage shed out back and started digging. He was quickly reminded of how rocky the North-Georgia terrain was just a few inches below the surface.

He spent the better part of four hours digging the hole, stopping every couple of feet to take a break and rest on his shovel while admiring the moon and the stars above. Then it was back to shoveling. He was aiming for a full six feet. He figured someone would come looking for the spook, and the closer he could get Tanner's body to hell, the better.

It was just before daybreak when Paul finished filling the grave back in. He found an old wooden headstone nearby that read, "Rocky." The name was fitting. He marked the grave and then went back to the farmhouse, exhausted from the hours-long ordeal. He figured Michelle and Aaron would be up soon. Then it would be time to head back into the city and meet with Claire and the others.

My, how quickly life can change, thought Paul. Last weekend he had been lining up a babysitter and planning a surprise Valentine's Day getaway for him and Michelle. It would have been their first official date night since Aaron was born. But instead of making love by the glow of a crackling fireplace in a romantic cabin in the hills, Paul would be spending this weekend–and likely many weekends thereafter–trying to figure out how to keep his family alive. All because of one little pill.

Paul was still coming to grips with the dreams, and their effect on reality. The skeptic in him wanted to believe none of the assertions were true, but deep down, Paul knew Ocula had unlocked abilities he couldn't begin to comprehend. The human brain was the most complex structure known to mankind, a high efficiency biological computer capable of using a network one hundred billion neurons strong to send signals across one thousand trillion synaptic connections. No way any scientist or neurologist or pharmaceutical company for that matter could account for every hidden road, side street, and alleyway that existed in the neural highway of our minds.

Did that explain how a pharmaceutically enhanced mind could influence the mind of another? Hardly. Humans had obsessed over the functions and faculties of the mind for millennia, with more mysteries remaining than would likely be solved in Paul's lifetime. But whether Paul liked it or not, there was no denying what had happened at the facility. The guards. The snakes. The shootings. Every detail was vivid, every image so clear. His mind's eye had painted a crisp and colorful scene, and it all played out in reality more or less the way he envisioned it in his dream.

Everyone needs a key to get into locked away places, Doyle had said. Funny that he never mentioned why some places in the mind were locked away to begin with.

What was going to happen when the drug went to market? Out of the original two thousand participants in the clinical trials, twelve had had side effects. Even if the number of outliers in the original trials had been a fluke, an FDA-approved drug would likely mean thousands more insomniacs would be afflicted by the pill.

The death toll would be staggering. Bosses choking on their T-bones. High-school acquaintances walking into heavy traffic. An epidemic of ex-spouses slipping in showers and drowning in bathtubs. And those would just be the affected humans. Paul's brother Alex was proof that Ocula's side effects could lead to much wilder encounters. The more Paul thought about it, the more he realized that putting Ocula in the hands of the general public sounded less like a dream, and more like a full-scale nightmare.

A nightmare he couldn't let happen.

Paul wished he had never heard of Ocula. He figured he should have been mad at Michelle for spiking his nightcap with the drug to begin with, but it felt wrong to bring it up now. There was no way she could have known an innocuous little sleeping pill would lead to a full-blown pharmaceutical conspiracy. Still, she should have talked to him about his insomnia. The ploy wasn't lost on Paul, and the conversation was one to be had in due time, but not now. Not after everything that had happened. Paul just wanted to love his wife, and was too busy thanking God his family was safe to worry about the alleged deception.

And, he was tired, or as Alex would have said, dog tired. Paul longed for the comfort of his own bed, but there would be no going home any time soon. It was too dangerous. If he was ever going to rest in peace again, it would have to be in a world where Asteria Pharmaceuticals ceased to exist. A small part of Paul wanted to take his family and disappear, but settling for a life of looking over his shoulder wasn't in his DNA. He had to help the journalist find the others. He had to help her see this thing through to the end. After all, a deal was a deal.

Paul looked over at his wife and smiled. It would have been easy for him to get lost in Michelle's doting hazel eyes, were not for the billowing cloud of trepidation looming over his head. Tanner was dead, and that gave him solace for the time being. But Paul also knew powerful forces were at work at Asteria, meaning any provisional peace was likely to be short-lived.

Paul eased off the gas and took his time driving his family back into the city. He reached over to Michelle, and she took his hand without the slightest hesitation. Then they looked to the road ahead. The highway stretched far into the distance, cresting a thinly wooded hill before disappearing into the rising sun. The light overwhelmed the horizon where the dark asphalt road met the bright yellow sky, stretching out from the sun and hiding the faraway landscape behind the blinding beams.

Paul knew in a minute or two the truth would be revealed; that the road would lead through the groves and the fields that were hiding behind the golden horizon. The sunrise blending into the distant countryside was nothing more than an optical illusion. Crystal balls and tarot cards. A convincing deception from a distance, yet easily debunked under close scrutiny.

Just a couple more miles. Then he would see.

And he did, though much to his dismay. Even though the white-oak groves and the hay-stripped fields he passed coming in were exactly where he remembered, a new horizon had formed. A new bright and blended landscape sat in the distance, out of reach and impossible to see, hidden away by the glaring, golden light.

Maybe I'll keep driving, thought Paul. *Right into the sunlight. Maybe then I could peek behind the curtain, like a snooping fanatic at a Donny Ford seminar.*

But that was crazy talk. Paul knew there was a simple reason for the eternally veiled horizon. It came to him when he thought about the dreams. Dreams that had led Tanner to torture and kill for the promise of a buck. Dreams that had pushed Claire to the brink of insanity. Dreams that could end countless lives and change the world, all because a drug company chose to meddle with a technology it failed to understand.

All because of one little pill.

The dreams were abominations.

And just like the horizon, they should have forever stayed hidden.

Because for this world to keep on spinning, Paul figured, some things were better left unseen.

The End

Resources

This novel is a work of fiction, but several of the themes covered in this book have real-world ties. The following list of resources was put together to help anyone interested in learning more about the science, history and current events behind the book.

Ban, Thomas A., MD, FRCP(C). "The Role of Serendipity in Drug Discovery - Ncbi.nlm.nih.gov." *Nih.gov.* U.S. National Library of Medicine, 8 Sept. 2006. Web.

Various. *Buchanan's Journal of Man.* N.p.: Project Gutenberg, 2008. Project Gutenberg, 24 June 2008. Web.

"Can Brain Waves Interfere with Radio Waves? | MIT School ..." N.p., 25 Oct. 2011. Web.

"CDC: 9 Million Americans Use Sleeping Pills - NY Daily News." *Nydailynews.com.* The Associated Press, 30 Aug. 2013. Web. 20 Oct. 2016.

"DNA, Genes and Chromosomes — University of Leicester." Creative Commons, n.d. Web. 20 Oct. 2016.

"Drug-Gene Testing - Mayo Clinic Research." *Mayoresearch.mayo.edu.* Mayo Foundation for Medical Education and Research, n.d. Web. 24 June 2016.

Edward, Mark. "I Was One of America's Top Psychics—And Like ... - Alternet." *Alternet.org.* N.p., 3 Aug. 2012. Web. 15 May 2016.

Extraordinary People: The Boy with the Incredible Brain. Channel 5 Broadcasting Ltd, 23 May 2005. Web. Retrieved from YouTube at https://www.youtube.com/watch?v=PPySn3slfXI

"FDA Drug Approval Process Infographic (Horizontal)." *Fda.gov.* N.p., 26 Feb. 2016. Web. 4 May 2016.

Harvey, Shannon. "How To Use Your Mind To Control Your Heart Rate." *Theconnection.tv.* The Connection, 3 May 2015. Web.

Various. "How Independent Is the FDA?, on the Frontline Site - Pbs.org." Frontline, 13 Nov. 2003. Web. 20 Oct. 2016.

Ingraham, Christopher. "One Striking Chart Shows Why Pharma Companies Are Fighting ..." *Washingtonpost.com.* The Washington Post, 13 July 2016. Web.

Innes, Emma. "Feeling Cold? Why Not Try Meditating? Scientists Prove You ..." *Dailymail.co.uk.* Daily Mail, 9 Apr. 2013. Web.

"Intro to Tibetan Buddhism - Jigdal Dagchen Sakya." *Www.sakya.org.* Creative Commons, n.d. Web. 12 Sept. 2016.

Kattalia, Kathryn. "Scans Show Liberals, Conservatives Have Different Brain ..." *Nydailynews.com.* New York Daily News, 8 Apr. 2011. Web.

"Personal Genomics: The Future of Healthcare? | Stories ..." *Yourgenome.org.* N.p., 14 June 2016. Web.

Pollack, Andrew. "F.D.A. Approves Genetic Drug to Treat Rare Disease." *Nytimes.com.* The New York Times, 29 Jan.

2013. Web.

Roberts-Grey, Gina. "Is Insomnia Hereditary?" *Sleepapnea.com*. Philips Respironics, n.d. Web. 7 July 2016.

Saez, Catherine. "Clinical Trial Reporting Biased; Full Disclosure ..." *Ip-watch.org*. Intellectual Property Watch, 30 Sept. 2016. Web.

Shreeve, James. "Beyond the Brain." *National Geographic*. N.p., n.d. Web. 11 May 2016.

"The Human Proteome in Brain - The Human Protein Atlas." *Proteinatlas.org*. N.p., n.d. Web. 3 June 2016.

"The Ten Worst Drug Recalls In The History Of The FDA - 24 ..." *247wallst.com*. N.p., 10 Dec. 2010. Web.

"What Is REM Sleep?" *Nih.gov*. National Institutes of Health, 9 July 2013. Web.

Zimmer, Carl. "Updated Brain Map Identifies Nearly 100 New Regions - The ..." *Nytimes.com*. The New York Times, 20 July 2016. Web.

About the author

J.M. Lanham was born in Georgia in 1983. He currently lives in Florida with his wife and son.

Be sure to stay up to date with the latest J.M. Lanham news by visiting www.jmlanham.com.

70379260R00194

Made in the USA
Middletown, DE
13 April 2018